Sir Tracy Calendar appeared riding a beautiful chestnut. Althea could feel Mr. Pendarly bridle nervously at her side.

"You are early out this morning. Allow me to compliment you: you have captured half the hearts of Bond Street already." Sir Tracy turned to Pendarly with a nod. "You must think yourself fortunate to have stolen the march on this lady's army of suitors."

"I doubt, sir, whether I have captured so much as one heart, let alone those of an army," replied Althea.

"Nonsense. In London hearts are given as lightly as air, and taken as freely at a moment's notice. Mr. Pendarly here may be at your feet today and on the morrow be dangling after the first fair lady with a fortune that he encounters."

Althea was startled. Was Sir Tracy trying to tell her something?

Althea

Madeleine Robins

A FAWCETT CREST BOOK

Fawcett Publications, Inc., Greenwich, Connecticut

ALTHEA

A Fawcett Crest Original

© 1977 Madeleine Robins

ISBN 0-449-23268-9

Printed in the United States of America

10 9 8 7 6 5 4 3 2 1

For Karen Beecher, 1956-1973
First audience, kindest critic, dear friend

Chapter One

Lady Bevan was discontent, peevish, fretful, tired, bored, irritated, and generally out of charity with the world. This was by no means an unusual state for this lady when awakened before noon, but such was her unreason that she felt inclined, at the very least, to throw something at someone.

So much had conspired on this particular morning to further her distress: Francis's gaming, which was showing signs, to Lady Bevan's eye, of becoming a "Fatal Flaw"; the dreadful spot on her chin, which seemed determined to pop out despite all her efforts to stop it; and the horrifying bill from her mantua maker, which had arrived only that morning with her chocolate. It was as she sat abed, sipping the brew and turning over the cards of invitation, that the loathsome thing came in sight: the third notice, after which a letter would be sent to Francis.

The thought of the scene that would ensue should her husband see that bill totally ruined her pleasure in several kind invitations, and in the letter from her best friend, Miss Iphigenia Prydd.

As she cast the dreadful thing away, her ladyship's dresser, Bailey, came in.

Lady Bevan shoved ineffectually at the tray on her lap. "This stuff is cold. Take it away!" she said in tones of distress. The long-suffering Bailey removed the tray and disposed of it, then returned with her mistress's dressing sacque.

"Put that thing away, too, and if anyone calls, say I am dead or gone away somewhere. I have the headache, and I expect I shall be quite dreadfully low all day, and all on account of that dreadful bill!" She sighed artistically and sank back into her pillows, looking hopefully at Bailey, who very often had helpful ideas about situations like this. Bailey pressed her lips together unresponsively.

"If you please, m'lady, there is someone already called. That is, ma'am, the lady says she is your sister, but I wasn't sure, as she looked—well, ma'am—" Bailey paused delicately, unsure of how to proceed to describe the disarray that the supposed Miss Ervine had arrived in.

"Piffle! Althea could not be here. It must be one of Francis's jests, for I doubt that Papa has ever let Ally go farther than the county border without dragging her back to Hook Well. And whoever it is below, I do not wish to see her. Besides, why should she come and not warn me in advance?" Lady Bevan was pleased with this stroke of reasoning. "Pray send her away and fetch me my salts. I am so miserable!" With a wave of the bill still clutched in her hand, Lady Bevan turned her face to the pillow, and Bailey, after placing the salts bottle within her reach, left the room, wondering all the while how to dismiss the determined-looking lady downstairs.

Downstairs, Debbens, the second footman, was polishing the already well polished handles of the front door in order, as he said to Mrs. Chaverly, the housekeeper, to keep an eye on the young person, who didn't look any better than she should, if he was any judge of the matter. When Bailey appeared at the head of the stairs and gestured to him, it was with reluctance that Debbens relinquished his polishing rag and went up to speak with her.

"Her ladyship says she's out and don't want to see no one, be they princess or long lost sister or the sweep." The lift of eyebrows that accompanied this declaration was considerably more emphatic than mere words at conveying the doom awaiting anyone who disobeyed her la-

dyship's orders. Debbens betook himself down the stairs
to where the young lady was seated, drew himself up to
his highest dignity, and was about to send her about her
business when the young lady herself stood and began to
address him.

"Well, then, is Maria prepared to see me? Keeping a
lady waiting in the hallway is the most rag-mannered
thing, and so I shall tell her, although in the state I'm in I
suppose you might have cause to wonder. I shan't steal
the silver plate, and you might at least have *offered* me
the parlor and kept watch on me there. Well?"

As the lady seemed to expect some reply, Debbens collected himself and said in his most reproving tone, "Her
ladyship is not within, madam. If you would care to leave
a card?"

His tone suggested that she should neither care to leave
a card nor to inquire further. He had badly misjudged his
subject, however, for the lady gathered her gloves and reticule but did not appear to be moving toward the door.

"Maria abroad before noon? If she was awake to tell
the maid to fob me off, I should be much surprised. Come
then, show me to her room, and I shall announce myself.
I have made a most tiresomely long journey from the
country and am in no humor to sit in the doorway until
my sister or her husband sees fit to acknowledge me!"

So saying, the young lady neatly sidestepped Debbens
and began to climb the stairs. Debbens, meanwhile, found
himself quite at a loss for what to do. Somewhere in the
back of his head, he entertained the suspicion that it
might just be her ladyship's sister now climbing the stairs.
She was stubborn enough, although there was not a look
between them to proclaim a relationship. Indeed, the
young lady would tower over Lady Bevan's fair head. By
the time Debbens had weighed his alternatives and decided that his position demanded he stop the intruder, she
had already reached the landing and turned, unerringly,
to the left, toward her ladyship's door.

In her room Lady Bevan had become aware of a row in the hallway. By now her imagined headache was becoming quite real, and she had begun to beguile herself with marvelous, improbable solutions to the problem of Madame Helena's bill, which solutions needed silence to be properly nurtured. When the noise began, Lady Bevan reached for her bell to summon Bailey and have the noise removed. But at that moment the noise obligingly walked in. In the doorway stood a tall, dark young woman, dusty and travel-stained, with her bonnet askew and a rent in her skirt, and a weary, humorous smile.

"Ally!" Lady Bevan flew across the room to gather her sister Althea in a strongly scented beribboned embrace.

Miss Ervine, who by this time was indeed beginning to feel the fatigues of her haphazard journey, could only murmur, "Well, Maria, *at last!*"

"But my dearest creature!" cried Lady Bevan. She led her sister to a sofa. "What on earth are you doing in town? However did you contrive to leave Papa? How very good it is to see you again, to be sure—you positively do my heart good—but, Ally, how in heaven did you get so sadly turnabout, and where on earth did you find that costume?" Lady Bevan rang for more chocolate and requested, with a wrinkled nose, that Bailey dispose of Miss Ervine's pelisse and bonnet. When Bailey had left on these errands, and to relieve the anxious Debbens as to the security of his position, Maria began her questioning again.

"No, really, Ally, it is simply too bad of you! Giving me no warning and all and simply turning up on my doorstep at this *indecent* hour! I would have had a room all ready for you, but now you must take one of the plain rooms until we can mend that. And that must be your punishment for the ill usage of your poor sister."

"One of the plains rooms will be delightful, my *poor* sister. In fact, any room where I may lie down and sleep the clock round will be more than sufficient. And, if I know you, having a room 'made ready' involves new paper and hangings, which is a great deal of nonsense only for me, Mary. But how are you? You write such wretched letters. All balls and assemblies and routs and new hats, and nary a word of my sister in them anywhere. Your poor footman must have thought me shockingly brazen, but I knew you must be at home at this *indecent* hour, and I was very firm in my desire to see you. He was equally firm that I should not. Do you know how I found you? I followed that dreadful scent of yours down the hallway until I came to your room. Now stop laughing and let me look at you."

Althea held her sister at arm's length and inspected her closely. "Well, still the family beauty. You look so much like dear Mama, Merrit looks like Papa, and I look like no one I can think of. But you look thin, Mary, and tired. Are you well?"

For a moment Lady Bevan trembled on the verge of spilling out her heart to her sister: Francis's gaming and her own boredom and fretfulness, and of course that wretched bill from Madame Helena. But she shook her head impatiently.

"Of course I'm well. And all the better for your being here. And my figure is much admired. Johnny Wallingham called me wandlike just the other night. But, Ally, will you please tell me how you got here and how you contrived to convince Papa to let you come? And, my dear, we simply must get you something to wear this instant! How very dreadful that gown is. Have you come all the way from Hook Well with your ankles showing thus?"

Maria shook her head: the gown Althea wore was of brown alpaca trimmed in black grosgrain ribbon, and the age of this venerable garment was such that the alpaca had taken on a very definite shine, in contrast to the grosgrain, which had lost its shine completely. Maria had noted the bonnet and pelisse that Bailey had removed. She devoutly hoped they would be burned. Althea was not used to dressing this way at home, Maria hoped, but if she was, it might begin to explain her unmarried state at the age of three and twenty. Certainly she was not homely or without grace, and Maria had to admit that, if her sister had not inherited either parent's spectacular looks, she had gotten her wit from another source as well—although this was a mixed blessing, as everyone *knew* men were shy of smart women as a rule. But brains or none, Maria was pleased as a child to have a new doll to dress.

"I am quite decided," she announced. "I shall take you in hand. And what is more, I shall make you all the rage."

"Very fine, Mary. But could I not have some sleep first?" There was submission in Miss Ervine's voice, and a sort of desperate laughter imminent at the corners of her mouth.

"Wretch, you're laughing at me. How very disobliging you are, to be sure. Now, for the third time, Ally, will you tell me how you are come here? Is Merrit with you? Tell me everything, for not a wink of sleep shall you have until I know what's afoot." Lady Bevan settled herself comfortably upon the sofa and waited expectantly.

"Well, you see, Maria, Papa's disowned me."

"Again?" Lady Bevan blinked. "What was it this time? Last time, as I recall, it was for that mad-dash ride you made across the hunt field to save that stupid dog that bit you afterward. I have always thought that a singular piece of ingratitude."

"In Papa or the dog? This time it was for scolding Merrit—deservedly, I thought—for riding through the rose gardens. John-gardener is almost eighty, and those roses are all he tends now himself—why, they're wife and children to him—and I cannot think it right to see Merrit chasing around in the roses as if they weren't there and breaking poor John's heart."

She paused thoughtfully. "No, I suppose he must have

known that they were there, for he surely felt the brambles. But in any case, Papa heard me scolding Merrit and told me then and there that I was an ungrateful hussy to be arguing with the heir to Hook Well and promptly disowned me."

"Althea, he never said anything so odiously familial!"

"He assuredly did, and my name has again been scratched from the family Bible, where he had written it in before, along with the text about the sheep returning to the fold. And since I had been looking for some excuse to come to you for an age, I promptly took to my heels and here I am. And oh, the adventures I have had, Maria. They would turn you old and pale!"

As Lady Bevan showed no sign of becoming either old or pale and signaled her sister to continue, Althea did— with the liveliest amusement.

"Well, the reason that I look as I do is that I was forced to make my escape quite stealthily—by dint of a ladder at midnight, no less. Oh, it was a fine adventure, Mary! I left the house and walked into Hooking by the light of the moon and sat on the steps of the bank until it opened the next morning!"

"Ally, you never did such a shocking thing!"

"Well, not quite that bad. I *did* use the ladder, but I went to Mrs. Greendragon's cottage and got lodging there for the night, and the next morning Davy Greendragon drove me into Hooking in their dog cart and I went to the bank and borrowed some money from Mr. Preake, giving him those awful ruby studs of Great-Aunt Amarantha's as security. Anyway, the walk to the Greendragons' is much harder than you would imagine, and dear Mrs. Green-dragon loaned me one of her dresses. I think it must have been her best, too, which is why I'm ashamed of its present condition. I must remember to send her some cloth for a new dress and my best apology. The dear thing thought it so very romantic to be helping me on an elopement, even if there was no one with whom I was eloping."

Maria puzzled. "But that does not explain how you came to look as though you had been savaged by highwaymen, Althea."

"I was as respectable as you please not three hours ago. But half an hour out of London, my coach was thrown off the road by a curricle and pair driving furiously in the other direction. It neatly hedged us into a ditch and then vanished into the distance. I was most distressed, and as for the post boy—I could only be silent and hope that he would not recollect that I, too, am a member of the same gentry he was villifying. It was all of half an hour before a dear, *kind* farmer and his three dear, kind sons came by and pushed us out of the ditch and we could be on our way. We had to stop at the first posting house and have some trifling thing fixed, but I simply hid away, buried in the coach, for fear that the post boy would think better of it and set me down there. As it happens, dear, I paid him off, and the farmer too, and thus I arrived here without a farthing to my name and wearing the rags you see. How is that for a famous adventure?"

"Althea, you spent all that time with an irate post boy and no maid!"

"Well, you must see that a maid would have been a dreadful encumbrance on this sort of journey, Sister. I could not invite Banders along, certainly, for, even discarding the possibility that she would be able to climb down a ladder in the dark and take a midnight stroll of four miles, I think that her first act upon invitation to such an outing would be to dutifully inform Papa. I did leave Papa a note, thanking him kindly for his care and support through the years—and suggesting that he might forward any communications to me through you. Do you mind?"

"Althea, it is beyond me that you could leave Papa

such a note, which is not to say that he didn't deserve it, for anyone can see that you had to break loose from your confinement at Hook Well after all this time. But to accomplish the whole thing by yourself in such a businesslike fashion! There is something quite unladylike about it. Did you really pawn Aunt Amarantha's studs?"

"Yes. Mr. Preake told me that he was not giving me a fraction of their real worth, for that would be pawning them rather than 'using them as security,' which is so very much more genteel. But I think, all the same, that I pawned them. I suppose that I must pay back the loan and get the studs back. But it is a shame, for they are in the worst of bad taste. In any case, I must wait until I have next quarter's allowance."

"Ally, Papa could not stop your allowance, could he?"

"I asked Mr. Preake just that question, but he says that it is impossible, for the money was Mama's fortune and is tied up so that Papa has no say in the matter at all. Else I daresay he would have put it in Merrit's hands by now."

"That is unjust!" cried Lady Bevan in tones of shock.

"No such thing. I don't say Papa is dishonest, just overzealous. You know that if Papa heard there was a chance of acquiring the English Channel for Merrit, he would do so. Therefore, Mary, here am I, disowned and quite willing to remain for the time being, at least. Will you have me?"

"Of course. And I suppose Francis will be delighted— not that I see him enough to know what *is* his delight these days. I think he will be glad to have someone who will amuse me," Maria said plaintively.

Althea did not reply to this speech but noted it carefully. She thought to herself: Plenty of time to smooth things out here. It is good I have come. Then she yawned. Maria, seeing that yawn, was instantly repentant. "You look fagged to death, and I keep you here talking."

"I admit that if I do not find a place to rest very quickly, I am like to fall into strong hysterics, or the vapors. I think the vapors, for they require far less exertion. And if I swoon away, perhaps you will be so good as to have me placed on a bed." Althea rose stiffly from the sofa and took a turn around the room, inspecting the portrait of their father that hung in an alcove: his wedding gift to his daughter. Lady Bevan lost herself for a moment in studying her sister—the tall, elegant figure in that ill-fitting gown; the strong, handsome face; the dark, thick hair coiled heavily atop her head; the graceful movements of her hands against the dark alpaca.

Her ladyship made plans.

"You shall rest immediately, but tomorrow we begin to make a woman of fashion of you, and I plan to enjoy myself very much!" She rang for Bailey. "Please take Miss Ervine to her room and see that one of the maids is sent to do for her until her own arrives—do you believe that Banders will come to London in the light of day, if she has no ladders to climb? Else we must engage you a new maid. I shall take you to my dressmaker and have Monsieur Philippe do your hair. Which is exceedingly kind of me, you know, for everyone knows that he is an absolute genius. No, go away and let me plan. This becomes so exciting!"

In the midst of visions of muslins, crepes, and lace, Maria patted her sister's shoulder absentmindedly. Bailey stopped at the doorway behind the departing Althea.

"If you please, m'lady, Mr. John Wallingham left his card and said that he would be back at two." Bailey hovered expectantly for the inevitable flurry of orders.

"At two! Lord, girl, settle my sister as quick as ever you can and come back direct. I've barely an hour to dress. At two!" As Althea left the room, it echoed with these sounds of dismay. Bailey followed after, and Lady Bevan rose to begin her daily activities.

Chapter Two

A perch phaeton came to an abrupt halt before the door of a large brick residence on Cavendish Street. A gentleman, swathed in a greatcoat with innumerable capes, fumbled briefly for his hat and alit from the phaeton, giving the reins to his tiger. The gentleman smoothed out the suggestion of a wrinkle at his shoulder, tucked his hat under his arm, and turned, before dismissing the phaeton, to address a question to the tiger.

"What was our exact time, Eustace—that is, what time did I tell Lord Quinlan?"

"I make it six hours and thirty-two minutes is what you told 'is lordship; but I still think as how it was six and seven and twenty."

"I admire your tenaciousness, Eustace, but I shall continue to believe my own watch in preference to yours, and in any case it is of no issue. I won our wager by a very safe margin. Thank you." The gentleman smiled briefly and waved a casual hand in dismissal; the phaeton started off at a sedate pace toward the stables. The gentleman then proceeded to enter his house, where he was greeted by a solicitous butler.

"Good evening, sir," the man said respectfully. "May I inquire on behalf of the servants' hall, sir, how your wager was concluded? There has been some consternation, I believe."

"The servants' hall can be at rest, Gergeley. I won the wager within very good bounds." He handed Gergeley his hat and coat and moved toward the stairs, but the *humpf* and stirring motion made by the butler stopped him, and he turned again with raised eyebrows.

"Excuse me, sir, but Lady Boskingram is here and is, I collect, awaiting you in the Green Saloon." The gentleman frowned briefly, then, as he continued toward the stairs, spoke over his shoulder. "Make my apologies to my lady and tell her that I shall join her when I have had the chance to rid myself of some portion of my dirt. Ask her if she will bear me company through dinner."

"I believe, sir, that she has formed the intention of staying for longer than dinner, sir. Her boxes have been removed to the yellow bedroom." A look of intense irritation crossed the gentleman's face, and then another thought seemed to strike him, for he raised one eyebrow in an exceedingly satirical manner, murmuring, "Indeed, Gergeley? How very unconventional of the lady. Be sure to tell her that I shall give myself the *honor* of joining her *very* shortly."

From the tone and the irritation in his master's eye, Gergeley judged that it was time to remove himself; he bowed and left the hall. His master, after a tentative start in the direction of the Green Saloon, decided that his first impulse had been better and that it would improve his temper to face Lady Boskingram after changing from riding clothes.

Some fifteen minutes later, the gentleman descended into the hallway again. The red coat and top boots were gone, and in their place was a coat of blue superfine, beautifully fitted to his form, faultless ivory pantaloons, a waistcoat of a very delicate shade of yellow, and a cravat tied in the intricate and trying fashion of the *Orientale*. Although extremely tall, the gentleman was blessed by nature with a figure and a leg to compliment even the trying current fashion; and although his hair was, undoubtedly, a violent shade of red, it was cut and brushed stylishly *au coup de vent*.

Altogether the gentleman presented a fashionable figure, but one dressed with such exquisite propriety as to refresh the eyes of any who might scorn the affections of the dandy set. He paused before the door of the saloon with a gesture suggestive of one facing an inquisition, and then proceeded inward. On the sofa was a very small, brightly dressed lady of some five and sixty years. She turned and smiled at the gentleman who, from the look on his face, made it clear that he had not expected *this* Lady Boskingram to be the occupant of the room.

"Aunt Peg!" He advanced toward her with both hands outstretched. "That wretch Gergeley gave me to understand that it was Amalia who was here."

"Well, Tracy, I am still *a* Countess of Boskingram, if no longer the sole possessor of that title, and you cannot think that people will always remember to qualify me with respect to dear Amalia," she said with some asperity. "Stand off, dear boy, and let me look at you. I am shocked to behold a man who has just made an eight-hour journey in less than seven hours. And still you look like *the glass of fashion and the mold of form!* But you must tell me all about it."

"There is not much to tell, ma'am. Quinlan bet me that I could not drive my phaeton to his seat and back in under seven hours. Said that it took him at least that—and he was no mean whip at that. So I proved that I could. Went to White's on my return, collected my thousand from him, drank a toast at his expense, and here I am, none the worse for the day's work."

"None the worse? No mishaps, Tracy?"

"What, I, love? I confess that I did have a slight turn-up this morning on my way out of town, trying to pass an abominably show chaise coming into London on a very narrow piece of road. Other than that, I had a most uneventful ride. After the first hour I became quite *ennuyé*."

"No doubt," the dowager agreed dryly. "I imagine that

driving for six hours at breakneck pace over uncertain roads must become dreadfully commonplace. What was this slight turn-up? I collect we shall find the victims outside your door in the morning, screaming for your blood—or at least restitution. You dreadful scapegrace, I am appalled at you."

She did not sound appalled, and Sir Tracy did not seem to feel that she was, for he answered quite cheerfully, "I doubt it not, ma'am. I finally passed the chaise, but I fear I may have forced it over to the side a trifle farther than the driver found convenient."

"I vow, Tracy, I daily expect to see a runner appear inquiring as to the whereabouts of one Sir Tracy Calendar, wanted for I know not what. But certainly something odious. You obviously forced that poor coach off the road." Lady Boskingram leaned back and regarded her nephew with a look that Sir Tracy returned quite shamelessly.

"Sorry for the chaise, ma'am?"

"Sorry for the occupants, you odious boy, and for the driver. I cannot but imagine how unsettling it must be early in the day to have a phaeton come charging up over the horizon and neatly nudge one into a ditch. You really should strive to develop a sense of shame, my dear one." Sir Tracy seemed to consider this suggestion for a moment, but it was obvious to his aunt that he was unable to summon up any truly repentant fervor. "You are abominable, Tracy. But tell me, why did you enter the room looking so ferocious just now?"

"Was I so, ma'am? I fancy it was merely exhaustion." He stifled an enormous mock yawn. "I thought I had myself well in hand, but I collect it is not so. My apologies. Do you mean to stay long in town?" Sir Tracy spoke lightly, rising from the sofa to take a turn about the room, thus rendering his face unreadable for a minute or so.

"You shall not distract me, Tracy. Even had I been Amalia, as you so obviously expected I must be, I see that as no reason for entering a room looking as though you were bent upon murder. Come now, has Amalia been quizzing you, or you her? Richard particularly asked me to question you while I was in town, and while I put no great faith in my son's judgments as a rule, I felt it was only wise to see whether there was some bad feeling between you two."

"I hesitate to speak ill of anyone, ma'am, least of all my cousin's wife—"

"Fustian! I have heard you speak quite savagely of many people, the least of whom was Amalia. What has she been bothering you with?" Lady Boskingram rearranged her skirts, tucked a cushion more comfortably around her, and assumed such an expression of rapt and sympathetic interest that her nephew could not refrain from smiling. He dropped into a chair on the other side of the fireplace and nodded his head in surrender.

"All right, Aunt Peg. I should know by now that you uncover all the family secrets sooner or later, and I'd as lief you know as anyone in the family. Liefer, in fact. Amalia's been matchmaking again. Every time I see her she reads me some fine lecture on my duty to the family and the eminent superiority and suitability of some chit she's uncovered, God alone knows where, and then, damme if she doesn't sit back and wait for me to woo the chit in form and fulfill all expectations. She has said to me, ma'am, in a manner I could call bold-faced in anyone but Amalia, that since she and Boskingram have found what she terms *the blessed estate of matrimony* to be so satisfactory, she is determined to see me settled in the same condition of bliss. Good God, if I ever allow myself to become leg-shackled, it will never be to one of those mawkish females who prates of *the blessed estate of matrimony* as if it were some decaying plot in the country!"

After this outburst Sir Tracy settled even further into his chair and attempted to regain his composure, allowing the dowager the safety to speak.

"Truly, my dear, there is nothing so terribly odious

about marriage. I myself have been married, which I consider most fortunate, since elsewise I should have had all Boskingram's children illegitimately, which does not increase one's social consequence one jot." Sir Tracy let out a delighted gurgle of laughter and reached forward to take her hand. "Aunt Peg, if there is another woman like you in the world, which I by no means believe, I might consider having some legitimate children myself."

"Have you any by-blows, Tracy?" Lady Boskingram asked curiously.

"None that I am aware of, madam," he said wickedly. "But at any rate, I do not feel at present any pressing need to secure my immortality at the expense of my freedom. I cannot see that I am at all called upon to present an heir to the world. Since Amalia has been so obliging as to secure the title for Boskingram's offspring to the tune of three heirs, that makes me fourth in line, and frankly I cannot feel at present that it would be any service to add another to the line of prospective heirs to the earldom. I think Amalia might let me go to the devil in my own way and content herself with matchmaking her own boys when they are grown."

"But only think, Tracy, Charles is seven, Frederick but five, and George barely out of leading strings. So, long must Amalia wait until even one of them becomes eligible for her matchmaking talents. You are a godsend to her. Let her content herself just now with this unfruitful pastime—it will not last long, I am sure, for I believe that Amalia is increasing *again*. By and by, love, even if you were hanging out for a wife, which you have made it abundantly clear you are not, you would certainly frighten off most prospects with that tongue of yours!" With an expressive *moue* Lady Boskingram rose stiffly from the brocade sofa and rang from Gergeley.

"You'd most certainly have my apologies, ma'am, had it not been you who taught me all those inelegant and ineligible expressions years ago. Amalia is increasing again?

Good God, married but eight years and she and my cousin already have six in the nursery. What can they be about?" The Dowager Countess of Boskingram turned a mild gaze on her nephew and raised one eyebrow expressively. The entrance of Gergeley forced him to compose himself under his aunt's ruthlessly amused eyes.

"Gergeley, I find I am shockingly famished. Will you see if there is any way that dinner might be moved up just a trifle earlier tonight? I am so rusticated of late that I fear we keep positively vicarage hours in the country."

"My lady, supposing this must be the case and that Sir Tracy would find himself hungrier than usual due to his—er—exertions, I requested Cook to have the meal ready earlier than usual." Although Gergeley's face remained impassive, his manner suggested that he considered this a master stroke. Lady Boskingram was sharp enough to give credit its due and ingratiate herself with the butler.

"Gergeley, you are a prize above rubies. Perhaps you might be so kind as to bring me a bit of sherry as well, for it has been a long day, and I think I need fortification."

Gergeley withdrew to return some minutes later with a decanter and glasses.

"This was an excellent notion, Aunt. I own that Gergeley was right as well. I am devilishly sharp set tonight, obviously due to what he calls my exertions. You have piqued my curiosity now, you know, for I shall probably go to my grave wondering who it was riding in that chaise."

"Like as not you'll know tomorrow, when the aggrieved occupants arrive and lay claims against you. Probably some tradesman's fat wife returning from the spas," retorted Lady Boskingram cheerfully.

"In any case, I won. It seemed a great deal more amusing to reach Quinlan's seat, return to London, and collect the fruits of my labor amid general rejoicing than to stop and minister to my victims, as you so obligingly designate them. I suppose I shall be haunted forever by the question of who it was I ditched." He yawned theatrically and passed a glass to Lady Boskingram.

"You have piqued *my* curiosity, Tracy. What is it that Amalia has been throwing at your head to make you so shy of women? I should have heard rumors had you started some great flirtation. I do hear these things, you know."

"I am firmly convinced that your spy network is even more effective than Bonaparte's. Amalia does not go in for perseverance; when she sees that I have no interest in one female, she procures another nearly identical in insipidity and narrowness, but fortunately, somewhat different from her predecessor in looks. That way I am afforded at least a changing prospect. I have toyed with the thought that perhaps Amalia keeps a store of eligible young women in the cellar against a surprise visit by me. She works on the principle, you see, that if she bombards me with hapless females, sooner or later I shall capitulate out of sheer weariness."

"I cannot believe that Richard would permit her to keep them in the cellar, dearest—they would knock his port and claret about shockingly, I am sure. When was the last instance of this bombardment? Surely the last time you were at Bosk the notice was far too short for her to procure anyone eligible, unless she truly had hidden someone in the cellar. What is wrong with these girls, outside of their insipidity and narrowness?" Lady Boskingram eyed her impatient nephew suspiciously as he shifted in his chair.

"Why should I shackle myself to some female I can barely countenance? All these chits are well enough to look at, educated, as they call it, and accomplished. (Lord, ma'am, but you've no idea how tired I am of accomplished females!) But not one of them has a jot of, well, let us say, your wit or charm, ma'am."

The sally and the flirtatious grin that accompanied it were unsuccessful: Lady Boskingram was not to be sidetracked. Tracy began again. "As long as I've a comfortable establishment and some good friends—"

"Among the muslin set?" Lady Boskingram suggested cheerfully.

"Friends with whom I can while away an idle hour," Sir Tracy finished quellingly. "As long as my situation is comfortable, why should I change for the stormy seas of matrimony? I have hardly seen so many enviable marriages that I should wish to emulate any of them with the first straw-witted chit who catches my eye. I will thank Amalia to keep her plans to herself."

Lady Boskingram shuddered slightly. "I hope you do not believe that all women are either straw-witted or straw damsels, dear," she murmured quietly. After a moment he looked up and smiled, the frown gone from his face, even from his shaded eyes.

"I shall suggest to dear Amalia that she curtail her efforts to find you a bride," his aunt continued and was again rewarded by that beaming smile. They were silent for a moment, and Lady Boskingram took the opportunity to observe her nephew as he sat, his brow lined again in abstraction. One carefully placed lock had come forward at the side of his face, disturbing the strict disorder of the *coup de vent* style, but adding rather more authenticity to it. Tracy's gray eyes were hooded at present by the slouch of expressive brows, and there was a mocking turn to his mouth. Striking, but not handsome, Lady Boskingram thought. And so like his mother—and her own husband. Not handsome in the way her son Richard was, but with a great deal more character and, she thought, more kindness and sweetness than was ever seen by ordinary acquaintances. She sighed briefly, and the sound served to remind Sir Tracy that he had a guest with him.

"But, Aunt Peg, you are still a mystery to me. You

have not yet explained why you have done my house the honor of this visit. Not that I am not delighted, but I must confess myself vulgarly curious. Have the Bosk tenants rebelled and turned you from the Dower House?"

"Tracy, after the dreadful happenings in France the last few years, I wonder you can speak in such a fashion!" His aunt was indignant.

"I have regaled you for quite half an hour with my trials. The only fair thing is for you to satisfy me with yours."

"Not trials, and so uninteresting—at least not so interesting as your reasons for avoiding Amalia, a project which on the whole I find myself approving, although I am sure it is scandalous in me to say so. No! It is simply that I have decided to attend some of the parties being given by some of my old friends for their own daughters, and—oh, mercy—their granddaughters. And since I was to be here, Amalia asked me to oversee the renovation of Bosk House, for she is not up to the exertion. It would be too dreadful to sleep amid all that paint and new paper, let alone to be awakened at dawn by the footsteps of workmen shuffling about under the window. So here I am settled upon you. I do not mean to be a charge on you, dear, nor to let you change your 'situation' one bit, so please treat your house as if it were your house. My only request is that when you hold your debauches you will warn me in advance, so that I may retire early and be out of the way."

"I am sure we shall deal admirably, ma'am." Sir Tracy took her hand, bent over it, and, as at this moment Gergeley arrived to announce the serving of dinner, tucked her hand under his arm and led her toward the dining room, making polite inquiries as to the nature of the renovations to be done at his cousin's town house.

After they had dined, Lady Boskingram excused herself and retired. Although Sir Tracy himself was feeling rather fatigued, he knew that it behooved him, on the evening of his triumph, to go abroad among his fellows and receive their congratulations, and to prove, of course, that he was none the worse for his day's work: that he was not as tired, in fact, as he knew himself to be. In consequence, he remained out far longer than he had intended, drank a trifle more than he should, lost one hundred guineas at one table, and made up the loss in double at another.

When at last he returned to Cavendish Street, it was nearer the morning than the night, and he sent his yawning valet off to bed, preferring to fend for himself than keep the man up. The process of disrobing was somewhat slower than usual, with no extra hands to pull off the hessians, and his own hands somewhat clumsy with fatigue and drink.

As he undressed, he thought of his aunt's comments at dinner and in the Green Saloon, and chuckled slightly at the sole of the boot he was just removing. His last thoughts before he was overcome by sleep were not for his luck at gaming, or even, really, for his wager. I suppose I shall never know who it was in that chaise, he thought, and was instantly asleep.

Chapter Three

Lady Bevan, suppressing a natural impatience to get at her project, allowed her sister to sleep the clock round and longer, so that it was not until the next afternoon that they ventured out in Lady Bevan's barouche toward Bond Street. After a good deal of sleep and an excellent nuncheon, Miss Ervine was in great spirits and looked, as

far as might be possible considering the necessary deficiencies of her toilette, very handsome. Regrettably there
had been no other dress to be found within the house at
Grosvenor Square that would come near to fitting Miss
Ervine, all the maids being too small or of an amplitude
that would have swamped her in folds of bombazine.
Despite the dismal quality of her wardrobe, Althea was
pleased to be abroad, taking the liveliest interest in all
that she could see around her, and enjoying, as she told
her sister, a most blessed sense of freedom from dear
Papa.

"What a scandalous thing to say, Ally. You must take
care now you are in my charge, for offending the proprieties I will not have. And do try to look around a little less
obviously, dearest. I know that London is very busy after
a town like Hooking, but everyone must think you are
some country bumpkin gawking at the sights, and if
you've no care for your own standing with the *ton*, have a
little care for mine! I am known never to have anyone
driving with me who is not of the first stare!"

"How boring that must be for you, Mary," her sister
said amiably, as she continued to gawk.

"And please contrive not to—oh, I don't know what it
is, but you do look so very large," Lady Bevan said
despairingly. "The fashion is to be small and delicate and
fragile, and you sit there looking as though you were a
housekeeper. It is of all things too bad."

"I truly cannot help my size, Sister. Perhaps you could
give up your idea of fashionable life for me and find me
some comfortable position where I can look as practical
and as *large* as I want."

"Now, Ally, don't be difficult. It is only that I cannot
see how we are to convince some man that he wants to
take care of you all your life when you look as though
you will be taking care of him. No, that's not quite right
either." Lady Bevan looked at her healthy sister in dismay. "In any event, Ally, contrive to slouch a little. Out

in public there is no reason for you to sit as though Miss Brandywine still had the broomstick tied to your back!"

At this memory both sisters dissolved into giggles, for Althea's deportment had been the despair of their governess, and it was only from merest kindness that Althea had finally given in and learned the schoolroom manners Miss Brandywine considered eligible.

"Just you wait, though, Ally, for when Madame Helena sees you she will know just how to treat you to make you perfect. She's a miracle who walks, although she is frightfully dear. I know that between the two of us we shall come upon something in short order." Althea found herself the subject of her sister's intense scrutiny, with which evaluative stare she was becoming very familiar.

"If I cannot go as a housekeeper, perhaps you had better let me start a vogue for tall country bumpkins. I do not intend to be made into a schoolroom miss at my age, Mary, so remember it. And in the meantime, whatever is that edifice?"

Having successfully distracted her sister's attention from herself, Althea spent the next few minutes quizzing Maria about the city and was stunned to find that her ladyship knew less than Althea herself about certain of the sights.

"I for one confess myself vulgarly curious about the city, and I shall think you to be the meanest creature on earth if you don't allow me some time to go about openmouthed and gaping at the Tower and the Houses of Parliament. As for the rest, I think the only thing for it is to start a vogue for dark ladies of height, for I'm too tall by far ever to learn to be a swooning maiden. And I fear that if ever I should faint away, I should carry some hapless bystander with me, and think how embarrassing that would be. If I find some man willing to marry me, Sister, I can only hope that he will not expect such a one as you detail, for that I shall never be."

"Althea!" Lady Bevan said in tones of the greatest horror. "You are not going to be strong-minded, are you? That would be too much! I beg you will not speak so before anyone else in London but me, and I hope you will not talk so even then, for I consider it excessively unbecoming. I have the most uncomfortable feeling you mean to be a fractious pupil, and I will brook no disobedience from you. But listen: I cannot think that Madame will have any but a very few garments ready within the next few days, if she takes you on as a customer, which she certainly will. So in that time I shall let you have your fill of London—it will be a fortnight before you are fitted out decently—and I will contrive to give you some notion of what you must expect in London Society. No, don't look rebellious at me. I may be a widgeon, as Papa says, but I know what's what in town, and you do not. Why, you might"—Lady Bevan paused to consider a social crime of dire consequence—"you might dance the waltz at Almack's before you had leave, or ride down St. James, or do any manner of terrible things."

"Better give me no leave to waltz at all, Mary, for I'm shocking bad at it and have had no practice since Miss Brandywine made us dance around the nursery in the arms of the rocking chair."

By the time this image and the other amusing remembrances it evoked had been duly examined, the barouche had drawn up to the door of Madame Helena's shop. And at that, Althea, having promised to behave herself in a decorous fashion, preceded her sister out of the carriage, and together they entered the shop.

Madame Helena herself emerged from the back rooms to greet the young Lady Bevan and her guest. Though Lady Bevan had a sizable unpaid bill to her credit, Madame was confident of eventual payment—whether from the lady herself or from her irate husband, Madame neither knew nor cared. She had a good eye for clothing and a genius for recognizing those garments and styles that brought out the best in her customers. Tiny and ro-

tund and sharp-eyed, Madame spoke her English with a
heavy French accent and muttered fluently to herself in
that language, but for all that she had been born in
Cheapside. Her success was due to the kind offices of a
former admirer who, at the end of their connection, had
given her the shop as a parting gift. Madame had made it
prosper, until it was said that she had as much to do with
making or breaking a young belle as Mr. Brummell or any
of his set.

Very conscious of this power, Madame Helena now
designed only for a very few, leaving the rest to her as-
sistants. It was only when her curiosity—or her rage—
was roused that Madame could be prevailed upon to
oversee a wardrobe personally.

One dowager had gone so far as to cross Madame, and
in retaliation, Madame had created for her a new ball
gown in the sublime shades of lime and chocolate, the
fold, flounces, and ribbons of which were designed to
show the Honorable Mrs. Laverham to the worst advantage. It was hard to believe that Mrs. Laverham did
not know the figure she presented when she wore that
gown, but she wore it frequently and even went so far as
to solicit compliments upon her toilette for the sheer joy
of explaining that it had been designed for her by Helena.
Madame's immense power could only be exposed by this,
so that both women were very happy at the transaction.

Althea was duly introduced to Madame, who abruptly
set her to walking about the room, then running, then
dancing. With a pair of scissors that hung about her waist,
Madame snipped off a lock of Althea's dark hair and
noted the color of the lady's eyes as gray. Maria, made
nervous by Madame's august presence, began to chatter
about white and pink and a girl's come-out; but one
glance from over the rims of Madame's pince-nez quelled
her. Madame condescended to give her opinion: no
whites or pastels or any furbelows suitable for debutantes.

"Mademoiselle is not in the common way, and it would

do her, and my toilettes, a disservice to dress her so." Althea made a face at Maria. "Mademoiselle will stand above the milk-and-water misses! I shall make her the storm of the town!" Upon which Gallic declaration of war, Madame shrugged, gave orders regarding fittings to the seamstress at her elbow, and stalked off.

Althea, as she was measured, made an effort to suppress her merriment at the spectacle of Madame, so tiny and plump, prepared to tackle all of the *ton* in order to make her new protégée the rage. The storm of the town, indeed! Maria was not so amused and begged her sister to smother her mirth, lest Madame become incensed and do something dreadful in retaliation—and then bill them for her revenge. Althea managed to control her amusement for the quarter-hour that the fitting lasted and then, safely in the barouche, gave vent to the fullness of her amusement.

"It appears that I must reconcile myself to becoming a diamond of the first water if you and Madame must have it so. Poor Papa little knew what a service he did me when he cast me on the mercy of the parish—and my competance." Lady Bevan eyed her sister wrathfully for a moment, but the wrath turned to inspiration, and Althea experienced a very low feeling at the look in her sister's eye.

"The very thing! We shall hire you a dancing master!"

"No such thing! I will, if I must, stand above the milk-and-water misses, although I think that to be a singularly ill chosen simile to apply to one of my height, but I will not consent to being led around the drawing room by some smirking fellow used to dealing with children half my age."

Lady Bevan could not answer this sally as she would have liked, for the carriage had now arrived at the door of her favorite milliner, and the conflict that seemed imminent would have to wait upon the delights of straw satin bonnets and ostrich feather festoons. The subject of a dancing master did not recur, for they were in and out of shops and stalls for the rest of the afternoon, inquiring after ribbons, shawls, fans, vinaigrettes, reticules, and slippers—all of which must accompany the toilette of any pretender to fashion. When at last, having exhausted the resources of the Pantheon Bazaar, Lady Bevan and Miss Ervine climbed into the barouche for the journey homeward, they both seemed to feel that the less said about the dancing master the better, so the subject was scrupulously avoided.

"Did your Madame say when I might have some replacement for this sad rag I wear now? If she delays much above a week I shall start to sewing myself."

"A week? Ally, you are in London, not Hooking. Madame's assistant said we might have the first morning gowns and the rose round gown within three days. She said that she could well understand our impatience to rid you of those garments. And I for one am not about to jeopardize my standing with the *ton* by driving out with you before you have something suitable to wear, so that means that for three days at least I am entitled to keep you locked up to consider your sins."

Althea would only smile and agree that this must be a very good idea indeed. It was almost the hour of five when they returned, and Maria said with a sigh that she feared she must miss her afternoon drive in the Park. Althea asked, in some confusion, how her sister could talk about driving out when they had only just returned.

"No, stupid! This is the social drive. All the world is out in the Park between four and six, but today I fear I could never be ready to drive before six, and that would not serve at all. So I must forget it, obviously." She sighed in heavy tones of self-sacrifice. Instead of driving out, they decided that a restorative glass of ratafia might be in order and repaired to the drawing room, where they discovered Lord Francis Bevan sitting at an escritoire, studiously not writing letters. When he saw them he dropped

his pen with a sigh of relief and rose to greet them. He
had an airy, casual kiss for his wife, and then he stood for
a moment and took in Althea's appearance. Althea,
hoping he would not start surveying her with that same
evaluative air Maria used, availed herself of the opportunity to examine Francis.

She had liked her pleasant brother-in-law from their
first acquaintance, the more because of his undisguised affection for Maria. He was slight and fair, had aristocratic
bones, and possessed a sweetness of temper and a not
overly clever mind. Althea was surprised to see that in
matters of dress, he had changed a great deal from the
man she had known on his visits to Hook Well, and she
concluded that in the country he had been dressing to suit
country notions of propriety. In London, while his dress
was really no more flamboyant (and indeed rather less
so) than that of most of the beaux she had seen from the
barouche that afternoon, it did display a marked tendency
toward dandyism. His collar points, although uncomfortably high, did not entirely impede the motion of his head,
and the shoulders of his coat, though padded, were only
of a moderate height. He wore only three fobs, which Althea had come to realize was a show of great restraint.
And if his hands could have done with some small attention from soap and water, his neckcloth showed not a sign
of having been tied by those smudged fingers.

"Ally! Good to see you here. Cheer Mary up like nothing else—loves to have you about, and damme if I don't
too. Letter for you and Mary upon the table. Must be
from your father, unless you've advised some others of
your arrival? Must be all done up if what Maria's been
telling me of your leaving is true." Althea frowned slightly
at her brother-in-law's foppish drawl. That, too, had
changed since his visit to Hook Well.

"I vow *I* am quite done up by this magnificence, Francis, for I think in Lancashire you were never used to ex-
hibit your full plumage. I am awed by your splendor."

She received his kiss on her cheek and stood for a moment smiling at him. Despite the foppery there was much to like in him. Althea resolved that if there was any trouble between her sister and brother-in-law, she would be the one to mend it.

"Althea, only come and read this letter!" Lady Bevan, her bonnet only half untied, stood staring at a letter with an expression that defied rational description. "Only look at this!" With a squeak that boded hysterics, Maria sank into the nearest chair, holding the offending notepaper at arm's length. "Althea, how ever came I to be your sister—or rather you mine, since I am the older, and you the last? But whatever have you done to poor Papa? Oh dear, I mean, did he do to—" Maria went into a fit of weak giggling while her sister rescued the letter from her clutch and spoke with some asperity to the deranged Maria.

"Maria, it is bad enough that I sit here in all stages of disarray, but the *ton* will know that the last trump has surely blown if Lady Maria Bevan sits about in such a sad case, waving her bonnet like a flag of truce!" Lady Bevan instantly snatched the offensive bonnet from its precarious position, while her sister sat and began to peruse the note. It was couched, as she knew it must be, in the most purple of prose, with a great many references to Christian Charity, Filial Duty, Forgiveness, and such like terms, but despite the volume of words squeezed in a tight hand upon the sheet of paper, there was remarkably little sense to be made of it.

It was some minutes after she had finished reading the letter before Althea could sufficiently recover her countenance, and then her thoughts were for her unfortunate maid, Miss Banders, who had been left behind to the storm in the wake of Althea's defection.

"Poor Banders! I infer from Papa's scrawling that she has been packed off to Suffolk to be a charge upon her father until I repent my sins and return to the fold. I shall have to send for her immediately. But only think, Maria, what sort of odious tasks you can set me to that might bring me to a full sense of my perfidy. Peeling onions in the scullery? Oh dear, a Viper in his Bosom! What a letter for Papa to write—the house must be completely beyond his management if he is so angered, and I only gone a few days."

In the following week Althea found herself under a more rigorous tutelage than any she had enjoyed in the schoolroom at Hook Well. She learned the rules of Almack's Assembly until she maintained that she could, and did, repeat them in her sleep. Maria's only sally was to inquire as to how her sister could know whether or not she did so, since she must be sleeping at the time. Over Althea's protests, a dancing master was found, and she began to relearn the arts of the quadrille, the country dance, and the waltz—this time without benefit of the chair.

"It is so very different when you are dancing with a real person rather than with that horrible chair. But then, the chair does not use oil of lavender pomade on its hair, which Signore Francesco regrettably does."

Although Althea justly maintained that she needed no schoolroom lessons in manners, she received them will-or-nil-she, and discovered what Maria called manners she would have labeled flirtation.

"For one thing, you must not laugh all the time. Some tender gentleman will believe you laugh at him, and who will offer marriage if he thinks to be made a guy of all his life—by his wife! A gentle laugh is very becoming, but you take such a pleasure in it, it is positively unladylike!"

And every day there were fittings and more fittings, until Althea's shoulders ached and she felt like a puppet jerked for the amusement of Maria and the indefatigable Madame Helena. Francis was likely to stroll in now and then to approve a new dress or take a turn with her while the dancing master yapped shrill instructions at her, but

Althea noticed that most of the time he was from the house, and she wondered if it was her presence that kept him away.

"Never heard such a deuced silly idea. Maria doesn't much like my hanging about, so I stay busy. There's Jackson's and Tat's, Manton's Gallery, Cribb's Parlour, the clubs—any number of places ready to entertain a fellow with some blunt to sport. Bought a stunning pair of matched bays last week. Prime blood. Like to ride, Ally? If you do, we can mount you and you can go out with one of the grooms. Mary doesn't care much to ride, but once you know some folk, there ought to be plenty of people who'll want to ride with you."

Althea smiled at this gentle compliment and would dearly have loved to take him up on his offer of a mount immediately, but to ride, one must have a habit. She suppressed her longing for one good wild gallop and submitted again to the hands of the dressmakers. It seemed as though she must escape to Hooking if she was ever to be allowed a moment's peace. But from what Althea had heard from Miss Banders, newly arrived from Suffolk, even at home she was not likely to find much peace. And despite Maria's halfhearted attempts on two occasions to satisfy her sister's curiosity as to the sights of London, Althea sighed and pined to see more. Maria threw up her hands and told her sister she would be taken for a country nobody, to which Althea replied that that was exactly what she was.

And still the fittings continued.

Lady Bevan arrived at her sister's door one morning, at such an unusual hour that Althea was still abed.

"What in heaven's name can you be at, abroad at this hour, Maria? I've not known you to rise so early since we all had the chicken pox, and that was all of fifteen years ago."

"Wretch! What an odious thing to remind me of, especially when I've come a-purpose to give you such good news." She held out a sheet of notepaper, but before Althea could begin to decipher the tiny scrabbled script, the paper was snatched away as Maria executed a neat waltz around the end of the bed. After another moment of dancing under Althea's sleepy but cheerful gaze, Maria came to a halt and said impatiently, "Goose! It is from dear, *kind* Lady Sefton herself, who has promised as a favor to me to procure for you a voucher to Almack's. It is of all things most fortunate that she should, for I am not wholly in charity with Sally Jersey just now, and the Countess Lieven is from town." She began her dance again. "Only behave as I have taught you to, and I shall be most proud."

"Maria, do you remember that you a speaking to a woman of three and twenty years, and not some schoolroom chit of seventeen? You sound as though I cannot be trusted out without Miss Brandywine! But I promise faithfully that I shall not arrive after eleven, dance until I have been presented, waltz until I am given permission, nor wear pantaloons in favor of breeches! See now, how well I have learned the codes of Almack's!"

"Pantaloons! Oh, Ally, do not dare to say such a thing at Almack's or anywhere else in company. I shall die!" cried the tormented Lady Bevan in despair. But she did settle herself at the foot of Althea's bed and begin to plan.

The following night was to mark Althea's first appearance among the *ton*, and Maria was full of dresses and Norwich silk shawls, jewels and Valenciennes veiling, and how best to wear one's hair. As she gabbled on happily, she was caught up by a thought of such apparent force that for a moment it appeared to have rendered her speechless.

"Althea, we have done nothing about your hair! We must have Philippe here immediately, for it is not something that can be done at the last minute. You must sleep upon it at least one night before going out in public, and

Banders must be taught to dress it between times. Oh lord, if only he will consent to come here as a favor to me!" Maria rang sharply and gave Banders orders to send the redoubtable Debbens in search of Monsieur Philippe, to entreat him to come at once, as a favor to Lady Bevan.

Some three hours later Monsieur Philippe and his small retinue arrived, and Althea was whisked from the arms and metronome of the energetic Signore Francesco and removed upstairs to Lady Bevan's dressing room to be abandoned to the hairdresser's hands for the better part of the afternoon. When at last he had departed, Althea had to admit that the transformation was quite astonishing. Her front hair had been clipped and curled to frame her large, steady gray eyes, while her back hair had been trimmed and swept up and carefully confined within a series of ribbons. "I hope you recall how all this was done," she said to Banders, who had spent an exhausting half-hour with the maestro, learning the styling of hair in the classical mode.

"I look like a figure from a Grecian urn," Althea said to Maria.

"Well, of course, as that style is called the Sappho, and I think that she must have been a Greek—Ally, whatever have I said to send you into such gales?" Lady Bevan was bewildered.

"Mary, I begin to feel that my education must be the death of me, but when you scold me for saying something as innocuous as 'pantaloons' and then tell me that this styling is called Sappho, I feel that it is just too unjust!" She gurgled with laughter. "Yes, my dear, the lady was a Greek, and a most improper one at that, and a lady author to boot! I was much given to reading at Hook Well, for indeed what else had I to do? And I came across some of her writings. I only thank God that Papa never came across *that*. No, dear, I've finished laughing, I think." Maria could only offer up a silent prayer that her sister would not alienate any possible suitors by laughing at improper Greek tales.

"Really, Ally, you must not appear a bluestocking. It would be the outside of too much after all the work I've done on you. You look quite ravishing as you are, and I am no end pleased with the way you have turned up."

"Of course, Pygmalion, how could you feel else? You and Madame have done nothing but predict my success from my arrival in town. I only wish that Helena could witness my triumphant entrance at the Ffyordings' ball tomorrow night. But was I really the rude barbarian you called me?" Althea's voice dropped a little on this last, for to be truthful, at times she reflected upon what had been so very ineligible about her former appearance and manners, that Maria had made all these efforts to change them. Maria assured her sister that she was her own dear Ally and quite wonderful. She, Maria, had only added the town polish to make her perfect.

"Even without Madame and Philippe and Francesco, you are something like, and besides that, you are the dearest sister in the world. Now, shall we consider your slippers?" With a decidedly businesslike air that was most becoming, Maria turned her attention to the matter of dress again, and of course Althea's attention must follow.

When the next evening at seven o'clock Maria knocked upon her sister's door, Althea was fully dressed and only wanted a decision as to which scarf to carry.

Maria silently owned herself remarkably pleased with Althea's appearance. While her sister's new style was not much to her own taste, it was decidedly becoming on Althea. Out of the common way. Althea wore an evening dress of cherry silk muslin over a slip of gray satin, sashed with gray ribbons and beaded at the hem with tiny crystal shots. The bright cherry of the dress brought out Althea's clear coloring, reddened her lips, and was a foil for the dark hair worn in its fashionable style. At her throat and ears were her mother's pearls, and on her wrist a set of silver bangles Francis had presented her that afternoon. Upon the dressing table lay a posy of flowers in a wonderfully wrought ebony holder, and spread across the bed was a profusion of silk and lace shawls and scarves that Althea surveyed with indecision.

"I think this is the best, do you not?" She held up a simple scarf of white silk. "Though I did consider the black lace mantilla."

"No, Ally, that is just right. You are a very picture! You *shall* stand over the milk-and-water misses *and* take the town by storm! Madame was quite right," Maria said with satisfaction and a little surprise. Busy with her own images of Althea as a debutante, she had never understood that Madame had been quite correct in dressing her differently from the schoolroom misses who flocked to assemblies in the shadows of their mamas. Althea was in no one's shadow.

"Well, Mary, have you not said I should all along?" Althea asked comfortably. "You look quite becoming yourself. That blue and white suits you admirably. What a pair we shall make of it: the Amazon and the Fairy Princess. Very like a sprite you look, too." With this exchange of compliments and another glance in the mirror for each, they left the chamber and descended to the drawing room.

Lord Bevan was awaiting them, and his reaction to their appearance was gratifying indeed.

"Here, you look grand out of all mention, Ally. Scarcely dare talk to you." He bowed in her direction.

Althea fell back a pace. "Oh, you'd do better to talk to my sister, sir. She's far better at your town talk than I." She slipped by him as he advanced to greet his wife and went to the bookshelf, occupying herself with the titles there.

"Looking devilish pretty tonight, Mary. Don't know why I haven't seen you in that dress before. I'll have the

best-looking wife at the ball." He bent his head attentively
and Maria, seemingly overwhelmed by this attention, for-
cused her gaze on the third button of her husband's coat.

"I cannot think why you have missed this rag, sir, for it
is quite an antique. But I suppose we so rarely go to the
same parties, and now, with Althea here, and—" Her
voice trailed off, and Lady Bevan found herself blushing
like a nursery chit.

"Must begin to frequent the same parties, then. Can't
have some other fellow dashing off with the most beautiful woman in London when she's my wife." Francis's
voice grew lower, his head dropped still more toward his
wife's, and there was no telling what scene might have
been enacted had not Debbens entered at precisely that
moment to announce the serving of dinner.

Maria and Francis looked up and realized that Althea
was still behind them, tactfully engrossed in a Latin gram-
mar. Maria was pale, Francis was flushed, but both were
in excellent spirits when he offered his arms to sister-in-
law and wife and the three went in to dinner.

Chapter Four

With an experience limited to the neighborhood of Hooking, Althea was totally unprepared for the rather vulgar
and very expensive furnishings of Fforyding House, and
for the very vulgar and rather expensive furnishings of the
Dowager Baroness Fforyding herself. She had followed
the classical mode in her decoration of both herself and
her house, and while the house withstood the treatment

tolerably, no one would say that Lady Fforyding had been so fortunate. This evening her ladyship wore a gown of yellow silk calculated to be trying to a woman ten years younger, considerably slimmer, and with a far better complexion. The toilette, completed as it was by a topaz set and knots of yellow and white ribbons, had the effect of making Matilda Fforyding look like a particularly ornate mushroom. Fortunately the lady was blithely unaware of this, and she *did* give excellent parties to which all the *ton* came. It was fortunate that Althea was to make her curtsy to Polite Society in those grossly overdecorated hallways.

After they had been kindly welcomed by their hostess and her oldest son, Lord William Fforyding, a plump and somewhat somnolent young man in the regimentals of the King's Guard, the Bevan party advanced into the hall. Maria and Francis were still mightily absorbed in each other, so that Althea was afforded an opportunity to gape at her surroundings without reproach. The main ballroom had been draped entirely in pink silk, the effect of which—though pretty—was to increase the normally warm atmosphere of a ballroom to hothouse proportions. By the end of the evening Althea suspected that most of the people present would be done in more surely by the heat than by the dancing or the ratafia punch. Lady Fforyding had added a few mock Grecian statuettes to the great room, cunningly draped in pink silk for the sake of modesty. In the arms of one marble nymph was a huge and wholly inappropriate spray of hothouse flowers. Althea rather liked the gesture, for it showed to her a rather whimsical mind. Turning from her perusal of the hall, she found her sister and brother-in-law still enthralled with each other. But as they stood directly in the doorway, blocking those coming to and from the room, she felt that they must be moved from harm's way—and said so.

At the sound of her voice, both Maria and Francis started guiltily. Maria recalled to herself as they moved across the room that she was here as chaperone to Al-

thea, with the result that she began, with Francis's inter-
jecting helpful words, to indicate notables present. Their
progress was halted by their hostess soon enough, as she
advanced upon them with a young man following close behind her.

"Miss Ervine, I hope you enjoy our little fete." Althea
owned herself privately amazed that a woman of Lady
Fforyding's imposing size and mien could contrive to appear so coy, but allowed that she was indeed enjoying
herself.

"But I should never call it a *little* fete, ma'am. Quite
the contrary. Of course I am but lately come to town and
so must be held unaccountable for these things." This answer apparently found favor with Lady Fforyding, who
drew the young man at her elbow forward. He was of sober mien, with that haunted look common to young men
wearing a dress suit for the first time. It occurred to Althea after a moment that perhaps he was not so much sober as shy, and this supposition was borne out when Lady
Fforyding spoke—for he blushed, painfully, from his collar points to the roots of his hair.

"Miss Ervine, may I present Mr. Jonathan Tidd to you
as a most desirable dancing partner? Mr. Tidd, Miss Ervine is but lately come to town, so surely you can entertain
her with an account of the doings here." As Mr. Tidd had
been standing not three feet away when Lady Fforyding
had learned this bit of information, Althea could not but
feel its redundancy a trifle foolish. But she smiled and
gave a pretty dip. Mr. Tidd bowed, struggled to say something about the honor Miss Ervine did him, and as he led
her out where sets were forming for the quadrille, fell into
an impenetrable silence. Althea made one or two attempts
to break that silence but then, realizing that he was taken
up with the steps of the *pas de zephyr*, gave up the project. She was quite startled when he finally spoke. She was,
in fact, forced to ask him to repeat what he had said.

"I am so sorry." He blushed vividly. "I only asked if you were well acquainted with the Fforydings."

"I am afraid I have only met the Baroness and Lord Fforyding this very evening. Are there more in the family?" Now that her partner had begun to speak, Althea did not intend to let him lapse into silence again. If a discussion of the Fforydings' genealogy would spark his interest, she was just as willing to listen to that as any other topic of polite conversation she felt him able to introduce.

"There are three younger sons and two daughters." Again that ferocious blush spread to his hairline and receded. Althea, fearing his retreat into silence, prodded him on, asking for specifics. "There are Giles and Miles, who are at Harrow, and young Frederick, who is, I believe, in the schoolroom still, with the younger Miss Fforyding, Miss Alice. There is also Miss Sophia." The blush reappeared, so vividly that Althea feared for her partner's health. After a moment, however, he appeared to control his evident fervor.

"I collect, then, that Miss Sophia Fforyding is present this evening? I feel that it would certainly behoove me to make her acquaintance," Althea said kindly. "I know next to no one in London, and indeed I am very eager to meet people. Perhaps you will be so kind as to introduce me to her, Mr. Tidd?" Althea was rewarded for this bit of tact by another of Mr. Tidd's blushes and a look of gratification. He all but pulled Miss Ervine out of the set, casting an eager eye throughout the crowd.

"I see her, just over there beside the columns." Althea's attention was turned to a passably pretty, very young girl dressed in white, conversing with a tall gentleman, next to one of those cunning pillars that were proving a sore hazard to enthusiastic dancers that evening. The Honorable Miss Fforyding, Althea realized, was one of Madame Helena's milk-and-water misses, over whom she would certainly tower, literally if not metaphorically.

Mr. Tidd did not seem to think that Miss Fforyding was anything but the pattern of perfection; he began to shoulder his way through the crowd with a mixture of determination and self-effacement that Althea, trailing behind him, found quite droll. When at last they reached Miss Fforyding and her partner, Althea let a sigh of relief escape, for in their dash across the floor she had been in constant terror that Mr. Tidd would step through her flounced hem.

For her part, Sophia cast a shy look of delight at Mr. Tidd, and a glance of admiration and awe at Miss Ervine, who observed the girl in friendly fashion. Sophia, Althea noted, did not share her mother's love of the unsuitable, and, aside from one beaded knot at her waist, was almost elegant in her dress. She had been conversing with a very tall gentleman some years older than herself, but when Miss Ervine and Mr. Tidd arrived, all conversation ended. Both Mr. Tidd and Miss Fforyding lapsed into silence and *blushed*. To Althea's intense relief, the tall gentleman very politely drawled, "Well, Tidd, are you going to present your partner to us?" Again Mr. Tidd flushed and turned to Miss Fforyding with abject apology in his eye. She blushed back, and, with an air of one freed to perform a necessary chore, he began his introductions.

"Miss Irving, may I present Sir Tracy Calendar and"—with an air of royal presentation—"The Honorable Miss Sophia Fforyding." Again his blush, hers, and the two of them stood wordless and bemused by each other. Althea caught Sir Tracy's amused eye over the top of the younger girl's head.

"Perhaps, Miss Irving, you would like to sit for a few minutes? The atmosphere in this room can most kindly be referred to as stifling. Why my aunt must drape the walls with that pink stuff . . ." He gestured to a few gilt chairs set some yards from their present position and Althea followed gladly. She noted that his dress, while far less extravagant than that of Lord Bevan or even Mr. Tidd, contrived to be far more elegant in its understatement. She decidedly approved of this control of fashion, and for a change it was a distinct pleasure to meet a man she did not look virtually in the eye.

"I must apologize for my cousin and her suitor, Miss Ervine. They are extremely tiresome in each other's company, but I assure you that they have both been heard to utter entire phrases when apart."

Althea darted a glance at her companion and wondered in passing if that red head betokened irrascibility.

"I am at a loss to know how you corrected my name when Mr. Tidd was most scrupulous in his mistake of it. I suppose he has been under a cloud all evening, and did not much attend when we were introduced."

"I saw you enter with Lord and Lady Bevan and had heard that Lady Bevan's sister, a Miss Ervine, was visiting. I concluded the rest from these facts."

"You are most perspicacious, sir." She glanced back toward the spot where Mr. Tidd and his lady were still engaged in that silent, blushing perusal of each other. "I must admit that I have never seen the like of it, sir."

"What, ma'am? The ball, or my cousin's infatuation with young Tidd?"

Sir Tracy took his seat beside her, folding those extraordinarily long legs neatly beneath him around the legs of the gilt chair.

"You cannot think me so rag-mannered as to say such a thing of a ball I have scarcely arrived at yet, let alone left. I was speaking of Miss Fforyding and Mr. Tidd. Their attachment appears to be like something out of a novel, or at least that is my opinion. Of course, where I am used to live I never saw anything of that sort. London ways may be quite different. Oh, I ought not to have said that!" Miss Ervine frowned at herself, to Sir Tracy's amusement.

"Why not, ma'am? The statement seemed unexceptionable to me."

"Sir, I will not scruple to tell you that for the past fort-night my sister has been contriving to teach me to behave like a gazetted belle, and the first thing she told me was that I must at all times appear as though I had lived in London all my life. I shudder to think what she would say had she heard me just then."

"Fortunately, ma'am, she did not, and I give you my word that I shall never betray your confidence." His eyes glinted under those dark brows. Althea smiled in return. This man did not seem shocked, as Maria had assured her anyone would be, at her mention of country upbringing, and Althea could not help but like him the better for it. He did seem to be laughing just a bit at her frankness, which did not please her quite so well, but she determined not to mind his teasing.

"How long will you be in our city, ma'am?" He put the question with such consummate propriety that Althea could hardly keep a straight face, and when a lifted eyebrow assured her that she was being quizzed, she permitted herself one gurgle of sheer delight.

"I have been here but a fortnight, sir," she said in tones to mimic his. "Though I have the strangest notion that I have met you before—which I am sure cannot be possible. I must say I had hardly planned to be so amused tonight, for to hear my sister speak, everything is done with such exquisite sobriety that all that is ever required of a lady is a genteel nod once in a while."

"People do laugh in London, ma'am, but seldom with such refreshing relish as you. I'm sure all of London will do all that's possible to keep you properly amused. For my part, you may call on me at any time and I will endeavor to contrive something amusing to say. My Aunt Fforyding introduced you to young Tidd, did she? Another of her ploys to keep her daughter from him. I never saw such a pair of ninnyhammers, and I am sure they will suit each other to a nicety." He wagged an eyebrow distastefully. "But I see your sister searching for you, Miss Ervine. Allow me to return you to her."

Over Calendar's extended hand Althea glimpsed Maria glancing through the crowd in a preoccupied manner. Sir Tracy offered his arm and began to steer her expertly across the room. They continued to speak as they went, and at some point something that she said so amused him that he threw his head back and laughed—Althea thought—with considerable relish. It did not change his face in any particular but made it easier, less hard. He felt her eyes upon him and smiled, disconcertingly, down upon her. Althea, accustomed as she was to look most men directly in the eye, found that she was blushing at the straightforward look in Sir Tracy's eye, his height, and his shameless use of it.

"Don't fear, Miss Ervine, no doubt your sister would disapprove, but I am said to retain some few of the social graces." He stopped, for they had almost reached Maria's side, took her hand and led her toward Maria, bowed, smiled, and strolled off.

"Lord, Ally, you begin well! First Jonathan Tidd, who is one of the richest young men in the City—but has a grandfather somewhere in trade, more's the pity—and then Tracy Calendar, who is all but a gazetted nonpareil! Oh, and several other young gentlemen have come up and begged introductions! I swear, I am as excited as if this were my own come-out ball! Sir Tracy is one of the smartest of the Corinthian set. Francis admires him no end." At the mention of her husband, something in her ladyship's manner became a trifle subdued, and her chatter ceased momentarily.

"I have the notion that Sir Tracy is here to look after his cousin, who is quite taken up with Mr. Tidd."

"Matilda Fforyding has been trying for years to get Calendar to fix his interest upon Miss Sophia, and now she is furious that the foolish girl has fallen in love with that boy. They shall make a fine match of it, I'm sure:

the two loobies will probably blush each other to death."

Althea was surprised by her sister's suddenly embittered tone, but there was no time to say anything, for one of the young men Althea had mentioned returned for his promised introduction and to beg the favor of the next dance. Althea naturally consented, and from that point onward had no chance to search out her sister and ask her the matter of it. What appeared to her an endless procession of honorables, sirs, and my lords seemed intent upon dancing with Miss Ervine, each begging an introduction from the other, and Althea found herself unable to remember the names of many—for since most of the syllables were swallowed up in shyness or in the imprecise drawl of the Pinks, it was hard to pick out a whole name from the lot. These gentlemen seemed to understand that Miss Ervine would prefer *not* to waltz until she had made a first appearance at Almack's, and there was always someone—or two or three—to sit beside her during these dances.

As Althea had not been promised before the ball for the supper dance, she found herself in the company of a Mr. Edward Pendarly during that dance, and afterward for supper. Some time before, Althea had espied Maria, whirling, in the arms of Mr. John Wallingham, to that forbidden waltz with a determined look on her face. Consequently, knowing her sister and that look, she despaired of finding her now. It was plain enough that Francis had wandered off and Maria was bent upon demonstrating that she had no need of his escort.

This turn of affairs fretted Althea, but Mr. Pendarly, aside from being almost garishly handsome, contrived to occupy her enough so that she forgot—or at least put in abeyance—her fears for Maria and Francis. When he sat her down on the corner of a settee and went to fetch her a plate and a glass of punch, however, she did make some effort to discover her sister or her brother-in-law. That effort was quite unsuccessful.

As Mr. Pendarly was still gone, Miss Ervine continued to amuse herself by watching the people about her. At one point she caught sight of Sir Tracy Calendar, and he of her. He could not approach, as he was cornered by two elderly gentlemen apparently intent upon having Sir Tracy's opinion upon some matter of taste; but he did not refrain from raising his glass to her and smiling slightly.

Althea was not unpleased by the attention, although Sir Tracy was not exactly to her taste; he was good company and, if all Maria said was true, a very important man in the *ton*. Mr. Pendarly returned with her plate and a glass of punch, drawing Althea's attention back to himself. To her surprise she found that she was quite famished and remarked as much to Pendarly.

"It must be the exertion involved in a ball, Miss Ervine. After dancing energetically for several hours, one's appetite is naturally aroused. I hope you are pleased with what I brought. Although Lady Fforyding keeps an almost awesome table for her suppers, I tried to restrict myself to the best—or at least the most readily digestible—foods offered." He smiled pleasantly.

"I admire your discretion and your choices, Mr. Pendarly. It would surely be foolish to indulge in lobster patties this late at night. I quite shudder to consider the consequences."

"How long will you grace our city with your presence, ma'am?" The words brought back Calendar's polite parody of similar questions, and Althea again had the irritating feeling of stifling her laughter as Mr. Pendarly continued. "Can we hope to have the luck of your presence for the entire Season, ma'am? If so, I shall hope to see you often. I collect you are at your sister's house?"

"Yes, sir. I cannot say for how long I shall be staying, however, for that must depend upon the good will of my sister and her husband, but I hope to make a long visit and then be banished back to my father's home."

"If your stay depends upon your credit with Lady and

Lord Bevan, I am sure that we shall have you in London for a long while to come. How could they tire of so charming a guest?"

"Charm has no bonds for sisters, sir. Have you no sisters or brothers of your own that you would know the bounds of filial affection?" Althea, rather overwhelmed by the compliments of Mr. Pendarly, sought to turn the conversation around to him. He was a pleasant partner, quiet but not sober, and unlike most of the young men she had met, given to neither overstatement nor inarticulateness. His admiration for her he displayed quite clearly, and Althea could not help but be cheered by the attentions of such an Adonis and to wish to know more about him.

"I have one brother, ma'am, who is my elder and with whom I confess I have never been on the best of terms."

"I understand you precisely, for my sister is reckoned to be the beauty of the family, as she takes after our mother, and when we were little she was used to positively twit me with the fact that she was fair and had Mama's features, while I had not. There was a long time when all I wanted from life were guinea-gold ringlets and the family nose. I have learned I shall never have either, and you can see that it has not permanently scarred me. Surely your brother has ceased to torment you now, since you are both grown."

"Jeremy seems to think any excuse quite adequate, ma'am. But why do we discuss my family feuds when there are other topics that must be far more interesting?" He smiled at her ingratiatingly. "What do you think of our city, ma'am? It is rare to meet someone who will admit that she is not city bred—or at least bored to distraction by city sights."

"In truth, sir, I have seen so little of those city sights that I cannot, in honesty, venture my opinion. My sister has kept me to the house almost since the moment of my arrival in town, and despite my pleas has done little more than to ride me around Hyde Park once and take me to a subscription library. Now that I am become a social creature, I do not believe that ever I shall see more than the outsides of people's doorways!"

"No, that is too bad! If you care to ride, I would give myself the honor of introducing you to the Park, for it cannot be properly appreciated from a carriage."

"Certainly not," Althea agreed demurely.

"Perhaps I could devise some sightseeing excursion for you, as well, for you must certainly see the Houses of Parliament and the Tower."

"Precisely what I have told Maria! I should dearly love to."

"Suppose we begin tomorrow, then? If I arrive to take you riding tomorrow morning, will you be able, after tonight's festivity, to accompany me? I believe that the best time to see the Park is in the early morning, before the crowds are come into it. Perhaps after that I could arrange some party for sightseeing. I have some friends who would be delighted to accompany us, I'm sure."

"I look forward to tomorrow. At what o'clock shall I look for you in Grosvenor Square? I will not balk at a little early rising." Mr. Pendarly took her hand for a brief moment.

"Ma'am, I should never think of you as so poor creature as that." He released her hand and continued. "At the hour of nine-thirty, if that suits you? You will bring new life to the jaded sights of Hyde Park." Althea, who had thought herself far beyond the age of blushing, discovered, to her horror, that she was doing just that and was almost relieved to see Maria and Francis, both looking remarkably grim, heading toward them. Maria seemed out of patience with even the smallest civility, which demanded that Althea take her leave of Mr. Pendarly. Once away from him, she turned to her sister and told her they must leave.

"I hate to drag you away from the ball when you are so enjoying yourself, Ally," (the merest emphasis upon the *you*) "but I have one of my dreadful headaches and I must get home. Perhaps it is better that you not tax your strength all in one night, dearest," she said guiltily. "You will be fagged out indeed for tomorrow, and I should hate to have you wear yourself thin at the beginning of your Season."

Althea agreed meekly, and Francis went off to procure their wraps while they waited in the hall. Maria quizzed Althea halfheartedly about her conquests, but when Francis reappeared, became silent altogether. Their quarrel, Althea guessed, must have been quite fierce to have brought on this reaction. Whatever it was, the silence, which lasted all the way back to Grosvenor Square, was so chilling that Althea could have sworn she could feel it through her shawl.

Once within doors Maria announced her intention of going directly to bed with a glass of hartshorn and water, and straightway marched up the stairs. Althea and Francis were left staring helplessly after her. When Maria had disappeared on the landing, Francis smiled weakly and told Althea he was off to a club, bidding her a good night's rest. Althea nodded absently and controlled the desire to ask what the matter was between them, since she could think of no way to do so but in the most officious manner. She sighed and retired to her room.

It was not in Althea's nature to remain glum, and after the success she had enjoyed that night, even a more depressive nature would have found it hard to refrain from smiling. It was only by main force, when finally in her bed, that she stopped herself from repeating bits of conversation in her head like a child of seventeen. If she was to be ready for Mr. Pendarly's call at nine-thirty, she would have to calm her overwrought mind and rest. This sensible but entirely impractical reasoning did not help her to sleep, however, and long into the night she stared, unseeing but quite happy, at the ceiling of her room.

Mr. Edward Pendarly, making his way home from the Fforydings' house, was embroiled in a piece of reasoning that he could not settle to his satisfaction no matter how he concluded it. He had gone to the party that night to fill an otherwise empty evening, and had found himself, as he melodramatically thought of it, smitten by Miss Ervine's beauty, wit, and all the various parts that could recommend a lady to a gentleman. In itself such an infatuation would not have been harmful, but Mr. Pendarly was, regrettably, very much engaged, and no matter how he reasoned, he could not imagine explaining to his fiancée, or worse, to her mother, why he had suddenly begun to find such amusement in *ton* parties while his betrothed was in the sickroom. Still less could he presently imagine telling Miss Ervine of his encumbrance—not if it would mean, as it certainly would, that the lady would banish him from the ranks of her serious admirers. For if Edward Pendarly was anything at any time it was serious. There lay the possibility, then, of prevarication, or at least omission. Which meant the danger of discovery and the subsequent wrath of Miss Ervine, Miss Laverham, and the Dragon, Mrs. Laverham. There was no question but that he must eventually be married to Miss Laverham: a man with debts such as his and a family full of expensive relations could not afford the luxury of wooing where he wished, and having found a financial prize like Georgiana Laverham, he could not afford to lose her. Without really resolving what his course of action would be, Mr. Pendarly decided that perhaps the morning ride would show Miss Ervine to be less attractive than he had thought. He slept very poorly that night.

Lord Francis Bevan, having said good night to his sister-in-law, left his house with no certain idea as to where to go. A turn in the night air cleared his brain somewhat, but also afforded some time for quiet reflection, most of which contributed to an already strong feeling that he should not return to his house just yet. In order to avoid doing so, Lord Bevan hailed a chair and gave the directions of Watier's. It was to be hoped that there would be some good play there, and the night was still relatively young. It was a damned shame that Maria had had to spoil Althea's first *ton* party with her willfulness, but Maria was not likely to consider anyone else's welfare above her own. The evening had started out so well, too, which only made Maria's behavior the worse. And his own, he admitted, had not been of the best.

By the time Lord Bevan reached Watier's he was in a state half of indignation, half of self-abnegation, a combination that had often proven fatal to his gaming sense.

On entering the club, he at once encountered several friends engaged in a hot discussion of the favorite in a private race to be run later in the week. Lord Bevan was welcomed enthusiastically and invited to take a chance on the race, which he gladly did, to the tune of five hundred guineas, placed on Ever Faithful. He knew nothing about either the horse or its rider but only liked the name, but this extravagance set the tone for the evening's gaming. By betting blindly where he liked, he managed to lose seven hundred at the dicing tables and a round two thousand at faro. When, some few hours later, he quit the faro room and sought *rouge et noir*, Lord Alvanley, who had been watching with a certain amusement young Bevan's attempts to throw himself to the wind, intervened, suggesting that Francis had done more than enough to impoverish his future heirs for one night. Francis, whose drinking had more than kept pace with his gaming, did not take kindly to the suggestion, merely said that he must be the judge of his own business. Alvanley sighed and nodded at the young fool, strolling back himself to the faro room. Francis's taste for *rouge et noir*, however, had deserted him, and he turned back to the hazard rooms with a look in his eye that boded ill for no one but himself.

At one table, Sir Tracy Calendar, having won a sub-stantial pile of money from Lord Sefton, was now en-gaged in conversation with him and Lord Petersham. As Francis Bevan entered the room, Lord Petersham had just finished one of his distracting daydreams about tea admix-tures, to the great amusement of his friends, and it was this momentary lapse in the conversation that permitted Calendar to notice Bevan's arrival. He also noticed the man's unsteady gait and flushed face.

Sir Tracy excused himself and approached Bevan. Francis, who expected to be reprimanded again as he had been by Alvanley, stiffened and glared at Calendar, who mildly asked if Lord Bevan was interested in a game of hazard. All Francis's stiffness relaxed so suddenly it was comical; he had expected a set-down and had received, instead, an invitation to play with a notable gamester! The wine and this particular new bit of consequence puffed Francis's confidence greatly, and he accepted with alacri-ty. Had he been more sober or less headstrong, he might have demurred, for he was too well acquainted with Calendar's reputation and with his own ill-fortune to chance such a meeting ordinarily. Tonight he was to be as unheeding as anyone—as Maria, in fact.

Tracy, for some vaguely philanthropic reason, found himself playing hazard with a slightly inebriated and moody Francis Bevan. From the moment he had seen Bevan's eyes across the room, Tracy had been sure that the man was set on some sort of ruin and was seized with an untraceable insight that told him it might be better for the young man to lose to someone less punctual in mat-ters of play and pay—to himself, that is—than to one of the professional gamesters present, who would doubtless bleed the young lord for all he was worth.

He was amused and pleased by the stoic way Lord Bevan insisted on taking his losses. For all he could do was lose, writing vouchers finally for large sums. Although Tracy thought it might be a good idea, he could not ask that no more wine be served without, he thought wryly, Bevan's calling him out. So on they continued, with the pile of vouchers growing as the night progressed, and Sir Tracy wondering what sort of despair Bevan must be feeling at his night's work.

Francis's elation at the very fact of Calendar's invitation very quickly subsided, leaving only a stubborn intent to continue playing. Francis was not a gambler by nature so much as by habit; as he was so shockingly bad at it, he was often scolded for his social gaming by his agent and his wife. Tonight, however, he was possessed by a need to gamble, not so much for the intoxication with chance as for the reckless feeling of abandonment it afforded him. It was very late when Calendar, pleading fatigue, suggested they end the game and gave Francis the total of his vouchers. Francis did not reply to the staggering figure but only turned pale. After a moment or two he said that he would send a draft on his bank the next day, to which Calendar replied that there was no hurry—thirty days was more than sufficient time—as it was only the beginning of the new quarter, he did not doubt but that Lord Bevan would be prompt.

Francis could only thank him and leave the club, his head buzzing and his heart sinking, as he repeated to himself the figure Calendar had given. He was not yet sober but was becoming so with disastrous rapidity. All that was left was to return home, submit himself to the ministrations of his sleepy valet, and fall into a deep, uneasy slumber, dreading tomorrow's reckoning and cursing the night entirely.

Sir Tracy Calendar, having left Lord Bevan, spoke for a few minutes with Mr. Brummell and Lord Petersham, then took his leave, preferring to walk rather than to call a chair or ride. He was surprised at his behavior tonight but felt he must not refine too closely upon it. After all,

Bevan did not ordinarily game so freely. It would seem that the young lord and his lady had had some sort of falling out: the seeds had been perceivable at the Fforydings' ball. Tracy thought to himself that it would be a shame if their infelicity should overset Miss Ervine and, on this notion, he smiled to himself, continuing up the streets to Cavendish.

Chapter Five

The atmosphere in the house at Grosvenor Square the next morning could only be said to be oppressive. Maria slept late, and even after she did awake, kept to her room, sulking over her chocolate and cards of invitation.

Since Mr. Pendarly was to call on her at nine-thirty, Althea, in her anxiety to be ready at that hour, found herself occupying the breakfast room with Francis. He wore a very drawn countenance and had that aversion to sudden noises that bespeaks too much wine and too little sleep. He did not eat more than a corner of toast but drank several cups of coffee; Althea felt for him deeply but could think of no words that would fit the occasion. His conversation was negligible, beyond inquiring of Althea how she had liked the ball. Then he did no more than sigh, sinking into his own miserable silence.

To Althea, sipping her second cup of tea, it was a relief when Mr. Pendarly was announced and she would go out to greet him. He allowed her a moment to adjust the very becoming shako on her dark hair and the folds of the matching gray and green habit before they went out into the street.

If Edward Pendarly had hoped that the attraction he felt for Miss Ervine would prove to be illusory, his hopes were to no avail. Miss Ervine was in splendid looks, her military-style habit and shako hat making the most of her height and authority. She held out her hand in the friendliest manner, waiting to be thrown into the saddle, and Pendarly knew that his case was lost.

"You are here in very good time. It is fortunate for you that I do not play the belle and delay you half an hour with changing my hat or some such thing, which my sister tells me it is every fashionable woman's duty to do."

"I cannot conceive that you would willingly inconvenience anyone, ma'am." He smiled warmly. Althea blushed but kept her tongue, waiting until they were some minutes along on their ride toward the park.

"I hope you know, sir, that I did not speak as I did to have you offer me the Spanish coin. I should hate to have you think so."

"I shall maintain, Miss Ervine, and not as Spanish coin either, that I should be much surprised to hear that you had troubled anyone unwillingly. One cannot, of course, be held responsible for those things that happen unavoidably." He spoke with some fervor, and the glow of admiration persisted still in his eyes. Althea felt the uncomfortable need to disabuse him of his illusions.

"You have never seen me in a temper, sir," she admitted. "I am told that I am altogether a termagant when I am angry. In fact, I am still at odds with my father, on account of my having scolded my brother for riding through the gardener's prized roses. When I am angry I do not think until after I have wrought, and by then it is often very late in the day indeed." Althea said all of this forthrightly, but tempered it with as much of Maria's smiling as she could; in any event the gentleman seemed unimpressed by her confession. He was, it appeared, determined to think well of her.

"The case you speak of surely is to your credit, ma'am. To incur your father's displeasure over another's sensibility—I collect those roses were something special to the gardener?—that surely indicates a great measure of consideration."

"I beg you will tell my father so, sir," she said dryly. They had entered the Park now, and Althea would have dearly loved a gallop, but of course this was London, not the long meadow at Hook Well, and such a display, she was persuaded, would ruin her credit forever. She contented herself with a sedate pace, keeping alongside Mr. Pendarly and enjoying the cool air of the morning. Mr. Pendarly kept up a flow of light, entertaining conversation, indicating places of interest that could be seen as they rode. There was no denying he was attractive and, in a subdued manner, quite charming. When the trees had hidden all but the Park itself from view Pendarly began to speak of the sightseeing excursion he had thought of, suggesting points of interest they might visit as a beginning.

"Of course, if you are determined to be a bluestocking, we will visit the Botanical Gardens, but I must inform you that unless you wish to be thought dreadfully learned or peculiar, they are not the place for a lady of fashion."

"Thank you for the kind warning. I will endeavor to cool my botanical yearnings, then, for my sister would never forgive me if I appeared a bluestocking after her careful tutoring. She labored hard and long to make me a paragon of presentability."

There was a quick look of something like disapproval at this flippancy, but the glance was so brief that Althea could almost believe her companion had not aimed it at her at all. She felt sure she could have said the same sort of thing to anyone else and received no worse than a question as to what she could possibly mean. Almost anyone she had met the night before—the tall man, Sir Tracy

Calendar, for example—would have understood the spirit of her remark. Surely she had only imagined the look from Mr. Pendarly.

As if the thought of him had conjured him up, Sir Tracy Calendar appeared from a side path, riding a beautiful showy chestnut. She could feel, or rather sense, Mr. Pendarly bridle nervously at her side, for what reason she knew not. She was pleased to see Sir Tracy, yet she would have wished for this hour with Pendarly alone if Calendar had some unfortunate effect upon the gentleman. Still, when Sir Tracy reined in beside her, she smiled cordially.

"Your servant, Miss Ervine. You are early out this morning, I see, and by the look of it, in excellent spirits after your triumph last night. Allow me to compliment you: you have captured half the hearts of Bond Street already." He turned to Pendarly with a nod. "You must think yourself fortunate to have stolen the march on this lady's army of suitors."

"I misdoubt, sir, whether I have captured so much as one heart, let alone those of an army. Some interest, perhaps, but hearts? Surely even in London that is a weightier business."

"Nonsense, Miss Ervine. In London hearts are given as lightly as air, and taken as freely at a moment's notice. Mr. Pendarly here may be at your feet today, and on the morrow be dangling after the first fair lady with china blue eyes and a fair fortune that he encounters. A sad truth, I'm afraid, to hand you on such a fair morning." Althea gaped at Calendar; this was strange talk for any morning, and she found the notion that any man would amuse himself with her until a wealthier woman appeared particularly repugnant.

Pendarly, during this speech, had grown pale, looking with angry eyes at Calendar. Althea was relieved to know that at least one of her escorts was sensible enough to find such plain speaking offensive. It might, she owned, be that she found the remark particularly obnoxious because she was its target, but still she could not repress the notion that it might well have been left unsaid. She would have glared in concert with Mr. Pendarly at Calendar's unrepentant head had not the gleam in that gentleman's eye warned her that he expected a reaction of that sort. If I strangle with it, I shall not give him such satisfaction, she thought indignantly. Sir Tracy—the man seemed a mind reader!—nodded as if he had understood this, too, and after a very long moment of awkward quiet, he politely took his leave and rode off.

"I thought him pleasant enough last night, but what a dreadful tongue that man has to him!" Althea remarked at the retreating back of Calendar. "It goes beyond anything."

"I am sorry that he should have had the opportunity to speak to you in such terms, Miss Ervine, and that I did not task him with it. But it is always so with Calendar, I believe. He has a reputation as a cynic, which he preens upon all occasions—I think it very ill bred of him. There is no accounting for the taste of others: some people find him most amiable." Althea wondered if there was not a touch of priggishness to Pendarly's speech, but at the moment a trace of priggishness seemed infinitely preferable to Calendar's odious plain speaking. Pendarly still seemed overset by Calendar's manner. She let him brood for a few minutes as they turned their horses back in the direction of the Bevan house.

"I cannot thank you enough for this morning's ride, sir. It has altogether cleared the cobwebs for me—I have not ridden in above two months, for my own hack at home broke its leg and was destroyed, and Papa has not been able to bear the thought of the price of a new mount for me."

"Why does your father deny such a request? Especially when you are such a good horsewoman?"

"My father has a particular dislike for spending money —except on himself and occasionally on my brother. He

does not intend to be mean—he simply forgets that I
have my little needs too. And there may be another reason in that a year or two ago I made rather a spectacle of
myself riding across the hunting field after a dog of mine.
Papa thought that so disgraceful that he"—she broke off
suddenly, knowing that being disowned, even so casually
as she had twice been, could not increase her credit with
Pendarly—"he scolded me quite dreadfully."

Pendarly smiled but said nothing. His mind seemed to
have drifted away and Althea, cursing Sir Tracy roundly
in her mind, kept silent for the remainder of the ride.
When they arrived in front of the Bevan house he bid her
good day and told her he would call again soon. Althea
did not like to be the one to mention their sightseeing
plans, so they parted in vague civilities.

It was barely eleven, and as she was informed that my
lady had not yet arisen and that my lord had departed the
house some half an hour earlier, Althea retired to the library where she discovered, after some browsing, a life of
Richard III, which she began with relish. How long she
sat reading Althea did not know, but when Debbens entered to tell her that Lady Bevan had awakened and was
inquiring for her sister, she whisked the book under a sofa
cushion, knowing what Maria's consternation would be if
she found that her sister had been reading a *history*.

Althea, on entering Lady Bevan's chamber, discovered
curtains drawn and her sister in high dudgeon, nursing a
cup of cold chocolate and shuffling through her cards of
invitation in the half-light.

"You'll never learn what is on them that way, stupid,"
Althea clucked at her as she lit the lamp at bedside. "You
look completely done up. Has that pretend headache of
yours become real?"

Lady Bevan sat bolt upright and tried to form her face
into a semblance of aggrieved self-righteousness, but gave
up at last when she saw no reaction from her sister.
"Very well, then, I should know better than to try to fool

you. But I *should* have had the headache last night, from the heat and the press and that awful champagne of Lady Fforyding's and from Francis's shocking treatment of me."

"And now you have made yourself ill in earnest from fretting. How silly you are, Mary. I must confess that I have no headache, for all I drank as much punch as you and was as long in the ballroom as you. Poor honey, had a turn-up with Francis, did you not?"

Lady Bevan considered denying the charge summarily, but another glance at her sister assured her that Althea knew almost the whole of it, and might as well be told now as later—before Francis had had the chance, in fact. When she spoke, there spilled out a torrent of recriminations, apologies, despair, all mixed with generous feelings of ill use. Althea found it a wholly unfortunate recipe. Maria ended her tirade with the matter of Madame Helena's bill—not the one incurred by Althea, for her sister was paying that out of her own income—but the one that had come on the day of Althea's arrival, and rested still, unpaid, in the drawer of Maria's chiffonier. Now the fear of Maria's heart was that any day the bill would come before Francis, and she was in a tremor, for she'd no idea at all what to do, and there was no possible way to pay it before the end of this quarter—nearly three months away—and what did her dearest Ally have to say to her sister's distress?

"Peace, Mary, and let me think. You've a rare muddle on your hands, but why are you so determined that Francis cannot know of it? Surely if you lay it before him and act prettily enough he won't scold you very much. No? Well then, perhaps you can pay part of it now and part later? If nothing else will do, I can advance you some money, although not so much. Since I received *my* dun from Helena, I'm none too plump in the pocket myself. Smile a little, Sis. The world will not come to an end. Try with Francis first, I say." Althea's faith in Francis's good temper added to her hope that he and her sister would resolve their difficulties.

"Ally, you cannot understand. I have not told you the whole of it," Maria wailed. "Before you came—oh, some months ago—Francis and I had the most dreadful row, and I said some horrible, unforgivable things to him about his gaming, and he was horrid about my extravagance, as he put it, and though we did make it up, it was never the same, although I promised to watch my spending and he vowed not to be so—so *profligate* in his gaming. I do not think he can ever truly love me after the things I said, and then last night I thought it was going to be all right again." Maria gulped miserably. "I began to think that he might begin to love me a little again, then everything was spoiled, for he went off to the gaming room and left me to amuse myself as best I might. I am so miserable—" She burst into tears and buried her face in the pillows. Althea gave her sister a five-minute pause to cry and recover herself before she attempted to speak to her. When the weeping had subsided a little and only an occasional gulp was heard from the pillow, Althea lifted her sister bodily from the bed, patted her shoulder, dried her tears with a ridiculously inadequate handkerchief, and refreshed her face with lavender water. Then she demanded an account, detailed and *truthful*, of the quarrel at the Fforydings'.

"Well, after Lady Fforyding came in and introduced you to that red-faced boy and the two of you strolled off together, Francis and I stood about just talking—just as if we were courting again. Then along came Johnny Wallingham and asked me to dance, and if *Francis* had asked me not to dance, of course I would not have, but Wallingham is perfectly unexceptionable—a little rakish, perhaps, but he is one of my cicisbeos, and very amusing. In any case, Francis made no fuss over it, so what could I do but agree, and when we came back after the two-third, he was gone! We found him, of course, but just when Wallingham had said the most amusing thing, so of course

I was laughing, and that put Francis in a terrible pucker. He only stood and *looked* at me. Such a look! And Wallingham excused himself, as well he might with Francis looking daggers. Then Francis turned upon me and said he hoped I would enjoy Wallingham's company, then walked off, cool as you please. I could not have chased after him in the middle of that crowd, could I? So what was there for it but for me to make a show of enjoying myself? And if John Wallingham and Hartington and Lord Sefton—did you meet him? the dearest man imaginable!—well, if people are pleased to be pleasant to me, then what can I do but be civil?"

"What a splendid mull, Mary."

"Well, I suppose that it was partly my fault, for I know Francis doesn't much care for Wallingham, and I suppose I could have refused to dance, but why should I when Francis said nothing to make me stay? In any case, that is all past, and we have said nothing to each other above two words since then. What an awful mess." As Lady Bevan showed signs of readying herself to plunge back into the pillow and her tears, Althea assumed a bracing manner.

"Yes it is, I don't doubt, but not so bad that I misdoubt we shall have you happy shortly. First, there is the bill from Helena. Once that is paid, you can go to Francis and beg his pardon very prettily—"

"*I* beg *his* pardon? When it was he who abandoned me all evening? Infamous! I'll not stand for it." Lady Bevan folded her arms and looked obstinate, but her sister could not be put off in that fashion.

"Mary, I beg you to believe me when I say that there is nothing to elicit an apology *like* an apology. It always works for Papa: all you do is to admit that you were wrong first, and a man will dearly love to be bountiful and forgive, and then turn about and lay his heart open to you in a veritable orgy of contrition. You would be shocked if I told you the ineligible things that Papa has

confessed to me after I have apologized over something—some of those things I hadn't the least idea of."

"You mean the hatmaker in the village?"

"Oh, that was long ago. There have been a few other
indiscretions since that, I can tell you."

"And you think that would work with Francis?" Lady
Bevan eyed her sister mistily, but with dawning hope.

"Of course it will. It does with most men, and I imagine that Francis is not any different from the common run
of men in this way. I will tell you when he has returned to
the house, and you may go down and beg his pardon very
prettily. Shall I sit on the stairs and shock Mrs. Chaverly,
who I think has distrusted me since I arrived in that very
irregular fashion, and watch for Francis, while you put on
something truly ravishing?"

Maria gave a watery chuckle. Althea rang for Bailey,
telling her sister to hurry with her toilette.

"Lord, Ally, will you manage your husband this way?"

"Lud, I hope I shall not, but then, since I've not met
the man, there's no telling. Who knows but what I shall
find him managing me!" Althea left the room to Maria
and Bailey, who considered Miss a godsend in handling
her fractious mistress.

Lord Bevan was harder to find than Althea had anticipated. When questioned, Debbens announced with a
harumph that considering the tearer the master had been
in when he left, begging Miss's pardon, he did not think
his lordship would return shortly, since it was his lordship's custom when overset to go riding, or pursue some
other, less suitable outlet for his temper, again begging
Miss's pardon. Althea, trying to conjure up the unsuitable
outlets open to a gentleman of fashion at high noon in
London, decided that either her education was deplorably
lacking, or Debbens had exaggerated somewhat. Upon
consideration, she attempted to understand what might
have put Francis into such a fury. The image of Francis
as he had appeared in the breakfast room that morning,

with his drawn countenance and sore head, was utterly irreconcilable with that of Francis in a rage. His anger, she was sure, must have had its source in some later influence.

Despite the hopes of the household, by four o'clock that afternoon Lord Bevan had not returned, and as his wife and sister-in-law were engaged to drive out with Mrs. Drummond-Burrell, the most imposing, unlikable, and critical of the London dowagers, Althea went up to her room to change, stopping on the way to admonish Maria as to the lateness of the hour. Maria was becomingly dressed but rather dispirited in appearance. She glanced up hopefully when Althea entered, but perceiving only her sister, shrugged impatiently.

"It's only I, love. I expect Francis has found some diversion for the afternoon and will not be home till later. Perhaps he will come back to change for the evening, and we can see him then. Debbens tells me that he was in a bad temper when he left, so perhaps it is a good sign that he has taken himself off, and he will return to you cheerful and ready to be repentant. You should only have seen him this morning, Mary! He was still a trifle foxed, and so sore in the head that he looked daggers at me when I only stirred my tea!" Althea had, during this, managed to bring her sister out into the hallway and down the stairs, and they stood now in the lower hallway, ready to meet the approaching Mrs. Drummond-Burrell. Althea reminded her sister that she must contrive to cover any and all *faux pas* her awkward sister might make, for she counted heavily on Maria's good influence with their hostess. Maria could only answer—a little tearfully—that Althea was a diamond of the first water, and if Mrs. Drummond-Burrell could not see it, she was a ninny indeed.

After a ride, which was rendered singularly uncomfortable by their hostess's well-known manner, Althea and Maria returned to dress and dine before going out to a rout party. As there was no word from Francis, Maria grew more and more dispirited, taking only half an hour with her evening toilette. They sat down just two to dinner that night, and until halfway through the meal, spoke only a few desultory words. Some fifteen minutes into the second course, however, Maria began to talk, swallowing a bit of turbot and then beginning a tirade against her own selfishness. After a few moments of this Althea had to break in and demand what it was Maria had done to justify her self-loathing.

"Why, goose, here I am with a reigning beauty on my hands, and I sit moping about some stupid quarrel I have had, totally ignoring your triumph. If you continue as you have begun, and Mr. Brummel shall not dislike you, then you will be toasted in St. James's, I make sure of it. Only think what a wonder we have wrought between us, Madame Helena and I!"

But the mention of the unfortunate dressmaker's name recalled Maria to her misery; she became very white, and again quietly tearful. Only after Althea had spoken at some length of Maria's part in the transformation (at no small cost to her own self-esteem, since she had to make herself sound like a very toad in order to suitably impress Maria) did she begin again to pick up in spirits. Her sister, recognizing this flower for the frail one that it was, carefully nursed it along through the evening.

Later that night, when they returned to the house, it was to find a note from Lord Bevan lying on a salver in the hallway. Lady Bevan tore the note open, read it quickly, reread it, and cast it to the floor with a sob. She gasped out something about Francis's cruelty and the injustice of it, and begged her sister to read the note while she sat and composed herself. She then dissolved into tears. Althea, with one arm about her weeping sister, did read Francis's note, which began hopefully enough with a plea for Maria's forgiveness for his behavior at the Fforydings'. It then changed its tone, and it became clear that the change was occasioned by the mail delivery, which brought the bill from Helena. That he should feel ill used in the light of his wife's animadversions upon his extravagances was not unreasonable, but Althea suspected that his head, and the precarious state of his relations with his wife, had made his reaction to the bill far greater than was necessary. That Francis, normally the mildest of men, and certainly not one given to literary extravagance, should couch his letter in terms of shameless duplicity, and in phrases such as "the extravagances you have attempted to hide from me by dint of rank untruth," and that he should end his letter with the sincere wish that his judgment should never again be so clouded as it had been when he had convinced himself they should suit!—this was above too much. The note was signed, coldly, "Bevan." And if it had surprised Althea to see such a letter, it had sent Maria into strong hysterics.

"His *judgment!* Why, he cannot chose his coat without I advise him, and then he must needs go about to his friends demanding do they like it. Ally, how could he write such an awful letter to me! We can never, ever be reconciled after this dreadful blow that he has dealt me." She rambled on in this manner for a few minutes more, until Althea could steer her up the stairs and ring for Bailey. When the maid arrived, Althea desired her to put Lady Bevan to bed, with a few drops of laudanum, if Bailey thought best. Bailey nodded and led her sodden mistress away, casting Althea a look of sage commiseration. Althea followed more slowly to her room, looking forward only to a long, mostly unsatisfactory review of the situation. Her thoughts were not very coherent—not surprising in one who had been dealing with a deranged sensibility all day. Althea felt she was responsible in some way, if not for the cause, then for the cure of the unrest in the Bevan household, but so late at night she could come up with no very good conclusion.

When morning came, Althea woke with her optimism full blown, and went down to her breakfast, only to be informed by the ubiquitous Debbens that his lordship had gone from town, sudden like, to meet some friends at a mill. Or so, Debbens remarked darkly, he had said. As this information had also been communicated to Lady Bevan, Althea found her sister in such circumstances as necessitated a great deal of soothing and consolation. At least to external view, however, the upset did not last beyond a morning's repining. In the face of her husband's absence, Maria became stubbornly insistent upon having the most enjoyable social time possible. If this behavior worried Althea, she should find no occasion to remonstrate with her sister, and as she, too, was becoming more and more drawn into the toils of social obligation, there never seemed to be time for more than a quick frown or a preoccupied thought.

Chapter Six

Maria, who cherished upon her sister's behalf the attention of any ummarried man, regarded it as the most delightful thing that Lord William Fforyding and his sister Sophia should find it convenient to call often at Grosvenor Square. Althea was better informed than her sister, and knew that Lord Fforyding was already betrothed to a Miss Westleid; she also suspected that Miss Fforyding found the Bevan house an easy place to encounter Jonathan Tidd, who miraculously appeared whenever the Fforydings called. William, with or without Miss Westlied, was a fair conversationalist, albeit a very conventional one, and Althea was pleased to welcome him and his sister whenever they came to call. She would divert his attention to herself and spend half an hour discussing estate management, or the proper way to deal with one's gamekeeper, while Sophia and Mr. Tidd sat and blushed at each other. On occasion, the party enlarged to include both Edward Pendarly and Sir Tracy Calendar, and while Althea fully appreciated the awkward humor of the situation, she could have wished that it were more humorous and less awkward.

This day Sir Tracy sat in conversation with Maria, who was, as always, almost entirely uncomprehending of his remarks. Edward Pendarly sat in uneasy conversation with Althea, and kept casting glances of dislike at Sir Tracy, which were matched in intensity only by the looks of trepidation Sir Tracy was favored with by Sophia and Mr. Tidd. Calendar seemed unaware of these speaking looks, but Althea could not so underestimate him as to assume that he was so. Only Lord Fforyding was completely at ease, listening to Mr. Pendarly's comments upon points of interest in the city.

"Then you've seen the Bazaar? Seen Lord Elgin's marbles, have you?" he questioned in his bluff manner. Althea admitted that she had. "Been to Vauxhall, of course, and seen Piccadilly Circus and the Botanical Gardens? I cannot think of anywhere else to suggest," Lord Fforyding conceded. "Unless you want to go gawk at HRH—Prinny's a sight to behold, ain't he, Pendarly?"

Mr. Pendarly conceded that the Prince's presence cast a shadow of awe over the lowliest proceedings.

"If you are tired of the city's sights, Miss Ervine," he continued, "perhaps you would be pleased with a country outing?" Pendarly fixed his beautiful, soul-filled gaze upon Althea with great fervor. "My cousin, Mrs. Abbot, is mistress of a very picturesque estate, Danning Hall, not more than one and a half hours from London. Perhaps I could arrange for a party to visit the grounds—I am sure it would cheer my cousin no end, since her husband is in the Navy and has been at sea this last year or more."

From across the room Tracy Calendar drawled, "It sounds delightful, Pendarly. Perhaps you could make up a party of those of us present who might wish to go. I imagine Miss Fforyding and Mr. Tidd would enjoy it immensely." His tone was dry, and he ignored the ashen color of Pendarly's face, and the indignant stare from Althea. Lord Fforyding, altogether unaware of these currents, announced that he himself would be more than delighted to go, and, if it was agreeable, would bring Miss Westleid to accompany the party. Maria said on her part that it sounded dreadfully dull, but if her dearest Ally wished to go, then go she must.

"But, ma'am, think of the disservice you do when you deprive us of your company," Calendar protested unheatedly. "We counted upon you to lend us your dignity."

"I thank you for the thought, sir, but I am truly as indifferent a traveler as you might find, and could derive no satisfaction from driving for three hours in total for a picnic that might easily be held in Richmond. Perhaps someone can suggest another who will play your chaperone," Maria said, a little miffed to be imputed with dignity.

After some minutes Jonathan Tidd shyly offered the name of his aunt as a possibility. Since no one was acquainted with Miss Agatha Tidd, this suggestion was hallooed in several corners as being brilliant, and Mr. Tidd was earnestly entreated to secure his aunt's company for the party. The Tuesday of the coming week was settled upon as eminently suitable for everyone—everyone being Lord Fforyding, who in some way had become the organizer of the excursion. Althea was certain by this time that Sir Tracy was as little pleased by the party as she, and that Mr. Pendarly was regretting the overturning of his plans and their corruption to the general use.

It had been arranged that all the travelers would meet at Lord Fforyding's house, and somehow it was Tracy

Calendar and not Edward Pendarly who appointed himself to deliver Althea there. He arrived just a little later than agreed, so that Althea had had ample time to complete her toilette. Banders, watching her mistress arrange the ribbons of her bonnet in the most suitable way, said that she would never have thought to see little Miss Ally become such a town damsel that it took her ten minutes to decide between one carriage dress and another. The delay and the effort were, to Althea's eyes, rewarded by the pleasing image in the mirror: she looked comfortable but not in the least dowdy, her honey-colored dress and spencer being of just such a cut as to set her figure to best advantage. After a brief farewell to Maria, still groggy in the darkness of her room, Althea descended to meet Sir Tracy in the hallway.

Calendar was unusually taciturn, barely uttering a good morning as he handed her into the curricle. Althea was not put off by his manner, and as the gentleman vouchsafed no explanation, she asked for none and they rode in silence to Fforyding House.

Outside the building the group was gathering: Lord Fforyding and Sophia, Miss Caroline Westleid, Edward Pendarly, Jonathan Tidd and his aunt, Miss Agatha Tidd, who was to lend the party her dignity. Except that "dignity" was not a word one would associate with Miss Tidd, who gave every indication of being a clutching, overdressed, romantic old maid. Sir Tracy and Althea immediately found themselves in the midst of a great to-do over who should travel with whom. As a result, it appeared that no one was greatly in charity with anyone else. Miss Tidd, in fact, was the bone of contention; having taken Lord Fforyding in considerable fancy, she strenuously objected to riding with anyone else. To this suggestion Lord Fforyding, with his fiancée standing near, was heard to mutter darkly that he'd be damned if he'd ride to Danning with those two moon calves Sophia and her Tidd, as well as that overdressed bear leader with the rabbity face. Even one so oblivious to other people's sensibilities as Miss Tidd had to realize that she would only be the cause of misery if she persisted in her planning; besides, she discovered that young Mr. Pendarly was really much more concilliatory than Lord Fforyding. She cast him such a glance of forsakeness that he could not but say, with almost passable gallantry, that he would drive her. With pleasure.

Althea and Calendar were informed of the driving arrangements. If Sir Tracy, standing with closed mouth and silent eyes near his phaeton, thought anything about the situation, he was mercifully quiet, and not even a sardonic eyebrow gave him away.

The party, with the Fforyding barouche in the lead, moved out onto the street. Once free of the worst of city traffic, however, the curricles gained the lead on the barouche. Mr. Pendarly's phaeton was kept to a sedate pace for the benefit of Miss Tidd, who loudly professed to be vastly frightened by fast vehicles and large dogs. Calendar, under no such restrictions, took his vehicle into the distance ahead of the others.

Althea had been philosophical about driving to Danning with Sir Tracy; at times the devotion of Mr. Pendarly wore a little thin, and when she looked for a spark of kindred humor in him, it seemed she was always disappointed. Even so, after fifteen minutes of deepest silence from her host she felt it behooved her to break that silence, however vulgarly she might have to do so.

"Do you know that you have a peculiar knack of putting me out of countenance? Every time I see you there is sure to develop some uncomfortable lapse in the conversation. This is the longest I have known you to maintain it: I am very impressed by your fortitude, but could we not talk now? Here I am, ready to hang upon your every word—ready to toad-eat you, if necessary! *I* daren't say a word for fear of sounding missish; it is dreadfully taxing upon a woman of my age." Althea sighed artistically and, after a moment or two, Calendar's face lit with a reluctant but very real smile.

"I suppose I shall have to humbly beg your pardon. Though you know that you have something of the same effect on me: I hold my tongue for fear you will think me merely a mindless coxcomb, which I know is your abomination. If I were to say to you, for example, that that particular shade of brown—or is it yellow?—is calculated to a nicety to flatter your hair and your eyes, would you not scorn my frippery remarks? So rather than endure ignominy, I will keep my silence."

"You cannot mean to tell me that you have been silent this while for fear of me. My brother would say that that is coming it much too strong—and so say I. We could speak of something aside from the color of my spencer without the least danger of my disliking your conversation—unless you should happen to lapse into Spanish coin again, which I trust you will spare me. I am not against a little rational conversation, you know, and I should hope that you have some thoughts on *some* subject."

"I suppose we could speak of literature, but that would only go on long enough to disclose that we both love Cowper, detest Pope, never read novels, and there you are! We would dive into abysmal silence again." Tracy's tone was mocking, but if he was prepared to be in an evil temper, then Althea was prepared to quarrel him out of it.

"You speak very freely of my preferences. The only statement you have made that I can fully agree with is that our silence is abysmal. As for your digest of a lady's literary taste, I loathe Cowper, think Pope almost as bad, read novels frequently, and have a scandalous preference for Sterne and Fielding over Mrs. Radcliffe and her ilk. Make what you will of that."

"This is mere defiance!" Tracy smiled. "You cannot be so different from the others of your sex as to truly hold those opinions. It would spoil a theory that I formulated with a friend one night over a bottle—several bottles—of his port: that all women below the age of thirty were born with the same taste in all the arts. You only deny it to annoy me."

"Not to annoy but to uphold the honor of my sex—and my own honor as well. But what of the women over thirty? How do you account for them? In any case, at least I read novels and admit my crime, whereas most people take *Clarissa Harlow* or *The Castle of Otranto* off to read in a closet somewhere, and then virtuously decry novels—wishing all the while to be Emily St. Aubert or the wicked Montoni. Novels are a great deal of fun," Althea said solemnly. "At least if your taste runs to the scandalous—as Mary says mine does. Lord, but I scandalized her enough with laughing over the name of her hairstyle—Sappho. I explained who that worthy lady was, and Mary begged me never again to tell anyone that I even read Greek, let alone that I had read such a poet." Althea could feel Tracy's eyes upon her in a look of mild astonishment.

"Have I shocked you now? I had thought you were above being shocked by such a one as I. I suppose I might as well have admitted out and out to being a bluestocking. It is all the fault of living so deep in the country, you see. I had nothing to do but study and keep my father's house—I even persuaded the dominie to teach me Greek and Latin when I was quite small. Maria would be furious if she knew that I had explosed my guilty secret to you."

Tracy was making a definite attempt to control his amusement. "Why would that infuriate your sister so?" he asked gravely.

"After all the care she had lavished upon me? Maria is not in the least bookish, and has the greatest horror that I will be thought so, since I do read a book on occasion." Calendar unmistakably grinned. Althea was pleased enough by the results of her fatal confession to continue amusing him with the details of her transformation. "Mary's greatest fear is that I should flaunt my—my dreadful deficiency at large," she said airily.

"What dreadful deficiency?"

"A deficiency of maidenly ignorance. She has said that when I am married, I may be as learned as I please, although she could see no point to it. But knowledge is unconscionable in a single lady, and so until such time as some hapless man shall take responsibility for my foibles, I am to appear as sweet and senseless as Mary herself." Althea laughed ruefully. "And all to catch some poor witless fellow so I may continue to study! All those years at Hook Well there was no need for the quadrille and the waltz and knowing how to discourage an overly amorous gentleman—if I should ever run into such!—for Papa never let me farther than the town of Hooking. I suppose there was no practical use for Greek or German either, but I have to read: knitting and keeping stock of the preserves do not fill up an ordinary day, unless one is a very *slow* knitter or stockkeeper."

"And so your sister undertook to educate you in all these sadly neglected points in your education? I thought you waltzed very nicely."

"And so I do now, but a month ago! It is all due to the work of a Signore Francesco, teacher of the dance. A splendid master whom Maria pressed upon me with the direst threats. And she instructed me in flirtation, court manners, the rules of Society—why almost all the schoolroom nonsense I ignored when I *was* in the schoolroom. I cannot wonder that with all the rules she has to remember she often cannot talk correctly."

"But tell me, how does one discourage the attentions of an overly amorous gentleman? Just in case I ever need to know such a valuable piece of information."

"I could not be so unfair to the rest of my sex as to give secrets to one of the enemy camp!" This broke through the last vestige of Sir Tracy's composure. He abruptly drew the curricle to the side of the road, and burst into a whoop of laughter, to the distress of his cattle and the interest of a farmer steering a dog cart in the other direction. When he had somewhat recovered, he calmed his horses and replaced the beaver hat that had fallen behind him at the first of his laughter.

"You are serious in telling me that your sister subjected you to these ninnyish teachings? Lessons in flirtation? thought every woman was born with that lesson engraved upon her heart!"

"Like literary taste?" Althea suggested.

"Confess that the whole is some fancy's flight you have conceived to amuse me from my sullens."

"You admit that you are blue-deviled! I thought so. But I cannot confess what is not so. Maria was most scrupulous in her teaching, and although I have ignored most of it, I cannot but be grateful for some of it. Who knows what impropriety I might have committed had she not explained the rules of Almack's to me, for instance. I might have tried to gain admission after eleven, or some such equally dire crime."

"You might, I collect, have had the temerity to wear pantaloons—" Tracy began.

"Instead of knee breeches," Althea triumphed. "Just what I told Mary, only she was vastly scandalized, and begged me never to say such a thing in company. I cannot thank you enough for relieving me of the necessity—there can, of course, be no objection to *your* saying such a thing." Tracy sternly controlled himself and asked meekly what other gems Althea had garnered at her sister's knee.

"Of the rules of things, not much more than that. She did give me the credit for being a good student, and able to pick up much from what I saw others doing. But when Banders—my maid, and my mother's before me—when she arrived in town, it nearly began all again. She treats me as the veriest babe, which I certainly am not at the advanced age of three and twenty. When I come in from a drive or a ball she is sure to ask if I remembered to make my curtsy to such a one. Oh, please do tell me if I ever should forget to make my curtsy to you, for I should hate to be backward in civility."

"Well, ma'am," Calendar said at length, "I know now that you dislike Cowper and Pope, read novels, and are undergoing, I make no doubt for the second time, the exigencies of the schoolroom."

"Oh, as soon as I made my first appearance before the *ton* Maria stopped tutoring me. I am now to rise or fall on my own. Although I regret to say that I misdoubt Banders will ever treat me as an adult. I must not mind that."

"Your generosity knows no bounds, ma'am. I honor you. You enjoy Fielding? Who else do you favor with your patronage? If you really are a bluestocking, as you claim, you must recommend me some reading."

The remainder of the trip was spent in a lively discussion of literature. Althea was pleased—although not very surprised—to find that Sir Tracy's cynical nature did not preclude a broad interest in love of literature, and a well-informed mind. He had done classics at University, "a fact I try hard enough to hide, since erudition of a serious sort is as little regarded in a gentleman of fortune as it is in a young lady of seventeen—or three and twenty."

"Your impersonation of a mere fop had me entirely fooled. I was convinced you had not two ideas to rub against each other," Althea said wickedly.

By the time they reached Danning Hall, far in advance of the others of the party, they had covered the more current authors and were deep in an argument over the respective merits of the Greek and Roman playwrights: Althea held staunchly for the Greeks, while Tracy defended the Romans.

At Danning they were greeted by Mr. Pendarly's cousin Mrs. Abbot, a lively, pretty, stupid woman with a warmhearted manner and no sense that Althea could discern. After pressing them to come see her house, a manor cottage indistinguishable from the common run of such edifices, she offered them seats in the garden, and tried to encourage polite gossip and chatter upon such topics as the weather, dress, and flowers, and children. Tracy, inexperienced with the last and uninterested in the first, soon wandered away. Althea found then, to her embarrassment, that Mrs. Abbot began to discuss her cousin Edward in the fondest, most flattering of terms, obviously with an eye toward making a match. The assumption on her hostess's part that a match could be made in no way encouraged Althea's feelings, and it was a distinct relief to her when Pendarly's curricle, with the sharp, peering countenance of Miss Agatha Tidd, came sedately up the drive.

Very shortly thereafter the Fforyding barouche arrived and the party was complete. Mr. Pendarly luckily was able to dissuade his cousin from her fixed notion of displaying the peculiarities of Danning Hall to the guests, explaining that he had so extolled the beauty of the grounds that he doubted anyone in the group could be persuaded to enter indoors. The party moved in a desultory fashion across the green, Miss Fforyding and Mr. Tidd choosing to become involved in an observation of the statuary, and Lord Fforyding and his betrothed finding it convenient to rest under a willow situated out of the common path. This left Mr. Pendarly and his cousin, Miss Tidd, Althea, and Sir Tracy to walk down the path toward the lake.

Since their arrival Miss Tidd had made some efforts to attach herself to Sir Tracy, since Mr. Pendarly had not, outside of common civility, shown the least interest in her fatuous ramblings. As their group approached the water, Sir Tracy found that not only was Miss Tidd attempting to fix his interest, but that Mrs. Abbot was equally determined to foster it. She suggested that Sir Tracy might be interested in seeing the rest of the topiary in the garden just beyond the bend in the path, or failing that, perhaps the boathouse. Sir Tracy considered being rude by simply refusing to do either, but Althea happened to cast a glance at him—a glance full of enjoyment—and he stiffly offered his arm to Miss Tidd and started up the path toward the topiary. Mrs. Abbot then discovered that she had left her reticule back at the house; she must go and fetch it at once. She turned and hurried up the walk, the forgotten reticule flapping against her skirts. Althea would have laughed, but she saw the pained expression on Pendarly's face and forebore.

"I apologize for my cousin's want of manners, ma'am," he said stiffly.

"Not a want of manners so much as a superfluity of goodness, and a real affection for you, I should think. It really was rather funny. . . ." She began to giggle, but as Pendarly was apparently unable to appreciate the humor of the situation, Althea began to quiet herself, and had succeeded to a nicety when the memory of Calendar's face as he had been dragged up the path by the ambitious Miss Tidd sent her into a gale of laughter.

"Only think," she gasped when she had some breath to speak with, "only think of poor Calendar's expression when Miss Tidd finally inveigled him into a walk in the topiary! Oh lord!" The laughter tumbled out again and Mr. Pendarly began to smile.

"But I collect that I must have looked much the same when she appointed me her driver. That woman has the most appalling manner—she spent the entire trip here detailing to me her beaux and her bonnets." Pendarly joined in Althea's laughter awkwardly.

"You know that you looked no such way. Sir Tracy is spoiled, used to having his own way in everything, particularly, I imagine, where women are concerned. When he cannot charm them, or charm his way from them, and has not the brazenness to be rude—no, I correct that—I think he has the brazenness and that Miss Tidd would never have noticed it. When he is foiled, he will sulk like a child. You are too good-natured for that." In justice to Tracy, he had not precisely sulked—although what else she could call the ferocious scowl he had worn Althea did not know.

"I am not schooled to hide everything," Pendarly was saying softly, with a look that made Althea blush. "I am sure you know that I could never hide everything from *you*." What Pendarly's intended disclosure was Althea would not know, for Miss Tidd and Sir Tracy were returning from one direction and Mrs. Abbot from the other. The glares on the faces of Miss Tidd and Sir Tracy plainly expressed their mutual displeasure. Pendarly cast a rueful glance at Althea and rose to take Miss Tidd's arm.

From this time on the party became more general. Sophia and Mr. Tidd arrived from somewhere, both blushing and speechless, and Lord Fforyding appeared some minutes afterward with Miss Westleid on his arm. The rest of the visit was spent in examining the boathouse, which was very like almost every boathouse any of the party had ever seen; in a visit to the ruins, built five years before to make the property more picturesque; and finally, in the nuncheon set out on the lawn before the house.

After the nuncheon everyone sat about feeling pleased, with himself if not with the party at large. At length Lord Fforyding announced that it was time they started back for town. Again there was the problem of who would return with whom, or really, who was to bear the responsibility for Miss Tidd. Althea reflected that it was fortunate that Jonathan Tidd was so taken with Sophia Fforyding, else he might have been hurt by his aunt's behavior and the treatment it occasioned.

The matter was settled at last. Sir Tracy, acting, apparently, out of some twinge of conscience, offered to drive Miss Tidd to town, but the lady declined his offer icily, stating her reluctance to ride with anyone as toplofty as he. She fastened herself instead to Pendarly's arm, considering it better to take her chances with one who could be depended upon to be passably civil. She cast a pitying eye on Althea as she mounted the curricle.

"What on earth passed between you and Miss Tidd in the topiary?" Althea inquired of Tracy when they had driven a mile or so from Danning.

"I was finally forced to observe to her—after she had hung on my sleeve in the most shocking manner—that I could no longer permit her to do so, for she would throw a crease into my coat, and not all my respect for her sex could permit me to allow that. It had an effect that was little short of miraculous: suddenly she was able to support her own weight quite easily; she delivered herself of a prodigious sigh and stalked off ahead of me."

"Poor woman. She has made herself universally disliked, I fear, and then to have you say such a cutting thing to her. I do not wonder that she opted to drive back with Mr. Pendarly."

"Which is where you should be, I collect," Calendar said quietly.

"Have I made a complaint, sir? I hope it does not incommode you too seriously to have me as your passenger rather than Miss Tidd. Do I imagine you would have preferred her blandishments to mine?"

"Infinitely. But I have lost her good will forever, I fear."

"And serves you right, you dreadful, unpleasant man. How does one have a serious conversation with you? Or do you eschew serious conversations altogether?"

"No, not at all. I thought that was the privilige of your sex."

"Doubly odious."

Calendar raised his eyebrow. "I'm sorry you think so."

"Well, sir," Althea said firmly, "we have exhausted literature. What clse have we left? Music? Art? Politics? Aesthetics? And after we exhaust those, we shall have to give up our acquaintance, since there will be no more we can discuss. I leave the matter to you." Althea settled back comfortably and observed how the countryside sped by the wheels of the phaeton—at an alarming rate.

"I don't understand why your sister has been in town these four or five years now, and yet you never appeared until this spring," Tracy said at length.

Althea looked up in mild surprise. "That was hardly one of the topics I suggested to you, sir."

"You will answer it just the same, will you not?"

"I suppose I shall. But a real explanation would tire you dreadfully—it has to do with my mother's family, and the state of our estate, and my father, and my wretched brother, and—oh, enough to fill a romance, and all of it boring."

"I will endure the boredom if you think that is what it will take," Calendar said equably. "Are you cold? There is a rug behind you if you wish it."

"Thank you, I am fine." Althea considered again, then began her story. "You see, my grandfather's wife died—"

"I am desolated to hear of it, ma'am," Calendar said gravely.

"You needn't be! She died in the year 1763. So then he married my grandmother—"

"Who thus became your grandfather's wife. Fascinating. Please go on."

Althea restrained an impulse to box the gentleman's ears and continued with an air of impervious serenity. "He wed my grandmother, who was Lady Anne Kendon. Their daughter was my mother, Lady Dorothea Merrit. She married my father—"

"A most fortunate circumstance," Calendar drawled blandly.

"You brought this upon yourself, you know, and I am not going to curtail the story simply because you have not the patience to hear it through. The point to this genealogy is that her title descended from her to my sister Maria. Mary was only sixteen when Mama died, and the fuss she made about precedence was dreadful: I was only thirteen, and a wretched beanpole with freckles and no countenance, and Mary had always had gold hair and china eyes and been the prettiest thing, and now she was a ladyship! She became quite insufferable."

"This is all interesting, but what is it to the point?"

"I am coming to it. Do please endeavor to learn a little patience. When Mary was seventeen my Aunt Barbara invited her to town. I suppose that she thought it would not hurt to be hostess to a pretty niece who had some little money. So Mary went, and met Francis, and they were married. A very simple story, if I leave out all the nonsense that passed before they finally did marry! As for myself, I was never appealing enough, or conciliatory enough for Aunt Babs to take up. And Papa and Merrit—my odious brother—did need someone to look after the house for them. You cannot imagine a greater pair of gudgeons. I really wonder how affairs at Hook Well are managing these days. It was not until I took it upon myself to escape that I had been out of the county."

"Probably a very wise thing. One question more, then. Who is this Aunt Barbara of yours who caviled at your presence?"

"Lady Shelbering. She married Shelbering some ten years ago—having disposed of three husbands previously. Aunt Babs is something of a family fixture. She does not go about so much among the *ton* these days, but to hear her speak, in the old days she quite made and broke fashion."

"Not quite so important as that, but I remember her. The most insipid, sly old woman—but I should not be speaking so of your family. Forgive me."

"Why not? I assure you that I have very little good to say about most of my family, and no one in the family has anything good to say for Aunt Babs, except for Mary, and that is only to be expected. But must we really speak of my fatiguing relatives?"

"What do you think of music, then?" Tracy surrendered.

"As a topic or an art?" Althea challenged.

Within five minutes they were again deep in discussion. They clashed cheerfully for the remainder of the ride over their taste in music.

"I conclude," Calendar said sometime later, "that you are not so much unappreciative as untaught. It is a mercy you did not stay in the country any longer than you did, or your ideas might be even more outlandish."

"You shall not quiz me and escape unscathed. But you must on no account tell Maria that I have been speaking as an intelligent person—that would throw her into a panic. She insists that men like their wives sweet and amiable and stupid, and that it is the first business of our lives to be wives."

"You tone is quite evangelical," Tracy scolded her gently.

Althea continued in a smaller voice. "You will pardon the ouburst. And I will say that while I don't approve of your taste for Italian music, I am glad to find you have some thoughts on the matter."

"I am generally thought to have some conversation, ma'am. And if *I* sounded condescending before, I humbly beg your pardon."

Althea felt herself blush at his look. "I am overwhelmed," she said quickly. "But now you are lapsing into civility, and that will never do from you. If I cannot sharpen my wits by battling with you, I shall suffocate. And I see we are here. I will not trouble you to see me in, but thank you for the enjoyable ride. Good afternoon."

Althea was swung down from the carriage by a lackey, cast Calendar a brief smile, and turned into the house, leaving him to watch after her with a very quizzical look indeed.

Chapter Seven

Mr. Edward Pendarly's company, his very evident admiration of Miss Ervine, had the effect of making that company, that admiration, and in fact, Mr. Pendarly himself, increasingly welcome at the Bevan house. From merely esteeming him as a friend (and enjoying the sensation that was caused by her friend's possession of a profile straight from a Grecian coin), Althea began to wonder if perhaps her feelings were not growing to greater warmth. True, Maria was not overpleased by his attendance, but as she was embroiled in her own heedless intrigues, she had little time to observe the pass to which Mr. Pendarly's particularity had brought him and her sister. It was her hope that sooner or later some more eligible male might be found to tempt Althea, one who would dislodge Edward Pendarly from his position as favorite. She spent some little energy toward this end, noting with pleasure that certain prizes in the Matimonial Mart were to be seen now and again in the drawing room at Grosvenor Square. She forever quizzed her sister if she did not think Lord So-and-So had a charming address, or if Mr. Such-a-One did not present a modish figure.

"Certainly he ties his neckcloth well," Althea would murmur to this sort of question.

Maria only threw up her hands in pretty despair, wondering what besides his beauty made Edward Pendarly superior in her sister's eyes to the luminaries she bludgeoned Althea with.

Sir Tracy Calendar came several times to call upon Althea. The first time after the outing in the country she was not at home. Since the conclusion to their talk on the return from Danning Hall, Althea had had mixed feelings about the gentleman, and her feelings were just so mixed when she saw his card upon the tray and realized she had missed him. Upon his next visit Miss Ervine was at home, but Calendar found himself rather coolly received: Althea, feeling awkward in speaking to him, was somewhat more reserved in her manner than she had meant to be. This Sir Tracy seemed to sense: he set out to charm her. Against her better judgment, she *was* charmed. By the time Calendar left, Althea was altogether in charity with him again, although she confided to Maria that he was still the most outrageous person in her acquaintance.

"Althea, that is certainly no accomplishment," Maria chided.

"I know it." Althea laughed. "But it seems that Sir Tracy does not."

Upon the next occasion of Calendar's calling Althea was invited to drive out in the Park with him. As the tiger, Eustace, handed her into the curricle, she remarked to Calendar that the only reason she had been persuaded to ride out with him was that she was sure that it increased her credit in the *ton*. Eustace was so scandalized by this remark that he almost dropped Althea down into the street again. A reproving look from Calendar sent him racing to his perch behind with a look of displeased wonderment upon his face. "There's mort's what's usual glad enough to ride with us," he muttered under his breath. "I seen 'em looking as how they'd cry for the 'onor we do 'em." One stern look from Tracy halted this dark muttering, however, and Eustace subsided, fixing his glare at the back of Calendar's neck.

Sir Tracy exerted himself to be as outrageous as possible with Althea for the sheer pleasure of stinging her into retort. His amusement was compounded by the fact that when he said something outrageous, she would cap it immediately, and only then recover her sense of propriety and blush. Althea caught on to this plot in short order, however, and soon adopted a trick of making her scandalous pronouncements in the tones of a respectful and awed schoolgirl. Eustace, who disapproved on principle of all women except possibly his mother and certain of the kitchen maids at his master's establishments, hid his displeasure as best he could, reckoning that this temporary aberration could not last with Calendar.

Within the week of her first appearance Althea had met Brummell and had appeared at Almack's, these two occasions marking the true arrival of a lady in First Society. She had been prepared to dislike Brummell, and had been rash enough to say so, which, since she subsequently admitted to him it was impossible to do, pleased the Beau very well. He was disposed, he said lazily, to bring her into fashion, if she was not very much opposed to the notion. Since his hints were kind—far kinder than most of the remarks Brummell was apt to make about his fellow creatures and their dress—Althea took them with good grace and appreciation.

Maria's pleasure in Brummell's approval was all but overturned by Althea's reciprocal statement that she approved of *him*.

"You are pleased with him? Better he be pleased with you—which, thank God, he is. Dear Ally, never let him hear you say such a thing. Of course you are pleased with him!"

"It is too late now, Sister—I told him when we met," Althea said gravely.

"Althea!" Lady Bevan said in tones of outrage. "Have you no idea at all what you are about? Oh, dear heaven, told him to his very face." Maria sank back gingerly into one of the gilded chairs Almack's provided for the discomfort of its patrons. "But you have taken, there's no doubt about it," she continued after a refreshing moment with her salts. "I am not at all ashamed."

"Thank you, Sister," Althea began. She was spared Maria's further animadversions upon this subject by Edward Pendarly, who advanced upon them and asked for Miss Ervine's company during the waltz. With relief Maria waved her sister away and sat, regaining her spirits, until Mr. Wallingham could advance and tender his admiration.

Maria was truly, if fitfully, pleased by her sister's success. When she remembered that Althea had been to a party or a dinner and had been much admired, she would fold her hands complacently and nod like the dowagers who sat at the sides of the room nodding and smiling benignly at their daughters. But most of her time was taken up in proving, or trying to prove, that Francis's absence meant nothing at all to her. She danced, flirted, gossiped, and generally worked herself into a state of feverish gaiety. Gentlemen called as often to see her as to see her sister, and she was as likely to be seen driving or dancing, usually with John Wallingham, the most persistent of her beaux. By the same token, Althea, who was equally absorbed in social pastimes, took time from her schedule to fret over Maria and her health, as she saw her sister grow pale and thin. When she suggested an evening's respite, however, she was repulsed in no uncertain terms.

Althea was speaking with Harriet Leveson-Gower one night, a little more than a fortnight after her first appearance at Almack's, in the Leveson-Gower box at the opera, where she was a guest. Harriet was directing Althea's attentions to the people her guest had not yet met.

"Who on earth is that quiz of a woman over there?" Althea interrupted, pointing to an amply built, hideously dressed matriarch.

"That is Mrs. Laverham. Dreadful, isn't she? Helena designed that dress for her—after she had a falling out

with Mrs. L. I cannot conceive why she continues, after
this time, to wear that rag, but I suppose that Helena
made it dear enough, and that woman is a tiresome
nipfarthing. She's rather a dragon—I don't think she's
very good *ton*, but she is received everywhere, and her
cook makes a lovely iced cup."

Althea, watching the figure in lime green and chocolate
satin stalk by, prayed that fate and heaven would deliver
her from every quarreling with Madame Helena.

"She's got a daughter, too," Lady Leveson-Gower continued with an odd look at Althea. "Miss Laverham isn't
at all in her Mama's style, and dresses to please herself—
that is the only thing I can imagine she disobliges her
mother in, such a weak-willed little thing she is. And now
these last weeks she has been laid up with the measles,
locked up at home, which I think is exactly like her."
Lady Leveson-Gower's attention was claimed by her
brother-in-law at that moment, before Althea could inquire what connection there could be between lack of
character and contracting the measles. She had stood to
consider this, smiling obscurely, when she was joined by
Mr. Pendarly, come to inquire how she liked the program.

The two of them enjoyed a few minutes of rational
conversation, as much as was permitted over the pleasant
roar of well-bred manners at an intermission; it was plain
to any and all interested spectators that Lady Bevan's sister and Mr. Pendarly enjoyed each other's company
greatly. After five minutes' exchange about the voice of
the diva, Mr. Pendarly noticed that his companion was
glowing from the heat. He immediately pressed her to sit
down and wait until he could return with a cup of punch.
Unfortunately this idea was scotched when, in retreating
toward the door of the box, Pendarly put a heedless foot
through the flounce of Althea's muslin skirt, obliging her
to go in search of a needle and thread. Mr. Pendarly
could not apologize profusely enough; after the third time

Althea told him good-humoredly that it was no great thing, and she would seek some aid in the retiring rooms.

Pursuit of needle and thread was less easy than she had imagined, for the crush in the hallways was shocking, and it was some minutes before she could find and retire to the powdering room, set aside for just those repairs a lady of fashion might find expedient within a night. An attendant was shortly engaged to mend the flounce, while Althea assumed a stance that put her forcibly in mind of the hours spent towering over Helena's seamstresses. It was as she stood there that she heard her name mentioned outside the door of the room by some unseen woman. Normally she would have retreated to avoid hearing more, but positioned as she was, she could hardly move without causing a commotion.

". . . think the poor chit has any idea of it at all. It is scandalous of him, certainly, but I don't think she knows of it," the first voice was saying.

"I don't know. She appears to be a rather dashing thing to me. Throwing herself at another's betrothed is certainly not a well-mannered piece of behavior."

"Throwing herself? Unjust, Selina. Would you say she was throwing herself if the boy were not engaged to Fulvia Laverham's daughter? It is my opinion that young Mr. Pendarly is relying upon his handsome face to get him out of the scrape of courting one while his betrothed is ill. I still maintain that Miss Ervine is not guilty."

Althea missed the next few words of the conversation. Her mind was clamoring for explanation. Edward Pendarly engaged to Miss Laverham? How he must be laughing at her gullibility even now. And what a jest to tell his betrothed when she came out of the sickroom. It was beyond belief.

"I am persuaded that Fulvia cannot know of his attentions to her, for you know she is not one to be backward in protecting her daughter's rights," the second voice cut through Althea's thoughts.

"She is all taken up with Georgiana's sickness, and if she has heard anything of Pendarly's defection, you may depend upon it she expects the money will bring him back soon enough. What with the debts his Uncle Paul and that poor dear Celicia have piled up—and heaven knows his brother will not give him any help—why the family is completely to pieces. No wonder he has to marry the chit."

The voices had become less distinct and Althea realized that now she was actively listening. She stopped herself angrily, forcing her attention back to the patch of carpet she had been studying while the maid mended the flounce, but she wore such a look of fury that the girl, on her hands and knees at Althea's feet, gave a yelp of terror and accidentally stabbed Althea with the needle. Althea forced herself to smile at the girl, and the flounce was hurriedly mended. It took Althea another few minutes to compose herself enough to face returning to the Leveson-Gower box.

Fortunately when she returned the act had begun and there was darkness in which she could sit and brood. Her dread was that at the next intermission Pendarly would return again and seek her out, and that she would be forced into a scene there and then, which would rival the scene on the stage. To her profound relief it was Tracy Calendar who approached her, armed with two glasses of lemonade. They spoke for some minutes, mostly indulging in the sort of commonplaces that allowed Althea's mind to continue its feverish considering. One thought in particular suddenly struck her with such force that she choked on her lemonade, causing Sir Tracy to cast her a look of concern, sympathy, and mildest amusement.

He knew.

In the Park, when he had spoken so peculiarly to Pendarly, he had been trying to warn her. And that was why Pendarly disliked his company. Althea was honest enough to admit that had Calendar just come out with the truth, she might have refused to believe him. Now, rather than be impatient with him for his strange behavior, she was grateful.

"Are you feeling ill, ma'am?" He took her fan from her hand and waved it a few times for her, gently, as if he were accustomed to fanning distressed ladies at the opera.

"It is the heat," she said weakly. "And the noise. Oh dear." The look of a moment ago had vanished; all that remained in his eyes was concern. He murmured something about the paucity of ventilation and the quality of the air in the Opera House, and Althea nodded gratefully, too low to rankle at the suggestion that she could be undone by a little heat. In the pause she tried to think of some way she could convey her gratitude for his warning without being too specific—but could think of none, and grew increasingly uncomfortable with his solicitude.

"You may stop fanning me now," she said sharply. "I am quite recovered. Undoubtedly it was the heat. And the punch *was* strong." She cast truth to the winds, since the lemonade served here was renowned for its insipidity. Tracy regarded her with a glimmer of understanding in his otherwise wholly polite, disinterested glance. The perfect calm of that glance irritated Althea, already full of irritation with herself and with Pendarly. The final knowledge that she owed Calendar every courtesy made her wish to box his ears, or do something to mar his imperturbable grin. She managed instead an almost creditable smile.

"I understand that you have Brummell completely captivated, ma'am," he said lightly. "It is not every woman who can say so. I suppose now, rather than my company increasing your credit, yours will increase mine." Althea's smile drooped; this sally did not amuse her. "How did you put him at your feet? He is said to be proof against mere beauty—it is George himself who says so—and God knows women enough have tried." The satirical quirk was in his brow now, and Althea recognized a strong urge to strike that red head.

"I captivated him with my respectable conversation, sir," she said shortly.

"Your respectable conversation? O happy Brummell to have heard such a thing. I have never been so privileged." His tone was dry, his manner aggrieved. The urge to hit him grew stronger and stronger.

"Perhaps that is because you rarely speak in a conversation that is respectable, sir, and do not recognize it when you hear it. When I was still in the schoolroom my governess told me that the wisest thing to do is to pattern one's conversation after that of the people one converses with. If you do not speak respectably, then I must try to speak as barbarously as you do, only to be polite." She wished that this were a ball where she might vanish into the crowd. She wished the entr'acte would end and the lights of the theater go down one more time. She wished she did not have the maddening urge to cry.

"Perhaps sometime you will honor me with a little of your respectable conversation, ma'am. If I called tomorrow, would that be too short notice?" Tracy asked humbly, his eyes gleaming wickedly.

"I regret I will not be at home tomorrow," Althea said stiffly.

"At any time? That is very sad for me, ma'am. Another day will do as well."

"Certainly." Althea resolved that no matter what day he called, she would not receive him.

"There, you see, I have quarreled you out of your sullens, as you were so kind as to do for me the other day when we drove to Danning. And I see the curtain is about to rise again. Good evening, Miss Ervine. And rest well. Nothing seems quite so grim by daylight." He made a polite bow and sauntered away, pausing to greet Harriet Leveson-Gower and a few of her party, who were just then entering the box.

Althea was miserable; now she owed that infuriating man even more—for he *had* diverted her thoughts for a few blessed minutes. And he knew, she was sure now, of all that had happened to her that evening. The rest of the opera went by uneventfully as she tried to piece together a scheme whereby Francis would return to Maria, and she would make her thank you to Sir Tracy (without having him laugh at her for it, which she suspected he might well do), and have five minutes alone with Edward Pendarly to tell him her opinion of men who made fools of hapless women.

When she returned to the house at Grosvenor Square that evening Maria was standing in the hallway, just back from a card party she had been promised for. As she chattered to her sister of the evening's gossip, they climbed the stairs and made toward their bedrooms. Just before they parted, Maria remembered something and turned back to Althea to rejoice her with this bit of news.

"What a triumph, Ally! Brummell told Sally Jersey that you have speaking eyes!"

"Oh, Maria, do please shut up!" said the triumphant sister miserably.

Chapter Eight

Mr. Edward Pendarly, happily unaware of Althea Ervine's discovery, sent her a note the next morning regretting the fact that he had not seen her again at the opera. He then set out, uncomfortably, for his daily call of duty at the house of his betrothed, Miss Georgiana Laverham.

It had ceased to be an article of wonder to him that he could pay such a visit and then go directly to call upon Miss Ervine: having resolved to hold, as long as he could, Althea's good opinion, he went after his foredoomed happiness without much thought as to how discovery might affect her. He had no great opinion of himself, and could not believe that the loss of one more admirer could cause her the slightest distress. Thus he persuaded himself that his behavior was not so very infamous after all. It was a matter of indifference to him whether Miss Laverham knew of his flirtations or not—at least he told himself this was the case—and he remained remarkably calm whenever he went to sit in the drawing room of the Laverham house. No sighs or lingering looks of reproach, however much he might have anticipated them, were forthcoming, so he really had no practical idea how proof he could be against such tactics.

It was only the night before that Fulvia Laverham, in company for the first time since her daughter took ill, had learned of Miss Ervine's existence. In fact, she might have remained blissfully ignorant had it not been for an obliging friend, who specifically sought her out to wreak what damage she might on Miss Ervine's reputation and Mrs. Laverham's peace of mind. When she was informed that Mr. Pendarly waited below, Mrs. Laverham excused herself from her daughter's bedside and descended to meet him.

She was in fine fighting temper. She had just spent an unpleasant half-hour with her daughter, whom she had apprised of Pendarly's perfidy. To her disgust Georgiana had not become enraged, but had merely subsided into weak tears and said that if her dearest Edward truly loved another, *she* would not stand in his way, although it broke her heart. Mrs. Laverham, no weak soul herself, was disgusted by this want of spirit in her only child, and resolved that the wretch should find no easy atonement for making her little girl so miserable.

In her own mind, she was Boadicea defending her kingdom; to Edward Pendarly, she appeared more like one—or perhaps all—of the Furies descending upon him. For the first time he wondered if perhaps his reserve was as strong as he thought.

They went to the drawing room, where he waited in polite silence until she had settled her considerable bulk into a chair, and then inquired after Miss Georgie's recovery. In the usual course of things Mrs. Laverham would have said that dearest Georgie was doing as well as might be expected. Today she drew a deep breath before she began to speak: Pendarly knew a second twinge of apprehension. Mrs. Laverham released the breath in a long sigh and stated that her daughter was Not Very Well At All.

Mr. Pendarly was properly sympathetic, asking what could be interfering with Miss Georgie's splendid recovery. His concern was sincere enough: he had no reason, except the desire to be quit of her (but not her considerable fortune), to wish her ill. Mrs. Laverham, however, did not seem to think his degree of regard was proper. She resolved to speak more clearly.

"No, I am grieved to report to you that Georgie is not well at all. Her poor dear spirits have been thrown quite low, and I am sure she would have lain there all morning weeping had I not told her it might distress you to hear of her doing so. She desired me give her best love to you." Pendarly acknowledged this with a smile. "Some dreadful stories have reached her ears from somewhere, although I cannot imagine who would tell such tales to my poor, sick darling."

Pendarly grew a shade paler, the lady noticed with satisfaction. She continued with relish: "I cannot, of course, say what these stories were, for such a sweet, honorable thing as my Georgie is, she would not tell me the whole of it, but only suffers in silence. I do know, however, that she mentioned your name more than once." Pendarly blushed at this, then grew paler still. "Have you been much about town these weeks, sir? I have hardly seen a soul these days, although I did get out to the opera last night. It does one good to be brought up to all the new faces that appear during such an absence. Georgie will be quite captivated when I tell her who I saw last night—if she has left off her crying." Mrs. Laverham allowed herself the luxury of a perfectly malicious smile at his confusion. He, in his turn, could only murmur that he thought Brummell had returned to town from the country, and that he hoped Mrs. Laverham had enjoyed the opera.

"Do you know, Vinnie Warin said she saw you there, sir, but I collect she must have been mistaken." There was a plain threat in the lady's voice now, and Pendarly's complexion rather compared to the color of a tallow candle. He said soberly that he supposed that Lady Warin must have been mistaken, but this admission did not appease his hostess. There was a slight lull in the conversation and then, once Mrs. Laverham had rallied her defenses, she inquired after the health of Pendarly's Uncle Paul (the profligate) and his dear Grandmother Celicia (a compulsive wagerer). Pendarly's speech was so reduced by this time that he could only choke out something to the effect that he believed they enjoyed tolerable health before the power of speech left him completely.

Half an hour after his arrival, when Edward Pendarly rose to take his leave of Mrs. Laverham, he was a chastened man. Mrs. Laverham, having succeeded in bringing him to reason, as she termed it, rose also, and graciously reminded him that he was always a welcome visitor, and asked if he had any messages to send up to the poor invalid. He stiffly sent his assured affection and inquired meekly as to when Miss Georgiana could see visitors. Mrs. Laverham informed him airily that it could be any day *now*, and Pendarly wished her a hurried adieu as cordially as any man so thoroughly chastened could be expected to.

Mrs. Fulvia Laverham, filled with the satisfactory

feeling of a job well done, ascended to her daughter's room to assure her that she need not worry: Mr. Pendarly's affections, as always, were hers. And would stay so, if the gentleman knew what was wise, she muttered, but not loudly enough for her child to hear.

Althea, along with her chocolate, received the day's complement of letters and invitations, including a note from her father, which she opened straight away, hoping that that, at least, would afford her some amusement. His usual pomposity, and the unusual talent he had for stating something three times over in flowing phrases, did much to render his letters unreadable. This morning's missive, however, surprised her in that it was written with a lucidity born of desperation: domestic affairs at Hook Well had apparently come to such a pass that Sir George was willing to admit some possible fault on his part, if that would speed his daughter's return to housewifery. All in all, Althea considered it quite the kindest, most liberal letter she had ever received from her father, and while she had no intention of returning to Hook Well until, she thought grimly, she had taken care of certain business, it made the thought of her eventual return that much easier.

After a few minutes' reflection on the infelicities of her father's epistolary style, Althea reluctantly turned to a note that bore Mr. Pendarly's hand. The whole tone of his address she now regarded with altered sentiments and felt to be entirely too familiar, however ordinary the sentiments might be. He regretted not seeing her again, hoped she had finished the evening happily, and suggested that he might like to call upon her in the afternoon. He was her most devoted servant. Althea crumpled up the paper and flung it on the floor with an imprecation that startled Banders, just entering the room. That he would dare to address her in such terms, she thought indignantly, forgetting that two days before she would have thought his terms quite correct: she was in no humor for reason. The trouble with rational-minded people, she reflected bitterly, is that when they wish to be unreasonable, their rationality gets in the way in the most unsatisfactory manner. Maria was never troubled this way, nor Francis, nor her father, nor Merrit. She wondered in passing if perhaps Sir Tracy Calendar had ever noticed this problem. That thought irritated her, too, and she called sharply for Banders to lay out her riding dress, saying the only thing for it (Banders had no idea what "it" was) was a good ride in the Park, and the Polite World, such as might be abroad at the unseasonable hour of ten in the morning, might stare at its pleasure.

Tracy Calendar, up early, gave his horse a run through the Park before making his way to Manton's Shooting Gallery for an hour's practice. He was in a state of contemplation and did not see Althea Ervine when she passed him, accompanied by a sour-faced, indignant groom. Miss Ervine saw him, was surprised that he did not return her salute, and, as he passed on and she continued, remembered with a blush the way they had parted the night before. Perhaps, she thought shamefacedly, he was so out of patience with her that he had resolved to cut her. When she considered the debt she owed him, a slow flood of color infused her face. A day ago she would have laughed off his cut as a jest or a simple lack of attention and counted it no matter. Now she found herself thinking in the most remarkably fusty, melodramatic terms: everything was a portent. The rest of the ride, intended to cool her charged emotions, was troubled by new worries over this incident, and she returned to Bevan House as troubled as when she had left it.

Sir Tracy, completely unaware of Althea's passing, or of her troubled thoughts, went on to Manton's and spent his hour there sharpening his already impeccable aim, then returned to his house. If anyone at Manton's noticed that Calendar was a trifle preoccupied, no one thought of asking him the cause: Calendar's regard for his own privacy was well known, and the sight of his targets, when he had done shooting, had the peculiar effect of making one undesirous of disturbing him. It remained for Lady Boskingram to ask the question. On his return to Cavendish Street he found his aunt in the library, reading poetry and sipping tea. When he entered the room she put away the book, drained her cup and put it down in a purposeful manner, and settled herself into the couch.

"You look as though you are setting yourself up for a siege, Aunt," he said lazily.

"How unbecoming of you to notice it, Tracy. And you look to be in a brown study. What occasions so much thought?" She watched the eyebrows take their sudden swoop upward. "There is your supercilious look again. Do you know, I feel almost married to you—dreadful idea—for I see you so little we are become like a fashionable couple, going our own ways."

"But you cut me to the quick, ma'am. A dreadful idea? When all that has kept me from sweeping you off to Gretna is the fact that we are related." He expressed his hurt by strolling over and kissing her powdery cheek lightly.

"Beside my well-known affection for you, scandalous Aunt, did you not say I was to treat my house as my own, so long as I gave you prior warning of any and all orgies, scandals, and similarly intemperate behavior I planned? In fact, I was sure I had been a model host, for I have foregone my orgies (which you know I hold on a regular basis), all so you might not be troubled to hide in your room." Tracy crossed his long legs and toyed idly with the fob at his waist.

"Since this is your house and I the interloper, I collect that you are trying to shame me into admitting that you are a very fine host to me. But you are dodging my question, which I greatly dislike. All your banter and foolishness may fool others. It don't distract me." She glowered at him sternly. "I demand to know what could possibly be more absorbing than fending off the complaints of your aged aunt."

"I am sorry, ma'am. It is abysmal of me, I know." Tracy smiled thoughtfully. "To tell the truth, I am planning something of a rather intemperate nature—at least something original. And I am not altogether sure of the propriety of my plans—not that I will let that stop me, but . . ."

Lady Boskingram was intrigued by this leading statement and demanded to know what was the ending to such a provoking beginning.

"I am contemplating matrimony," Tracy threw into the silence and sat back to admire the dramatic effect.

"Don't try to fool with me, Tracy, for I'll have the truth from you sooner or later, you know," his aunt warned. After a moment or two, during which he regarded her solemnly, she gasped, "Don't tell me that Amalia has finally converted you to husband by dint of one of those infamous schoolroom misses with all the accomplishments!"

"Not at all, I am thankful to say. She is no schoolroom miss, and I owe no thanks to Amalia for her discovery. She—the lady—has, if I understand it, divided her last few years between managing her father's house and much of his estate, and studying classical literature. She is rather an exceptional woman, Aunt."

"I collect she must be if she has gotten you to moon after a bluestocking. How very unlike you, Tracy. And what a change from your adulation of Bessborough's girl. That's the only other female I can remember your having admired in all these years."

"I beg you will not bring up attachments I held when I was only in short coats, ma'am. And you know well enough that if she were merely a bluestocking, I would not have found her so enchanting." He paused, saw she was about to speak, and began again. "I will withdraw the last word, for I can see it leaves me open to all manner of your disparaging remarks."

"Well, you have told me that she is a learned woman but not a bluestocking, that she managed her father's estate (what was her father doing in all that while?), and that she is enchanting. Do you think you could now tell me her name?"

"Why, had I not? Her name is Ervine, Aunt, Althea Ervine."

"Ervine. Is it possible I saw her at Esterhazy's drum, talking to George Brummell quite as if he were not the God of Fashion but only an ordinary mortal? But Tracy, that girl's not beautiful—taking enough, I warrant you, and she dresses well enough, but I would have thought that for you—"

"For me she does excellently well, thank you. I can find nothing wrong in her appearance, and as for her character! She is bright and maddening and wise as a sage about some things, and the greenest green head about others. And what a tongue! I don't doubt but that she will lead me a dance if ever I can persuade her to wed me, but I am ready to wed her and welcome the dance, her flighty sister, her overbearing papa, and all."

"You love her!" the dowager accused.

"Did I not say so?" he asked lightly.

"I only hope that she can appreciate your finer qualities, buried as they are under that dreadful dandified exterior and your shockingly disrespectful manners to you elders." Sir Tracy shook his head in bereaved denial. "I hope she knows you're worth ten of the grandest beaux in town."

Lady Boskingram paused to wipe her eyes, while Tracy refreshed himself with a walk the length of the room and back.

"You said *if*, Tracy. Is there any question that she won't take you?"

"Not everyone is so kind as to see me with your affection, Aunt. It is possible that her affections are permanently attached somewhere else."

"Nonsense. If the girl you described to me ain't got the sense to leap at you, then you described her very ill," Lady Boskingram said fondly. This assurance did not seem to cheer Sir Tracy greatly.

"Ma'am, I could only have understated where Althea is concerned. But you know that I am not the only male on the Matrimonial Market, and there have been others who have evinced the same interest as I. I fancy that one of them—just the wrong one, too—was on the point of making her—of fixing his interest with her. And while I deplore her lack of taste, she may still prefer him to me. The devil is in it that the fellow—Pendarly—is contracted to Georgiana Laverham. You remember her? Tiny fair thing, pretty in a dollish sort of manner, with no conversation and little countenance, Fulvia Laverham's daughter. I see *that* rings a bell for you. The man has been paying Miss Ervine as formal a court as any I've seen. You know Mrs. Laverham. I cannot believe that he has been released from his betrothal just to suit his own convenience or Althea's happiness—not by her."

"And your Miss Ervine knows nothing of all this?"

"I have a notion that she learned of it all somehow last night at the opera. Fulvia Laverham was there, and I would not put it past her to have accosted Althea and apprised her of the situation in no uncertain terms. If Althea—Miss Ervine—knows, then she will put an end to her attachment to Pendarly at once. I know that. But I am not sure how deep her affection for him goes, and I know that he is much smitten with her, for all his responsibilities to Miss Laverham. I did try, once or twice, to hint him away or give Althea some notion of how the land lay, but I could not say 'This man is betrothed—best keep your distance!' So I fear that she has taken me amiss and all I have done is to alienate her from myself."

Calendar smiled bitterly. "A charming state of affairs, is it not?"

"You have made a fine mull of it, haven't you, my dear?" Lady Boskingram admitted comfortably. "But it may all come aright in the end with some patience from you—not that you have overmuch of that commodity."

"I expect to be, let us say, rather *impatient* this afternoon."

"Tracy, do please restrain yourself from dropping mysterious hints. I am on tenterhooks. Have a little pity and tell me straight out what you mean."

"I intend to offer for her this afternoon."

"Just out of the other fellow's arms? Dear boy, if you have any sense about military campaigns, you should know not to rush the enemy that way. Or a woman." Lady Boskingram shook her head in bewilderment.

"That's just the thing, ma'am," Tracy insisted. "If I don't make sure of her now, I may never have the chance again. You have no idea the ways we contrive to stay at odds with each other, but if I approach her the right way—and God knows what that is—it may suit her down to the ground to be betrothed just now. If I wait until her temper is cooled, why then she will probably be rational and say we should not suit, and we should quarrel over *that*, and so you see I should never win her to me."

This tangle of logic so exhausted Tracy that he dropped back onto the couch and spent some minutes scowling fiercely at the andirons.

"I seem to recall that we did things more simply when I was young," his aunt offered weakly.

"I collect I have been trying to convince myself more than you, Aunt, but if you only knew the way I affect her now—it will change, I'm sure of it, but good God, ma'am, now! There seems to be only the method I plan to try. And," he added softly, "as you surmised, and for all and no good reasons, I do love her."

"Well," Lady Boskingram sighed philosophically, "if

you know that much, I suppose I must leave you to your own affairs."

Three-thirty that afternoon found Althea awaiting inspiration to govern her actions: should she go out in order to avoid a visit by Pendarly, or stay in to receive Calendar should he call? Fortunately, before inspiration arrived, Sir Tracy himself did, and Althea was happily absolved of concern for the matter. He had called to ask her driving, and if during the Promenade he said nothing to her of the cut he had given her earlier in the day, Althea regarded it as hopeful that he had called at all.

They drove silently for a few minutes: Tracy was unsure how to preface a proposal of marriage to such a reluctant idol, and Althea was worrying over the fancied slight she had received that morning. She would wait, she resolved, to hear him speak of it in order to forgive him handsomely. Strangely, though, he did not speak of it, and she grew more stiff and the resolve to forgive handsomely grew less handsome and less firm. Tracy, for all his noted address, found himself completely at a loss to begin; he could not even think of a plausible excuse to send Eustace away to afford them some privacy. Eustace himself, sitting glumly behind, reflected that it was probably the gentry mort what had the master so terrible blue-deviled, and he heartily wished them rid of her.

Althea finally took matters into her own hands and said the first thing that occurred to her. "That is the most beautiful pair of horses I have yet seen in London, Sir Tracy," she began inconsequentially. Tracy, relieved by the introduction of the topic—or any topic at all—delved into it wholeheartedly, with rather more fervor than he was wont to expend on such a discussion.

"I am judged to be a tolerable critic of horseflesh, Miss Ervine," he said enthusiastically.

"Tolerable?" Althea laughed brittlely. "You are known to be top of the trees! I have often wished I could have a

phaeton, especially in town, but my fortune will hardly
admit of such an extravagance."

"You tell me that you drive, Miss Ervine?" Eustace,
divining the inevitable outcome of this discussion, cow-
ered in the back, glaring at his master's neck. Tracy, mer-
cilessly unaware of the grimaces aimed at him, continued
to drive on as Miss Ervine elaborated.

"Certainly I do. My brother taught me, back in Lancashire, and I have always wished I could do so in town;
there is something very striking about a smartly driven
phaeton. And Mr. Brummell told me that I should never
be backward in doing what is striking."

"I would never dare quarrel with Brummell's taste,
ma'am. But I would add that there is generally something
striking about *any* carriage that is smartly driven: the
number of gentlemen who think they can drive to an inch
and are really quite ham-fisted would shock you, ma'am. I
would have thought, from your descriptions of him, that
your brother would not prove a great driver or a patient
teacher."

"He had ample motive for patience, sir, although he
would never be my instructor of choice. But with that motive he became a satisfactory teacher. You see, I black-
mailed him—is that the word?—into giving me lessons,
some three years ago when Papa had gone visiting."

"Your methods are a trifle unorthodox, certainly,"
Calendar said dryly, with a twist of that speaking brow.

"Oh, I know it. You see, Merrit had been sent down
from university for some prank involving the chancellor's
nightcap and a lady of—of—somewhat *generous nature*,
known as High Flung Jenny. Merrit feared Papa's reaction to his mess no end, and I was entirely ruthless in
using it against him for my own ends. Yes, I know exactly
how sordid it sounds, and it was rather."

"It sounds like excellent romance, Miss Ervine, but did
you learn to drive, in truth?"

"Oh yes, for while Merrit is too racketty for anything,

and cannot chose a horse but it must be some mean, showy nag, all chest and no breath, he is a good driver. And I am a better, I think, for at least I respect my horses."

Eustace, feeling the shadow of ignominy hovering over him, sank down as low as he could, hoping the world would not connect him with this obviously deranged pair in the curricle.

"If that is the case, ma'am, do you object to showing me your prowess?" Tracy asked, heedless of Eustace's now audible groans. "I will ask you to relieve me while I recover my strength." The exchange was made, and Calendar turned to give Eustace one exquisitely quelling glance before they were under way again. Althea, sensing that mutiny had been put down, flicked the whip expertly out over the heads of her leaders, caught the thong neatly, and proceeded forward. A very few minutes in this fashion convinced Calendar that she had not exaggerated—she was a good driver, needing only a little experience with town traffic to sharpen her nicely. Even Eustace, who for the sake of his reputation had slid his head so deep into his collar that he began to look deformed, grumbled less loudly than before. Althea took the phaeton once around the Park, to the admiration of several acquaintances, who understood better than she what a signal honor she was being done.

After a circuit of the Park Althea was content to return to being a passenger, with only a small, but sincere, show of reluctance. "I could continue for any length of time," she said happily. She turned and addressed Eustace sharply. "You may come out from your coat now. I have quite done for today!"

Tracy gave a shout of laughter, to the consternation of his bays. Eustace had to jump down and go quickly to their heads to quiet them, while Althea and Tracy regained their countenances and Eustace some of his dignity. The strain of conversation had vanished, and they could discuss any number of unimportant topics, each seeking to avoid what most interested him. As the conversation again came around to horses, Althea found herself with an opportunity to discuss his behavior that morning.

"I greatly admired the horse I saw you on this morning, you know. I thought it was you, in any case, but I could not be certain, since you did not seem to recognize me."

"I cannot think you could mistake me for anyone else with this crop of mine, but I had no idea that we met—I assure you that I did not mean to be rude. It must have been when I was on my way to or from Manton's. I was rather in a study, you know, and may have passed through the entire Park without once seeing a tree in passing. If I cut you, please put it down to my befogged mind and bad manners, not my intentions." Althea emitted a sigh so profound that it surprised her: she had not realized how much importance she had placed upon his good will.

"I make no matter of it, sir," she said lightly. "And I know enough from Maria's teaching to say that your manners are *never* bad. You are odious, certainly, but that is required for the position of social arbiter, I imagine. You see how I have benefited from my sister's tutelage?"

"I cannot believe that it is all her doing." He smiled.

"That is quite the nicest thing I have had said to me today. Should my partners tonight prove less inspired, you will have delivered the most memorable *mot* of the day!"

"You collect them?" he asked.

"Of course. Women do, although few are so honest as to say so. Pretty words are counted up and written in diaries, or traded over teacups. I have always thought it unfair to the competitors that they do not know they are in a contest. But the compliments I have heard repeated over teacups would astonish and bore you, sir. They do me, I know." She laughed wryly, looking up from under the rim of her bonnet, an effective but altogether unwitting gesture. Tracy, himself laughing, was confronted by eyes teasing him, a full mouth curved in a generous smile, the whole effect framed by the brim of her bonnet. He drew a sharp breath and turned to look straight out at the road ahead of them as he turned the horses toward Grosvenor Square.

"Althea," he began. He stopped. There was a slight snort of disgust from Eustace in the back.

"Yes?" She had no idea what had made him so suddenly serious.

"I have been considering a great deal," he began again. "No, damn it, that's not right. Devil take it. I wish you would come to think of . . . no, that's wrong too. *I* have come to . . . oh hell!" he said in exasperation. "Will you marry me?"

There was a long silence in the phaeton. All of the occupants had been struck momentarily dumb with surprise.

"Oh hell, will you marry me?" Althea repeated at length. She began to giggle. "For a man famed for his address, Sir Tracy, you make an abysmal offer. Oh lord!" She was overcome by it, unable to gasp out a few jumbled words. In a moment she was joined by Tracy, then Eustace too. The phaeton rolled sedately down the street, occupied by three apparent lunatics, to the consternation of passersby.

At last, a little more rationally, Althea considered the proposal. It was wholly absurd, of course, albeit very flattering. One person at least had enough kindness to be concerned over her feelings, and that added to the debt of gratitude she owed him. But she did not love him, and of course he did not love her. She was not so far gone as to sell herself for an establishment. Besides which, she reminded herself sternly, we should probably kill each other within the week.

"I cannot wholly believe that you are serious, sir," she began slowly.

"That much, at least, is evident," he said ruefully. "You know that it is only to retrieve my honor, don't you? One does not make a man behave like a zany in his own curricle during the Promenade and then dare to refuse to do the honorable thing. Will you consider the suit, Ally?"

Althea looked about her in confusion, unreasonably affected by his use of her name. She could think of no reason why he had made the offer, unless it was all of a piece with his concern over Pendarly's defection. No, that was too brown. And I will not say that he is doing me too much honor, she thought furiously, for he would plague me with it no end. The curricle continued to pass through the street, and in her attempt to look anywhere but into the interested eyes of her companion, Althea saw another form with which she was familiar: Edward Pendarly's. He was strolling along beside a lady of uncertain years and considerable girth, the woman described to Althea the night before as Mrs. Fulvia Laverham.

Her hands tightened convulsively in her lap, and she found it necessary to struggle to keep her teeth from locking as she replied to Calendar's flattering proposal.

"Yes, Sir Tracy, I will marry you," she said flatly.

Calendar, who had seen, over her shoulder, exactly the spectacle that had affected her so, replied lightly, "I am delighted."

Chapter Nine

Within an hour of the event Sir Tracy Calendar had informed his aunt of his engagement. They sat together in the sitting room of his aunt's apartments, Lady

Boskingram listening while Sir Tracy related the precise and peculiar circumstances that had induced Miss Ervine to answer him affirmatively.

"But why you *will* offer for the girl if she's got a *tendre* for someone else is what escapes me, Tracy. You don't seem like a fool, though God knows my own brats are foolish enough, and why should not some other branch of the family carry some of the taint? I simply cannot see the necessity of such hugger-mugger, let alone that it will prosper. Still, it is all very amusing to hear you speak of it—poor Eustace, I hope you pay him well, for that man has gone through fire for you." She became serious. "You are sure it is your feelings that are engaged? I shall want to meet her...."

"Aunt, you have only to say the word and I will deliver her up to you at once!"

"Bring her when you will, boy, when you will, so long as I've a moment's notice to brew up a pot of tea or some such thing. Bring her of an afternoon, then disappear and watch the muslin set air themselves in the Park." Lady Boskingram gave a pronounced snuffle. "You're probably the only bright child among my relations of full age and more, but I forbid you to go off marrying anyone until I have met her."

"I would never conceive of doing otherwise. I will bring her tomorrow then, if that is suitable, and if she is not already regretting her hastiness."

"Tomorrow, certainly, and I will put on my most formidable purple and endeavor to look as fierce as I know how, and if I don't scare her into vapors, I shall think her much in the way to being a good sort of girl." She studied her nephew intently for a moment. "I hope to find her so, boy."

"Rest assured you shall, ma'am. In fact, you will like her." The seriousness in his tone seemed to relieve her.

"Well, I suppose your famous good taste cannot have gone too far astray." She signaled in her peculiarly royal manner that the interview was over and Tracy, trained in his aunt's ways, took his leave.

Lady Maria Bevan was apprised of the engagement the next day as she lay abed watching Bailey parade a variety of morning dresses for her selection. Althea knocked timidly on the door and entered, darting behind Bailey's substantial form and settling herself on the sofa next to Maria's bed. Maria made an exasperatingly long job of choosing her gown, then sent Bailey off to search out the necessary accoutrements to the sprigged muslin with lilac ribbon.

"There, I am ready for a coze. You look very serious for such an hour of the day, Ally. How fatiguing. Oh, but I must tell you what Mr. Wallingham said last night. . . ." Maria was off, and Althea had a job to recall her sister's attention and, when she had done that, make her understand the seriousness of her situation. This was all complicated by the fact that Althea had no idea, once she *had* Maria's attention, of how to inform her of the engagement. Her explanation finally dwindled into a mutter of incoherent statements regarding Calendar, Pendarly, her own resolve to be a "gentleman" come what might. Maria finally gave up trying to elicit any sense from these ramblings and sat bolt upright, demanding a simple explanation.

"Well," Althea took a long breath and continued slowly, "when I was out driving with Tracy Calendar yesterday he offered for me, and the devil's in it that I accepted him."

Maria fell back into her pillows so far that when next she spoke her words had the effect of coming disembodied from that pile of lace and linen. When finally she surfaced, she gave her sister a look of mixed awe and admiration.

"You have really accepted an offer from Calendar? Sister, all the mamas in this mart have been trying to catch him these last ten years! How did you manage it? You say he really accepted—I mean *you* did—without any idiotishness about too much honor, or whatever else? Of course he is far too smart for me, but I imagine you will suit nicely, and even if you don't, it makes no matter. And I thought it was that parsonical fellow with the beautiful face you fancied. You are the slyest thing in the world. How Francis will laugh when I tell—" Her face fell and her blue eyes began to fill with tears.

"You're not to tell *anyone* for the time, Mary, do you understand? I told <u>him</u> I wish this to stay a secret for a time—to think about it. I am not sure that Calendar didn't offer for me out of pity—yes, there is a reason why he might take it into his head to do so, though I think it very nonsensical, to be sure. I will not plague you with the whole of it now. I have had barely any sleep for thinking of this mess—dear heaven, how we laughed when he offered for me. I am not even able to tell you what I saw acted at Covent Garden last night, for I was in a fog then, too."

"You laughed at Calendar's proposal? Ally, I shudder to think it. Oh, I don't care for Sir Tracy much, I know—I suppose he doesn't care a rub for me, and I know I'm not clever enough to understand him," Maria said proudly. "But no matter, a man like Calendar doesn't offer for a lady of quality and then decide otherwise. And you did accept him? You're sure?" A note of trepidation came into Lady Bevan's voice. "Only to think of having you so remarkably settled, and in your first Season, too."

"It were probably better if I had said something missish and put him off—except then he would have laughed at me for it. But I've done what I've done, and I shall play an honorable part in this if it means—oh, anything!" Althea looked forlornly at her sister. "He's not so impossible—I suppose we could live very well together if I thought that we could keep from tearing at each other's throats for more than five minutes at a time." A sigh.

"Please, Mary, let me beg you not to tell anyone of this yet. I am dreadfully confused, and I don't know yet what is the right thing—I only said I would because I was so—"

To Maria's surprise her sister crumpled to the arm of the sofa and began to sob miserably. Maria, who had never seen her sister in such a state, could only pat her shoulders and whisper vague, clucking sounds, better calculated, one might think, to comfort a three-year-old than a lady of three and twenty. But the treatment proved efficacious: within a moment or so Althea sat aright, straightening and smoothing the folds of her gown.

"That is enough of my silliness for one day, at least. I cannot think what has made me such a deplorable peagoose. I suppose it is that I have had so little sleep. In any case, Calendar said he would call this afternoon, so I shall learn then if he was jesting with me. See, here is Bailey with your gown."

With a shaky sort of composure Althea left the room, watched by the bewildered Maria. What thoughts her sister might have entertained upon leaving the room Maria could not know, but for herself within minutes of Althea's departure, she was planning the most splendid celebratory ball of the Season, to be held at some unspecified time when Francis had returned to town.

When Sir Tracy arrived in Grosvenor Square that afternoon he found his betrothed in a state of nervous anxiety, engaged in beading a reticule in an appallingly ugly pattern. Althea had obviously been awaiting him; Lady Bevan, although he had not seen her, was, he felt sure, waiting in some hallway nearby. Althea rose as he came toward her, smiling tremulously, with her hand outstretched. He returned the smile and took the cold hand between his two warmer ones with a gesture that made Althea blush (to her fury) and look away in confusion.

"I have no intention of biting you," Sir Tracy said conversationally. "You may relax." Her breath came out in a gasp; her smile became more natural.

"Well, thank heaven for that," she said. "How are you today?"

"Tolerable, thank you, ma'am, tolerable." He looked down at her from that disconcerting height. "What concerns me more at present is how you feel today. Do you regret your words to me yesterday?"

"I have been asking myself the same of you: were you regretting your offer."

"Never," he said firmly. "And now, I have an invitation from my aunt: she is visiting with me until my cousin Boskingram's house is refurnished, and as she is a notorious busybody, she has desired me bring you to tea this afternoon. If I give you twenty minutes, can you make any changes your vanity may require and be ready to make the call?"

"Oh, I think so," Althea said bravely. Tracy noticed with amusement that when his betrothed left the room, the anxious form of Lady Bevan bore down upon her purposefully.

Less than ten minutes later Althea presented herself to Calendar, dressed in a walking gown of blue muslin, clutching a pair of York tan gloves very tightly in one hand. This was the only outward sign she gave of inward turmoil and Calendar, helping her into the phaeton, amused himself with the thought that he had grown very charitable of late, and refrained from mentioning her nervousness entirely.

"What is your aunt like, Sir Tracy?"

"Under the circumstances I think you might use my name now," he said mildly, "and that is Tracy, without benefit of Sir. I should like to hear you become accustomed to saying it."

Althea blushed.

"My aunt will try to intimidate you at first, but I suspect that you two will get on famously once you've begun.

She's as sharp as can put together, is Aunt Peg, and she fancies she has a proprietary interest in me, especially because since my parents died five years ago she has been most of my family to me. She makes it the point of *her* life to be the bane of *mine*, as well as the delight of my soul. For the rest, she is just a meddlesome old woman who thinks I live an entirely immoral life, and wishes she might do so, too."

"So we are exactly calculated to suit one another? What a strange notion you have of me, to be sure."

"I expect she will admire you greatly. She has a weakness for people who are not in the common way, and you, whatever you may say to the contrary, are not in the common way at all. Besides which, as a pattern of propriety, I hope you will undertake to give a good example for my errant aunt."

"You are the most insufferable man I ever met," Althea said slowly, "or else you are a wit." He made a small bow. "I collect then that your aunt dreams of dancing masters and gypsies or some such thing."

"I rely upon you to cure her of the trait, and to cure me of being so poorly mannered as to be insufferable during an afternoon call," Tracy said lightly. "And here we are. I was instructed to find you, deliver you up, and then—er—go ogle the opera dancers in the Park. Now, your bonnet is on quite straight, your gown is perfectly charming, and there are no wrinkles in it. Come, ma'am, I should never have thought you a coward."

"I shall undertake that it shall never be known, sir. We Ervines are renowned as fools and madmen, and known to rush in where any other would stay safe behind, but we are no cowards. Lead onward."

"Bravo! See, Aunt Peg, here we are arrived."

A small lively looking lady met them at the door, elbowing the scandalized butler out of the way. She took Althea's hand in a firm grip and cast a baleful look at her nephew.

"Tracy, did I not give you your orders? Go and do not darken my door for an hour or so. I shall make this child's life miserable enough without she has you tagging at her sleeve. Go along, kiss and say goodbye, and if you see Monkshood, tell him I daily expect to see him here." She fluttered a peremptory hand in his direction, to which he replied with a bow. He took Althea's hand and, to her surprise, drew her close.

"I have my orders, ma'am," he said lightly, and brushed her cheek with his lips. Althea was conscious of a glowing sort of shock in her midsection, as well as the blush that was becoming more and more apt to appear in his presence.

"Call that a kiss, do you?" Lady Boskingram said scornfully. "You young folk are a lily-livered lot!"

"My apologies, Aunt Peg. Your most obedient in all things," Tracy replied mildly. Pulling Althea closer still, he kissed her gently, but with some warmth. Althea, after a moment's shock, found herself returning this kiss with rather more interest than form, until she remembered that they still stood before the Dowager Countess of Boskingram. At that point she broke free, a little unsteadily. Tracy, unfazed, gave her something like a grin and left the room.

Lady Boskingram did not give her visitor time to consider her nephew's strange behavior. The older woman took the girl by the wrist and led her firmly to a sitting room, where a fire was laid and service for tea set out. Lady Boskingram settled herself comfortably in a large elegant thronelike chair, and motioned to Althea to take a smaller chair near the fire, watching all the while from under her speculative lids.

"You know, ma'am, you have much the look of your nephew when you—observe that way? It can be very unsettling." To Althea's fury, she was still oddly breathless, and the strange feeling in her stomach persisted.

"There is no real resemblance, child, although it is

quite possible that Tracy picked up that glare from me. He is my husband's nephew, you see, and even at that, I'm told he takes a great deal from his father's family."

"Who are the Calendars, ma'am—so then Lord Boskingram's family is something else? He has never told me anything about his family, except that his own parents had died. You did not know Tracy's father?" Althea unseeingly accepted her cracker and a half-cup of lukewarm tea.

"Didn't know Arthur Calendar until he was older and sickly, so I can't see any resemblance to Tracy at all. Tracy's mother was a Blakneigh—sister to my husband William. Of course I knew her—Tracy's mother, Anabel—pretty well, before William took me off to the Continent on one of his everlasting excavations. A sweet, pretty widgeon without two words to rub together, and close friends with Henrietta Bessborough and that crowd. But I bore you with all this family."

"Not at all, ma'am, although I confess I cannot follow you entirely. William was, I collect, the late Earl of Boskingram."

The Countess sighed. "He was, and to my mind the best of the lot of Blakneighs, but you will say I am prejudiced at least until I tell you that my own two children are the stupidest offspring God ever inflicted upon woman. I rather count upon Tracy to make up to me for all the disappointment I have had in my own two sobersides children. Perfect Blakneighs. Thank heaven Tracy is a Calendar."

Althea nodded helplessly, and tried to finish the tepid tea.

"He was the most *provoking* child, with a trick for imitation when he was young, and I think he has probably adopted that look from me. I wish you would cure him of it: that sort of inscrutability unnerves me in others."

"But not in yourself?"

"When you are as old as I, my dear, you'll look however you want to, and what's more, not a one will have the spine to scold you for it. Tracy wants to marry you."

Althea looked up hurriedly. "If you say you disapprove, ma'am, I am sure he'll promptly toss me back into the ranks of the unfortunate and tell me to go along about my business."

"And why should I disapprove, girl? Madness in your family? Can't be any worse than the collection of nitwits in his own. Poverty? That boy has enough to make you a household twice over, and still keep several expensive ladybirds on the side. Fortune is of little count." She looked hard at Althea. "Beauty? You're not a diamond of the first water, certainly, but you're like I was—you've got spirit, which makes people think you're a beauty even if you ain't. Why should I fret of it? And besides all this, even if I did disapprove, which I by no means do, the boy would take no more notice of me than if I were in China. Tracy knows his mind, girl. Be warned of that." The dowager wagged an admonitory finger at Althea.

"But now," she continued, "I am going to play my game with you. I cannot place your family, and it will plague me beyond anything until I can. Indulge me if you can. Ervine. Where do your people come from?"

"We come from Lancashire, ma'am. Hook Well, near Hooking, a village some few miles from Lake Windemere."

The Countess nodded intently. "Your father's name?"

"Sir George Ervine. My mother was Lady Dorothea Merrit. Does that help at all?"

"Admirable! You don't mince words, do you, nor flutter about in maidenly confusions. I think your mother must have been some dozen years younger than I, but I was good friends with her sister Ellen when we were young. Your mama was which one: the spotty one, the bookish one, or the sickly tempered one?"

"I believe it was my Aunt Lydia who had the spots, ma'am, and I know it was my Aunt Babs who was sickly," Althea said delightedly. "Aunt Babs has outlasted three husbands so far, and looks like to outlast the fourth, so I suppose the sickliness took no very serious course."

"I never supposed that it did, but poor Ellen was forever being plagued by Babs when the child had one of her earaches. Imagine sitting at home nursing a sister with a roasted onion at her ear rather than going to a Vauxhall masque! I am ashamed to say I cannot recall your father at all."

"How you would desolate him, who is convinced that only the Royal House of Hanover is so distinguished as that of Ervine. You might be like to remember my Uncle Ambrose, who had the bad taste to be killed in a duel over a lady some ten or fifteen years ago."

A light came over the dowager's face. "Of course!" she crowed. "Got into a brawl at White's over some chit's fair name and settled it with pistols. They were both dead foxed anyway, but I suppose that Ambrose was the drunker of the two. So now I know just who you are."

"Does my family make such a matter, ma'am?"

"As to your marrying Tracy? Ask Tracy that, girl, but don't be such a nodcock as to suppose I have any say in it. But it is my passion to place everyone I meet in some sort of place: I shall quiz you shamelessly and you shall answer patiently because I am a mad old woman, and then I will release you to go about breaking hearts again. You know all about that, I suppose."

"I fear I know less of breaking hearts than of Roman poets. Hook Well is a very isolated sort of place, and my papa did not approve of the young men who tried to call upon me, so I became more accustomed to read than to flirt."

Lady Boskingram was fascinated by this glimpse of rural tyranny and begged to know more. Under her prodding, Althea fell into the story of her life at Hook Well and her escape to London, her tutelage under Maria's stern eye, and the long hours of subjugation to Madame

Helena's underlings. Lady Boskingram seemed immensely amused: when Althea had done, she announced triumphantly that she understood exactly whom she was entertaining: a heroine. Althea demurred, but Lady Boskingram would have it so.

"It is most depressing, when all my life I have longed for a little adventure, and then you appear, and things happen to you as if by magic. Midnight escapes! Dancing masters! Pawning jewelry! I wonder if I could rid myself of a few pieces that I truly hate by pawning them? I certainly cannot give them to my maid, for the wretched girl would wear them in front of me, and I would be plagued by them all over again.

"It might be easier to have the stones reset," Althea said amusedly.

"Such odious practicality in a girl of your age!" Lady Boskingram said disgustedly. "Here I look for romance, and instead find housewifery. I don't want to be *practical* about it, goose."

"It cannot be a romantic impulse if you plan for it so, ma'am," Althea reminded her. "And at that, impulse is not always a happy thing."

"Regretting your answer to Tracy, child?"

Althea looked up wordlessly. The dowager nodded sagely. "I know what caused it—Tracy explained the whole to me—and while I can think of better reasons to accept an offer of marriage, I can think of many worse. Let me only say that I can think of no one better calculated to make him comfortable, and I think he will be a very good husband to you. In all events, he won't be a dull one! And I am so glad that it is you, rather than one of Amalia's chits that she keeps in the cellar."

"I beg your pardon, ma'am?" Althea asked weakly.

"My son Richard's wife Amalia has been trying to marry Tracy off these five years, and to such a collection of unsuitable insipid misses that I should not have wondered had he been put off from marriage forever. Tracy finally told me that he suspects Amalia keeps them in the cellar alongside Richard's port, and both are brought up when Tracy stays to dine. No, it is time that Tracy took his responsibilities seriously, for even if he's not close in line to the title, there is his own name to be considered. Of course Richard will doubtless live forever, and there are three boys, as well as the child Amalia is carrying now—that girl is indefatigable! Six children inside of eight years, and all of them revoltingly healthy. I cannot think what Richard and Amalia are about—well, that is hardly true either—" The dowager broke off at the sight of Althea's face.

"Poor child, I can see that I have entirely confused you. All I meant was that I feel better for knowing Tracy is to settle down at last. I have a certain affection for him, you know."

"Your secret is safe as houses with me, ma'am. But if I marry Sir Tracy, I shall trust in you to help me go on. And will you some time tell me something of Tracy's family?"

"If you are so forgiving of an old woman's crotchets that you can bear it, I'll tell you all the stories I can think of!" the dowager promised happily.

When Calendar returned to his house sometime later, he found his aunt and his betrothed deep in some scandal involving the Blakneighs, the Calendars, and the Fitzalans, Lady Boskingram's own family. Interrupted, the older woman looked up and snapped at him, "I see you mean to drag her off home, and just when we were to the most interesting part."

"Did you not specifically tell me to make sure you remembered that you are to dine out tonight?" Tracy protested. "And I am sure Miss Ervine has some appointment for which she must prepare also."

"I hate to admit it, for it spoils him dreadfully, but he is right," Lady Boskingram sighed. "You must be off, then, for I make no doubt that you have more invitations than you know what to do with. There's two times of life, my dear. Yours, when you are invited everywhere for your beauty and your wit and your fortune, if you have any, and mine, when you're invited because no one dares not to invite you. I'll not keep you longer, then. Your patience with my stories gives me some faith in your racketty generation." She stretched out a hand to draw Althea close, and stood almost on tiptoe to kiss her cheek.

Althea received her pelisse and turned once more to thank her hostess for her kindness. Lady Boskingram waved her hand irritably and insisted there was no kindness to it at all.

"Only idle curiosity. But Tracy, I would not have thought it possible that any of the Blakneighs, with the exception of William, could have had such good sense. Goodbye." Waving her hand absently, Lady Boskingram dismissed them and went to collect her charts and wander bemusedly up the stairs with her arms full of them.

"What have you found to discuss so weightedly this hour and a half?" Calendar asked as they settled into the phaeton. "I would swear that you both wished me at Jericho when I arrived. Has Aunt Peg been telling you dire stories of my extreme youth? Don't believe 'em, for she did not know me then."

"You are shockingly conceited if you think that we discussed you all that while," Althea retorted briskly. "Lady Boskingram was engaged to show me why you are your cousin's third cousin twice removed, as well as first cousin. She is quite amazing. But how does she know these things?"

"She asks," Tracy said dryly. "She has gone so far as to tell me that she loves her stories because they give her a license to ask whatever she will, and all the time with the most angelic look on her face."

"She has a look of you, you know." Althea smiled. "Not angelic, of course: that would be altogether impossible. But that supercilious eyebrow—yes, that's it—you share that eyebrow with your aunt, as well as that trick of observing everything about a person when it is least expected you could do so. You have no idea how disconcerting that is."

"You spend a great deal of time telling me what in me you find disconcerting. Is that in the hopes that you can reform me when you and I are wed?"

Althea moved uneasily on the phaeton seat. "I would never presume to change any part of you, least of all the affectations that make you such a figure in the *ton*."

"You mean that my height and this crop of carroty hair do not make me remarkable enough without some affectations? A fine, carnival place this London is come to be these days." He looked at her gravely. "I should never have thought to hear myself accused of affectations. Next you will have me a dandy."

"I confess that the thought had once or twice crossed my mind. . . ."

"Never say so, ma'am!" Tracy groaned. "A Corinthian, perhaps. A whip, or a Trojan, or even a swell I could permit with no great fear for my reputation, but a *dandy!* As soon call yourself"—he paused to think—"no. Perhaps you had better not call yourself *that*, but . . ."

"Oh, I stand corrected," Althea said unrepentantly. "And in your excess of emotion you have driven clear past my house. No, don't bother to go back." She gathered her reticule and gloves in her hand. "I am not daunted by a walk of some hundred feet or so. I am so glad that I met your aunt, Sir Tracy."

"I thought you agreed that I was to be Tracy from now on. You cannot go on speaking of me as if I were only another of your flirts, my dear." He took her proffered hand in his large, firm clasp. Eustace leapt down from the curricle and stood ready to help the lady descend. "I see I am to have no more conversation with you tonight, but I will do myself the honor of calling on you tomorrow.

Good night." He held her hand a moment longer, then released her, and Eustace swung her down to the street.

Althea was admitted to the house by Debbens, who motioned her to one side of the hallway and said, in a conspiratorial whisper, "Ma'am, his lordship's back again. Just thought you'd be wanting to know." Since their initial, unfortunate meeting, Althea and Debbens had become something like friends, or at least conspirators. Althea thanked him in the same melodramatic whisper and, seeing Maria approaching, dismissed him. Debbens winked in a distressingly familiar fashion and went off.

"Well, returned at last, I see," Maria said a little too loudly. "What did you think of Lady Boskingram? Did she prose you or try to scare you or both? I hope you gave her a smart set-down. You have been gone the longest time! It was quite unfair of Sir Tracy to demand you meet his aunt on such short notice."

"I liked it very well. I'm glad to have met her and made her my friend. But you, Mary. Has anything happened while I was gone? Did anyone call?"

"Call?" Maria looked up quickly. "No, no one called. I took my tea all alone. Oh, there was one thing."

Althea looked up too quickly. "Yes?"

"Your new gown was sent from Helena's, and there was a note from the shoemaker's about my sandals. Oh, and I got a note from Harriet Leveson-Gower about her aunt's *bal masque* next week. But no one called." The kerchief was almost irredeemably contorted by now. "We are to dine at Cousin Anne's tonight, so hurry and dress."

Althea, fearing that there was no way to bring Maria to own up to Francis's arrival, started up the stairs for her room to begin her delayed evening toilette. Maria's choked whisper stopped her.

"Ally?" She motioned her sister to rejoin her, and her voice dropped to the tiniest whisper. "Francis came back this afternoon. I haven't yet seen him, but I heard his voice." Her face hovered uncertainly between joy and misery. "Do you think he can forgive me, ever?"

"I am sure that he can, Sister, but this is no place to be discussing it. Go dress and then come see me before we go out." Althea patted her sister's hand and continued up the stairs.

"Ally? I'm so happy he's back. . . ." Maria stood alone in the large hallway, rather small, and looking anything but happy.

Chapter Ten

As events transpired, the reunion between the Bevans was neither so dramatic nor so painful as Maria, Francis, Althea, or any of the servants had feared (or hoped). Lord Bevan had simply become tired of life at his shooting box and lonesome for Maria. There was, after the first day or so, no decent wine to be had there; his housekeeper had no idea of how to sustain a gentleman above three days; there was no one within proximity of the cottage who was in the least amusing. In short, everything there seemed only to increase his longing for the warmth and well-ordered comfort of Grosvenor Square—and for Maria.

They did have a short bout of mutual self-recrimination; while Maria accused herself of being cowardly and deceitful, of willful behavior and flirtation aforethought, Francis spoke of his wretched temper, his violent jealousy of any man who so much as looked at Maria, and finally told her the story of his gaming debts with Calendar. Each was generous with absolution and loving words, and when the emotion of this charged scene had dissipated, they found that they had slipped back into their accustomed style of living.

Althea watched her sister's happiness with preoccupied pleasure. She had sworn Maria to secrecy even from Francis on the matter of her engagement, and was trying to work out her misgivings for herself. To be practical, although it was not generally considered the business of young ladies to be practical in the matter of marriage (that was for fond mamas and doting papas), Althea knew that marriage to Calendar could only improve her lot socially. To marry an acknowledged Martrimonial Prize, a rich man and a noted figure of Sport and Society, to be no longer a millstone around Maria's neck or responsible to her father—all of this was, of course, desirable. Still she retained an abhorrence of marriage to a man who merely wanted a wife and a mother for his heirs, and who had shown no sign of affection for her. Had not Lady Boskingram intimated that marriage was Tracy's duty?

Althea tossed the positives and negatives of the marriage—or any marriage at all—back and forth, without reaching a conclusion and without being able to banish the thoughts from her mind for longer than five minutes at a time. She was unable to read or sit alone without falling into a brown study, and no matter what hour she retired or what her exertions had been, it took her hours to fall asleep, during which time she was unable to divert her thoughts from the problem.

Francis and Maria were not normally perceptive, and just after Francis's return they were more besotted than usual. After a week or so, though, Francis remarked to Maria that he had noticed that fellow Calendar was much about the house these days, and also that Ally seemed set about in some fashion. She was surely not going into a decline, he hoped. Maria did not betray Althea's confidence, but gave her husband a look of great portent, saying that she thought Ally must be only a trifle fagged with all the unaccustomed gaiety.

Francis was not well pleased with Calendar's calls at his house, for every sight of that visitor reminded him of the shocking sum he still owed Sir Tracy for that one ill-advised night of gaming after the Fforydings' ball. To be sure, Sir Tracy had, in a note, written to Francis saying there need be no hurry with the debt, but the fact that there was walking about in London a man to whom he owed considerably more than his year's income made Francis very uncomfortable. He would have been surprised and a little indignant to find that Calendar, in the times he had seen Bevan since his return, had only looked at him in the light of a future brother-in-law, never as a man who owed him over ten thousand pounds. On all occasions his behavior was cordial, almost friendly, and entirely perplexing to Francis, who knew nothing of Althea's affairs. Tracy had assumed that Bevan had been told, and was himself a little surprised at Bevan's standoffish manner. All in all, everyone was a little less than certain of exactly where matters stood with anyone else, and Francis, like Althea, had thoughts concerning Calendar that took up entirely too much time and effort.

All this preoccupation did not keep Althea from enjoying, or at least from participating in, the usual gaiety around her. When, as she thought was more and more the case, she saw Sir Tracy out in company, he was very likely to monopolize her entirely, so that for the first few days after their engagement was contracted, she felt constricted and confined by him. So enclosed and caged did she feel by this flattering attention that she found herself becoming unappreciative of what she elsewise might have thought of as Sir Tracy's kind consideration. By sticking so close to Althea, he was insuring that Edward Pendarly, still happily unaware of Althea's discoveries, could not approach her until she was ready for such a confrontation. Observing the lady's distraught manner, Tracy was not likely to permit this to happen too soon. Another thing that escaped Althea's preoccupied notice was the gossip that was occasioned by Sir Tracy's attentions. Tracy was himself well aware of it. He had been used, for the past ten years, to hear his name tied to some female's, be she on the right or wrong side of the social pale. Now, although he knew that overreaction would only worsen the talk, he had a dislike of hearing Althea's name spoken in the same way. It was an effort to ignore his own inclinations and keep from placing a notice of their betrothal in the *Gazette*, but that, he knew, Althea would not forgive.

Despite an air of distractedness that was so interesting that certain young ladies had begun to copy it, Althea was conscious soon enough of some of the talk regarding her. At Almack's one evening she heard two of the patronesses discussing scandals, and was appalled to hear her own name mentioned by Lady Jersey, who said solicitously to Lady Caroline Lamb that she hoped the young Ervine was not going to have her feelings hurt by Calendar, when all the world knew that he had a heart of stone. Caroline Lamb, somewhat piqued by this (Calendar had long, if speciously, pronounced himself her devoted slave) lisped charmingly that Miss Ervine seemed entirely able to fend for herself. "And besides, until Tracy started to beau her around, wath she not busily engaged in winning Fulvia Laverham'th thon-in-law from Mith Georgiana? Exactly the thort of country behavior one might expect from such an amathon!" Sally Jersey twittered nervously and wondered at Calendar being so particular in his attentions.

Althea had been waiting for Maria when she caught this snatch of speech, but she moved immediately away from the area, determined rather to seek her sister out than to stay and hear more. If Lady Jersey or Lady Lamb noticed her, she gave no sign, and Althea, wishing herself away on the instant, instead found her arm taken by Sir

Tracy. His expression was inscrutable, but she wondered if he had heard.

"You needn't pay any attention to them," he said. "Caro is spiteful these days—restless—and I expect she'll wind up ruining herself with one of her mad starts some fine day. I used to fancy myself quite dreadfully in love with her when I was a boy."

"What happened," Althea asked coolly.

"She threw a Sèvres jug at me when we had an argument, and from that time on—" He looked down apologetically at Althea's amused eyes. "I didn't so much mind that she had thrown it at me, but what a deplorable waste of a beautiful jug. Unconscionable." He settled Althea on a very uncomfortable chair and allowed himself to lean on the wall next to her. "And Sally is called Silence for good reason: she has an unreasoning fear of allowing her tongue to grow still. You see, you are quite silly to heed them. And besides that, they are all wrong as well. My intentions are quite honorable. Are yours?"

Althea flushed, but said lightly, "I had no idea that a woman's were required to be, sir." She felt a flash of resentment: when he had first appeared, she had wanted to hit him, and now, against her judgment, she was being charmed from her sullens. It was hard to stay resentful, though, for the only time she found herself unplagued by doubts and indecision was when she was in his company.

"I imagine you are right," he was saying. "I think it rather unfair, though. Do you enjoy this crush tonight?

"What a terrible trickery question! If I say yes, then I admit to having the sort of dreadful, plebian taste that delights in assembly, when I know it is far more fashionable to abhor but endure it. And if I say no, then I am shockingly uncivil, and you may report me to your Lady Caro."

"Not, I beg you, *my* Lady Caro," Tracy said in accents of pain.

"Well, certainly not much William Lamb's! But here I,

too, am gossiping, which is the thing that men affect to hate above all else in a woman."

"Only affect?" The cynical eyebrow jumped up wryly under a shock of red hair that had slipped from its careful combing.

"Nonsense, Sir Tracy."

"Tracy. I thought we had settled that matter."

Althea ignored that. "Men are the worst gossips alive, and the more so for being so sanctimonious about their virtue. Oh dear ..." Althea turned a little white and her words trailed off indistinguishably. Calendar turned and saw Edward Pendarly bearing down upon them determinedly. Without a pause and without a ruffle Calendar asked Althea to dance. As he led her to the floor Althea cast him a look of intense gratitude that he affected not to notice. Edward Pendarly, behind them, cast a speaking glance at Calendar's retreating back and returned to the side of his fiancée and her mother.

"Mr. Pendarly," began Mrs. Laverham in a voice that oozed portent, "who is that amusing looking creature dancing with Tildy Fforyding's nevvy?" She snorted briefly. "Maypole-looking thing, ain't she, Georgie?" Georgiana, at her mother's side, knew exactly who the lady was, and colored with embarrassment at her mother's manner. Pendarly looked extremely uncomfortable, but admitted that it was Miss Ervine, sister to Lady Bevan. This speech did not please Georgiana, but her mother was well pleased by it, smiling broadly until her chins stretched almost to meet her ears. Pendarly swallowed three times and asked his betrothed to dance. A little distance between himself and Mrs. Laverham was the only solution he could arrive at for immediate relief to his discomfort.

Georgiana, aware though she was of his unhappiness, could not conceal the fact that she enjoyed his company. The motion of the dance precluded any close conversation, which in the run of things suited them both equally well. With all his other problems, Pendarly was finding that while he had once been able to talk to Georgiana on a variety of insipid topics, now even the merest vestiges of conversation deserted him. He could not tell if this was a product of his feeling for Althea Ervine, his guilt over his treatment of Georgiana, or his increasing feeling of impending doom in Mrs. Laverham's company.

Georgiana, only recently released from the sickroom, had looked avidly in the past few days for Lady Maria Bevan's sister, Miss Ervine. When she had at last attained a glimpse of that lady, her spirits had dropped sharply. Miss Ervine was all that she was not, and apparently all that Edward Pendarly found most admirable. Being slight, shy, and unassuming enough to be blind to her own prettiness, Georgiana found it altogether reasonable that Edward would prefer the striking, charming, sought-after Miss Ervine to a little mouse like herself. She was not stupid, nor was she blind. She knew of her mother's machinations to ensure Edward's continued attendance upon her, and while the results were highly gratifying, she had to admit that the methods were deplorable.

Lady Sefton remarked from across the hall that little Georgie Laverham was in looks tonight, and seemed quite recovered from her illness. In a gown of pink gauze trimmed in blond, she was pretty enough even for Pendarly to realize it. He also realized that a small stir of admiring comment was being made about his partner, and this lifted his spirits so much that he forgot to watch Althea from across the room as she whirled in Lord Hartington's arms, and to curse his relatives for putting him in a position where he could not approach her.

Sir Tracy, having relinquished Althea to Hartington, leaned against the wall and scanned the crowd lightly, noting who was there and speculating upon those darlings of Society who were not in evidence. He was aware of his aunt's entrance immediately and made his way through the crowd to join her.

He made her a courtly bow and she wagged her fan at him delightedly.

"Excellent! I have not seen so stylish a curtsy outside of Drury Lane, dear boy. You may fetch me some iced cup."

"You would not send me through that crowd again, would you, dearest of aunts?" He smiled. "Send another."

"Shocking crush, ain't it, Tracy? But your disrespect is equally shocking. Who shall I send to fetch me some refreshment before I die of thirst? Oh, see, here is just the man." She smiled agreeably at a fat corseted gentleman who approached. With a few words, the amiable Mr. Courtney had been sent upon Lady Boskingram's errand, leaving her once more with her nephew.

"Well," she said briskly, "where's my little friend Althea?" She chuckled. "Yes, dear, I know she'd make two of me, but still I claim the rights of my advancing age and call her my dear *little* friend."

"I find you in depressingly high spirits tonight, Aunt." Tracy said dryly. "As for Ally, she is dancing at present with Hartington, over there." He gestured.

Lady Boskingram totally ignored his indication and continued to scan the crowd. With an air of elegant distraction she began to quiz Tracy on passing couples.

"Who's the gal with your Aunt Fforyding's boy?"

"Miss Westleid, Aunt."

"And that one over there, isn't that Ponsonby's boy and his fiancée?"

"And well you know it, Aunt," Tracy said, wondering what his aunt was driving at.

"And the little one there in the pink is Laverham's daughter, ain't she? Who does she dance with?"

"Unworthy, Aunt Peg," Tracy snorted. "You might have asked straight out if Pendarly was here tonight. That is the villain, and an evil sort he looks, doesn't he?" Calendar sneered. "He seems to be pretty happy with his *own* fiancée tonight."

"I cannot understand a lively girl like Althea finding anything to admire in a pretty, parsonical fellow like that, Tracy."

"I think it may have been the attraction of being admired so excessively, Aunt, coupled with the fact that the man is rather handsome. I have nothing against him but that he made Althea very miserable for a while. But you are not to stir up any trouble. I see the dance is ending, and I intend to rescue my fiancée from any of Hartington's gallantry, and, unless I mistake my man, here is Courtney, and you are to be entertained by another of his interminable stories about last year's hunting." He nodded to the advancing gentleman, who had somehow contrived to get through the press with two full glasses of punch. "One last thing, I beg you. Until I give you leave, don't disclose my engagement to anyone—Ally requested we keep it close for a time. And especially," he whispered wickedly, "don't tell this loudmouthed bag-pudding!" He turned and greeted Mr. Courtney cordially, leaving his aunt to regain her countenance alone.

True enough, Mr. Courtney led Lady Boskingram to a chair, found another for himself, and proceeded to regale her with a very long winded tale of a hunting box, a left-handed gamekeeper, and his right-handed wife. Lady Boskingram soon lost the trail of this confused narrative and amused herself by watching her nephew and Althea from her vantage point. They were engaged for the waltz, skimming through the crowd skillfully. A very handsome couple, she decided with satisfaction: Althea in primrose muslin and champagne lace, Tracy severe and elegant in a blue Bath coat and the required knee breeches.

Georgiana Laverham and her partner swung past Lady Boskingram and her swain, and the dowager turned a quick eye in that direction. She looked with displeasure at Pendarly; handsome he certainly was, and with some imagination the Countess could conceive of him carrying on a worshipful enough adoration to sweep even a girl of sense such as Althea off her feet. As for the rest, she pronounced him a fine, prim sort of fellow, and probably a dead bore. In the long run Althea would have found out that they would never suit, and Lady Boskingram was pleased to believe that Althea was genuinely disaffected. As for the girl, she was presentable enough, if rather shy. That was allowable in a girl just out, but this was Miss Laverham's second Season, and she should have outgrown it by now. Lady Boskingram discovered in herself a lively desire to meet Miss Laverham. When the Princess Lieven drifted past in a cloud of patchouli and a rustle of silk, the Dowager Countess reached out an imperious hand to stop her. The Princess was not noted for her affability, but agreed readily enough to send one of her court to seek out Miss Laverham and present her to Lady Boskingram. When Miss Laverham appeared in the tow of a young man in wasp-waisted coat and paralyzingly high collar points, Lady Boskingram dismissed him and her own Mr. Courtney, who rose from his seat to do her bidding with creaky good will.

The dowager patted the vacated chair beside her with a smile, speaking kindly to the girl. "You must not look as if I shall eat you. It is true that I am a dragon, and have a pint of the Princess's blood to drink at my breakfast every morning, but I do not harm little slips of things such as you after dinner. And in front of this crowd, too. Think what a taking that would make."

Georgiana smiled a smile with much nervousness, much shyness, and a spark of quick, intelligent amusement. Lady Boskingram rapidly changed her notion of the girl.

"You are wondering, and rightly, why an old woman has called you away from your dancing, when I should be at my gossiping and my cards. Do not bother to deny it. I excuse myself by admitting flatly that I am the worst busybody in all London, my dear, and sooner or later you would have met up with me, so thank your lucky stars that you are about to have the interview over and done.

When I saw you dance, I knew at once that you must be related to Jessy Spote; that's Lady Jessamyn Spote to you, I suppose. She'd have been your father's second cousin"

Georgiana was half at ease by the end of this curious speech, and was able to answer composedly, "Yes, ma'am, I think I am connected with Lady Spote. At least Mama has always spoken so." It was just like that Fulvia Laverham to drop the name of her husband's connections to her own advantage, Lady Boskingram thought wryly.

She continued to quiz Georgiana for ten minutes or so, until Tracy appeared, his hands full of punch glasses. He bid Miss Laverham a polite good evening and offered her some punch. She thanked him a little tremulously and accepted the glass. She was not much interested in Lady Boskingram's prattle of old families, but liked the old woman herself.

"Miss Ervine has asked if I could permit her to pay you her respects, ma'am," Tracy said casually, trying assiduously not to observe Miss Laverham's reaction. "I told her she was foolish to stand upon ceremony with my rapscallion aunt, and she was absolutely violent in your defense."

Georgiana stirred uneasily and found her cold hand taken in Lady Boskingram's papery, strong one.

"Bring her straight away. I have never heard such fustian in all my life." The dowager clucked. "Hurry now. I can see Hartington is trying to fix his interest."

"No, Aunt, I should think that to be the least of her trials." Tracy smiled thoughtfully. He turned on his heel and faded into the crowd again. Georgiana began to collect her wits, framing in her mind some polite excuse to return to her mother. The hand on hers tightened.

"Don't think it, my dear. Your Mama has no need of you. Unless I miss my guess, she is happily engaged in losing her shift at silver loo. You must meet Althea Ervine sometime if you are to go about in town, and it might as well be under my wing. I think you might even like her, although perhaps she is just a trifle madcap for your disposition. A heroine, in fact. I see they come now. Quick, smile and look as though you enjoyed this—don't be so chicken-hearted. She don't want your parson anyway."

Georgiana was confounded by this rapid, whispered speech: was it possible that Althea had not, as her mother had intimated, shamelessly enticed Edward from her? There were Althea and Sir Tracy before them: Tracy rather bemused at the situation, Althea flushed and merry from heat and dancing. The look of unholy appreciation in Lady Boskingram's eyes was, to Georgiana's unpracticed sensibility, altogether indescribable.

"Good evening, child," the dowager purred, offering her cheek for Althea's salute. "I see you enjoy yourself as much as one can in this cesspool of virtue that Almack's is become—well, at least to appearances. One can hardly keep from being bored to tears. It is different, of course, when one is your age and has the world at her feet."

Althea cast a mischievous glance at her feet and assumed the demure mien of a governess as she assured the dowager that she saw no unfortunate males languishing there. "And you have the unkindness to accuse this lady and myself of being so shabby genteel as to enjoy ourselves, ma'am." Her look invited Georgiana to take up the teasing. Georgiana stirred fretfully in her chair, unused to this sort of jocularity before her elders.

"I am always unjust when I can get away with it, child," the dowager admitted equably. "It is one of the few compensations one receives for achieving age and losing beauty."

"And I promise you, Lady Boskingram, that whenever I hear you speak so fetchingly of the advantages of your advanced age, I am altogether green with envy, and long to be a grand old matron and wreck reputations with a blow."

Georgiana suppressed a strong urge to giggle at this exchange.

"I am unconscionably rude," Lady Boskingram was saying. "Althea, my dear, I must make you known to a new young friend of mine, who has been listening patiently to my nonsense. Althea, this is Georgiana Laverham." The dowager paused a moment for effect. Tracy choked slightly and looked away as she continued: "Georgiana," she said affably, "this is Althea Ervine."

Chapter Eleven

Althea suppressed a strong urge to run away. Georgiana, with a little more warning, had her feelings well in hand, and of the two of them presented the braver front. Lady Boskingram sat and watched the two girls with a smile of delicious amusement. Tracy stood by without comment, conscious of a tightness in his usually comfortable neckcloth. It was the Countess who finally broke the silence she had produced.

"Well, Althea, where are your manners? Make your curtsy to Miss Laverham!" Althea obeyed blindly, and in another minute was sufficiently collected to be able to say how do you do as well. Georgiana replied in kind and then there was nothing else to say.

"Tracy, go give my compliments to your Aunt Tyl—no, pray do *not* bring her to me here. Just the sight of her in that dreadful violet gown is almost more than I can stomach. Go, boy. Out of my sight." Tracy obeyed with alacrity, noting that his collar grew looser as his distance from the uncomfortable scene he had just witnessed grew greater.

"All right, then, you ninnyhammers," the dowager said with some asperity. "I have told Miss Laverham that you have no designs upon her fiancé, Althea, so I really think that you might prove it and act a little more kindly toward her. After all, it is she who will undertake to wed the indecisive Mr. Pendarly, so you can certainly afford to feel a little pity for her." Georgiana started indignantly at this. "Quiet, child," Lady Boskingram said indulgently. "You cannot expect me to appreciate your betrothed as I do my own nevvy, can you? I am sure that *you* and *he* shall do together *à merveilleux*."

Althea, who had been stiff and wary throughout the interview, began to be overwhelmed by the ridiculousness of her situation. She began to giggle, and then to laugh. Georgiana, not so accustomed to finding humor in her own discomfort, stared at Miss Ervine for a minute before subsiding into a weak chuckle.

"I declare, ma'am," Althea said chidingly to the dowager, "you must be the most outrageous person I have ever met." She turned to Georgiana. "Now confess, are you not shocked at her treatment of us? She sits there trying to make a battle royal from us, and the only thing for us to do is deny her the satisfaction—at least within her view. Do you know, I think I have been dancing this hour and more. Will you sit a while with me?"

Georgiana nodded mutely and Althea turned toward a row of empty chairs well to the rear of the room.

"By your leave, of course, ma'am!" Althea called back to Lady Boskingram, who waved them away helplessly and groped for a handkerchief to wipe her streaming eyes.

"What a dreadful old woman. I enjoy her no end."

"I have never met anyone like her," Georgiana admitted as she settled her skirts primly about her. "I rather wonder what she would be like if she met my mama."

"I do not know your mama, but I should think Lady Peg must conquer all."

Georgiana did not know what to make of Althea's free manner where Lady Boskingram was concerned. "Lady Peg? Well, in any case, you certainly cannot know my mama—she is something to be reckoned with. Brummell told someone once that she was like Mrs. Drummond-Burrell for her hauteur and like Mrs. Fitzherbert for her determination. I am afraid Mama assumed that it was a compliment. Last year the gentlemen at White's had a bet on the book as to whether or not Mama would capture a title for me within the first Season—and I understand that the betting was heavily in her favor. I was a sad disappointment to her, I fear," Georgiana said glumly.

Althea observed Miss Laverham with rather more interest than she had before: the girl was shy, of course, and given the overbearing manner of her mother, this was perhaps not much to be wondered at. But certainly she was not stupid, nor as insipidly dishonest as most schoolroom girls were wont to be: she knew her mother's quality, knew her own character. Althea found herself warming to her companion.

At that moment the "shy white mouse" was scanning the crowd, hoping for a glimpse of her Mr. Pendarly. Althea saw, and saw the blush of gratification that greeted her new friend's success.

"Lady Boskingram was right, you know," she said gently. "I did not know that Pendarly was betrothed to you, or anyone, in faith. I do now, of course, and I am not pining for him or plotting to wrest him from your arms. You are quite safe from me. I should have learned soon enough that we should never suit."

This speech had the effect of utterly undoing Georgiana's composure. She did not burst into tears, but looked very much as if she would have liked to, and her voice, when she spoke, was tremulous.

"You are so pretty," she began. This excellent beginning degenerated as her voice sank lower and lower and her words became a mumbling. "So pretty . . . and Edward—I mean, Mr. Pendarly—is so . . . and Mama told me . . . and I supposed that anyone, most of all Edward, would see . . . you have conversation and I have none . . . and how could Edward—I mean, Mr. Pendarly—resist . . . and I have been so miserable!" Althea reached for Georgiana's hand and thought wryly that it was indeed fortunate that they were situated so far from the common eye. After a while Georgiana looked up apologetically.

"I am so sorry," she gasped. "I have been ill, you know, and then to have all this to worry over—but I should never have bothered you in such a fashion. It is the most dreadful sort of imposition, and exactly what you must deplore. But when Mama told me that Mr. Pendarly seemed to have a partiality for you, I was . . . I was quite overset. Mama is not so very tactful, and she pictured you to me as the most awful, managing hussy with a fatal beauty, which is what I know well enough I shall never have."

"But here you see me, Miss Laverham, with two eyes, a nose, a mouth, a quantity of hair, and no fatal beauty at all. I spent my young years wishing *au désespoir* that I had charming yellow hair and a straight nose like my widgeon sister. I doubt that anyone with sense ever thinks she looks the way she exactly ought, until she has disposed of silly notions like that."

"I suppose Mama has the most improbable notions in London—for I know that she fancies herself monstrous attractive still, and has hopes of catching a husband for herself when I am safely wed away."

"Heaven save me from such a fate," Althea muttered devoutly. "But you are not such a ninnyhammer as to worry over such things seriously, are you?"

"You know, that is the first time that anyone has ever told me that I am *not* a ninnyhammer?" Georgiana said shyly. "I never thought that I was, but it can be hard to keep believing that when everyone seems to insist that you are."

"Well, you are not," Althea said sharply. "You want a little bringing out, but you are certainly not a fool, except in letting yourself be named so. But I see that my sister is making griffon faces at me, which I suppose to mean that she wishes to leave. Stay a moment. Will you come and call upon me? I will try to see that Maria is elsewhere, for while I do love her dearly, she does get in the way of a rational conversation. I would come to visit you, but I confess that I am vilely afraid of your mama."

"If you would like me to, I would be pleased to come," Georgiana said slowly. "You know, Miss Ervine, I was prepared to be afraid of you, or at least to dislike you, but I think you are quite the nicest person I have met this age—always accepting Edward, of course." Althea winced at the company she was put in, but smiled at Georgiana anyway as she rose, dimpled with a deep smile, and was gone from her chair, threading her way through the crowd toward her mama's chair. Althea, staring after her a moment, shook her head ruefully and returned to Lady Boskingram's side to take leave of her. From there Tracy gave her his arm to Maria.

Bearing each other company on the ride home, both girls, for differing reasons, were in cheering spiritis. Since Francis's return, Maria seemed to see everything with a slightly roseate halo, and chattered away to her sister like a pretty magpie. Althea had a tendency to stare into space and dissolve into chuckles, which Maria assumed were a response to the witty stories she was telling, until a particularly raucous burst of laughter made her tax her sister with her unreasonable hilarity. "Whatever possesses you? Have you reconciled yourself at last to being Lady Calendar?"

"I suppose I shall have to marry him," Althea answered. "If only to make sure I have his aunt on my side of any argument. What a devil that woman is, to be sure."

And she began to detail the whole of her introduction to Georgiana Laverham.

"Do you mean to say that Lady Boskingram placed you in such a position and all you can do is laugh about it? And in front of that condescending man, too. I know he is your fiancé, but he condescends to me—at least I think he does. I wish you would let me announce your betrothal to the world, though: if you should lose him through your peculiar treatment of him, I should never forgive you."

"Sis, *all* I can do now is to laugh at it. Once it is known that I am to marry Tracy, people will have their nine days' wonder and then they will forget how I threw myself at the head of an impecunious younger son with nothing to his credit but other people's debts." Maria, engaged again in the glories of a dream of Althea married to a Matrimonial Prize and queening it over Society, entirely missed the bitterness in her sister's voice.

"I am sure you are right, Ally." She sighed. "And once this annoying affair-of-honor thing with Francis and Sir Tracy is concluded, I am sure I shall be able to like him as well as Merrit, or even Papa, I suppose." She settled back into the seat lazily. "Mmmm. I wonder will Francis be home when we arrive."

"Maria," Althea said slowly, "what affair-of-honor thing? You cannot mean that Francis is to meet Tracy." Her face had gone very white as the images conjured up by that appalling phrase presented themselves.

"Ally dearest, don't faint. We are almost home, and think what a to-do it would make. There is no duel, nor is there like to be. Do please be calm and don't look so—so dreadfully white." Maria chafed her sister's hand and made motions of searching out her vinaigrette.

"I will not faint, provided you do not assault me with those dreadful salts," Althea said grimly. "Don't flutter about so, Mary, but tell me, if you please, what you *do* mean by such a Cheltenham phrase as an Affair of Honor? What am I to suppose if you use such a term?"

But the barouche was coming to a halt. Maria refused to tell her sister anything until they were safe inside and Althea bestowed in her room.

Upstairs in the dressing room of her apartments Althea at last turned and ruthlessly demanded of her sister that she stop tormenting her immediately.

"There is nothing to be so excited about, Ally." Maria pouted. "All it is is that Francis owes Sir Tracy some money—a dreadful sum, to be sure, but he shall be paid, never fear for that. You understand, don't you, dearest, that it makes Francis just the slightest bit nervous to be much in company with Sir Tracy until it is paid. That was why Francis was so dreadful put out over Helena's reckoning: he had lost that horrible amount to Sir Tracy only the night before, and when he got the account from Helena, well, of course, you see how he was placed. So you see, it is all the most natural thing in the world, and there was no reason why you should look so stricken."

"I am no longer stricken, Mary, I assure you," Althea said quietly. She bade Maria good night in the same subdued tones and retired to her room, leaving her sister to puzzle over her strange behavior.

Blessedly alone at last in the dark, Althea tried at first to calm herself. She realized that she was still in a rather hysterical state from the sudden meeting with Georgiana Laverham, and the subsequent discussion of it with Maria, and she did not really want to consider this latest piece of news while she felt so. When she thought her head a little cooler she began to calculate: Francis had left the house the day after he received Helena's bill, and that had been the day after her own first appearance, at the Fforydings' ball, which meant that—what it meant was that Sir Tracy had gone direct from the Fforydings', where he had met her, to some club, where he had won a prodigious amount of money from Francis. What was a prodigious sum of money? Maria's ideas on the subject were notoriously inaccurate so that she could not judge. But for the mild Francis to rail at Maria for extravagance while worrying over his own debts argued that the sum must be enormous indeed. And all the misery it had caused her sister and brother-in-law! It was not as though Tracy were in need of the money. The very night they had met he had won it. Maria's face when she read Francis's note about Helena's bill. Her own voice saying to Georgiana Laverham, "I would have learned soon enough that Pendarly and I should not suit." Tracy's cynical smile that infuriated her so—at least she assumed that it infuriated her. A prodigious sum of money. Tracy was—Tracy was—Tracy. . . .

She did not know when she fell asleep, and perhaps if she had known what an uneasy, tossing sleep it would be, Althea would have pressed harder to remain awake.

The next morning Francis observed to his wife that Ally seemed a trifle out of sorts. Maria, not considering what she said, assured her husband that she was sure her sister was fretting a trifle over Sir Tracy.

"Got a *tendre* for him? That could be bad business, Mary."

Maria stirred uneasily and decided that she felt absolutely unnatural in keeping a secret from her husband. "I told Ally I'd never tell a soul until she gave me leave, but surely you don't count in that. It is so famous! Calendar has asked Althea to marry him!" Maria wore a pretty air, so full of triumph that Francis rewarded her with a kiss. Then his expression sobered.

"That why we've had him underfoot these weeks? Really think you might have told me, Mary. Can't allow Calendar to go on waiting for the blunt I owe him if he's to marry Ally. Damned bad sport."

"But Francis," Maria protested in agitation, "can we afford to pay Sir Tracy such a dreadful lot of money?"

Her husband, who in certain moments could summon a manner almost paternal in dealing with his wife, patted her shoulder comfortingly. "Mean a little tightening of the belt for a while, but I fancy we shall be equal to that, hey?" Maria nuzzled the hand with her chin and smiled in a manner that indicated that, had she anything so unlikely as a belt, she would gladly tighten it and follow him to the ends of the earth. "Clear this thing up this very day," Francis said purposefully. He paused only to refresh himself with an embrace from his dutiful wife before he plunged out the door and down the street. He had gone some hundred yards in the wrong direction before he realized it, righted himself (to the consternation of several passersby), and charged off in the direction of Cavendish Street.

When he arrived at Cavendish Street, still full of fervent resolve to rid himself of debt and become, if necessary, poor but honorable for his sister-in-law's sake, he was informed by Sir Tracy's butler, the efficient Gergeley, that the master was out. Further inquiry fixed Calendar's probable whereabouts as Jackson's Saloon or Manton's Gallery, at either of which places Sir Tracy was often wont to take his exercise of a morning. Francis had by now discovered that walking purposefully for some distance over a short period of time could be fatiguing to a gentleman who had not retired until four in the morning. He hailed a chair and gave the direction for Manton's. He did not find Calendar there, but as he arrived at Jackson's, he found Sir Tracy, just upon the point of leaving, drawing on his gloves.

"Morning, Bevan. I don't believe that I can recall ever having seen you abroad at this hour," Calendar drawled politely.

"Not much for these damned early hours myself. Something unnatural about wandering around at such an hour in town. Uhh, I say, Calendar, could I have a word with you?" Now that he was face to face with the object of his search, Francis was a little less sure of how to proceed with this embarrassing matter.

"Come up in my carriage, then. If what you have to say will take longer than the distance from here to Grosvenor Square, I can always take my cattle around the Park a time or two. Which shall it be?" Eustace handed his master the whip and ribbons and stood from the leaders. Francis shocked out that it had better be the Park, then fell silent while Eustace clambered up to his place behind.

"Bevan," Calendar suggested gently after a time, "I believe you have something to discuss with me?"

Francis came perilously close to blushing, and began falteringly to speak. "Understand that you've fixed your interest with my sister Ally. Felt I ought to—" Francis began, before a choking sensation halted his progress.

"Are you come to inquire as to my intentions? I assure you they are of the most honorable. I only wait Althea's leave to post the notice of a betrothal in the *Gazette*."

"Good God," Francis cried, honestly revolted. "You don't suppose I'd take it upon myself to manage Ally's affairs, d'you?"

"Then what are you broaching," Tracy asked with visible patience. Behind him Eustace was listening to the conversation with some interest and little comprehension; at this point he abandoned any attempt to make head or tail of what was being said and instead occupied himself with ogling the passing females.

"Still have a debt outstanding to you. Never would have kept it outstanding this way, but things are a trifling bit tight just at present, and you did say that there was no press about it. Now that I know how things are between you and Ally—well, of course it won't do to have it unpaid. My man of business will take care of it tomorrow."

"I am afraid I cannot even recall what the sum was anymore, Bevan. I must apologize for my poor memory, but since we are, I hope, to be brothers, and since I obviously cannot have attached too much importance to the debt in the first place, what d'you say we call it settled? Now if you could perhaps persaude that devilishly stubborn *belle-soeur* of yours to allow me to make our engagement public, I would be much in *your* debt."

"You mean Ally doesn't want to marry you?" Francis asked in some surprise.

"Oh, she wants to. The trouble is that she doesn't know it yet," Tracy said grimly.

Francis, like his wife, was fully aware of the coup Althea had pulled off in snaring Calendar, and it was beyond him that Althea could not appreciate it as well. The sort of subtleties Sir Tracy was suggesting were beyond Francis. "She doesn't know it yet?" he echoed weakly.

"You were from town while all this happened, but she took a fancy to a man who was already betrothed, and when she discovered her mistake, she became engaged to me instead. I think it suited her purposes just then—except that the fellow doesn't know of it, so I cannot see what good it does her. You look confused, Bevan. Can't say that I blame you. Trying to keep track of Althea's whims may occupy the rest of my life. It is fortunate that I have the inclination to do exactly that. In any case, I asked for her hand and she said yes—with a little provocation of a not exactly romantic nature. But let me assure you that she does want to marry me. She doesn't know it yet, but she does. Or she will, I hope."

"I see," Francis said, who did not see at all. "But are you serious in that you are willing to cancel that debt?"

"I should think it only good taste," Tracy explained with a little less patience. The phaeton was now making a second circuit of the Park. "It seems rather uncouth to dun one's brother-in-law for some trifling gaming debt." Francis, to whom the debt was by no means trifling, thought this the most beautiful sentiment he had ever heard. "Now," Tracy continued, "with that business completed, do you think that I might return you to Grosvenor

Square? And would you please give Althea my regards and tell her that I regret I shall not be able to call on her this afternoon, but will look for her at the play this evening."

Francis agreed meekly. With dispatch Sir Tracy returned his prospective brother-in-law to his house, paused long enough to recall Francis to his message for Althea, and then, with Eustace hanging on behind, left the vicinity.

Maria was waiting in the doorway, very fetching in a morning gown of blue crepe, with a look of wifely anxiety on her face. As nothing was better calculated to make Francis feel that he was master of his kingdom, he immediately and gratifyingly undertook to assure his wife that all was well.

"Francis, will you for pity's sake speak to me! Are we quite poor? Did you speak to Sir Tracy?" Maria's face spoke of a determination to be bravely poor, no matter how much (and she was sure it would be a great deal) she disliked it.

Francis, with the air of one who has brought off a coup of some magnitude, announced that Sir Tracy Calendar was a Trojan. Maria, not sure how to handle such a declaration, demanded a clarification.

"Like a man and a brother, Calendar has canceled the debt. Said he could not think of that kind of debt between us—not to start anyway. He made no promises about after he and Ally are leg-shackled. So you see, you may continue to buy yourself as many geegaws as you like, with my blessing."

"And you will try to be a little more circumspect with your gaming, will you, my dearest?" Maria entreated sweetly. Francis suppressed a moment's annoyance at this mild scolding from his wife, and answered that he would make an effort in that direction.

"Oh, and will you tell Ally that Calendar sent a message to her? Said he couldn't come round to call this afternoon, but presented his compliments and hopes to see her at the play this evening."

"What a provoking man. How did he know that Ally and I were engaged for the play tonight? And will you please come with us, dearest? I will not think on what a trial that man is, but be happy for Althea's sake—and, Francis, do you mean that he has forgiven you that entire enormous amount of money? I am in transports!" The full impact of Francis's announcement had at last struck Maria: she sat down very hard on the nearest available chair.

"Well, of course, goose, did I not say so? I don't mind saying that it would have set me back considerably to have had to pay the debt right away. I call that right brotherly." Francis was infected with his wife's amazement, infused with giddy elation, which led him momentarily to dispose of the fortunes of others with the same abandon he had used in nearly divesting himself of his own. "After all, Mary, Calendar can afford to make a pretty gesture, he's rich as Croesus! What's a piddling sum of ten thousand pounds to him? Especially when he's to marry Althea. Nothing less to be expected of a gentleman."

Maria, to whom the sum of ten thousand pounds was so ridiculously high as to be incomprehensible, fell from her gasping silence to a slightly hysterical giggling, which mingled with Francis's own chuckles. He lifted his wife from her chair and, holding her considerably closer than the twelve inches prescribed at Almack's, began to whirl her around the room in a waltz that seriously endangered the well-being of the furniture.

To Debbens and the second housemaid, lingering outside the door, the sounds that issued from the morning room were altogether incomprehensible.

"Gentry!" Debbens snorted to the maid, who greeted this statement with a nod and a look of definite admiration. They turned from the door to find Mrs. Chaverly glowering at them; the maid went about her business with chastened alacrity; Debbens returned to his work and went through the day with a peculiarly harried look.

Chapter Twelve

Financial difficulties dissolved, Maria spent the afternoon at Madame Helena's warehouse, and saw neither her sister nor Miss Laverham when she came to call. This time it was Althea who had the advantage of Georgiana, who stood, tentative and chilled, in the doorway of the Bevans' drawing room.

"We shall have our tea straightway, and that will help to warm you," Althea greeted her sensibly. A maid appeared and was told that Banders should send down a warm shawl for Miss Laverham, and that tea should be brought immediately. That done and the topic of the chill in the air having been exhausted, Althea was disgusted to find that conversation had ceased between them.

"This is dreadful. I cannot fathom why we find it so hard to hold a rational conversation in simple insipidities like everyone else," she cried at length. Georgiana, who had been studying the braid on the shawl Banders had provided, gave a start and colored. "What is the worst of it," Althea continued after the tea tray had been delivered, "is that there is not the least reason in the world for *us* to feel awkward together. We certainly have been more sinned against than sinning."

Georgiana considered this. "But who *has* done the sinning?" she asked. "I could not help it that I was ill, and if

you did not know of Edward's commitment to me, you
could not be blamed. Is it all Edward's fault?"

"Well, you can hardly cherish the idea that I am a fatal
beauty anymore, can you," Althea snorted. "I am all put
out of patience with the race of men. My father was so
unreasonable that I ran away from him—and my tiresome
brother. And Francis—that is my sister's husband
Bevan—has treated my sister very shabbily, along with
his gaming, which has gotten him very heavily into debt.
Oh dear." Althea shook her head angrily at the thoughts
that whole imbroglio conjured up for her. "And then your
dear Edward comes and makes me believe that he is unat-
tached, and genuinely fond of me, which I know now
must have been the greatest piece of flummery. And finally Tracy! Oh, it is beyond anything dreadful."

Georgiana stared at Althea with fascination. "Are you
not, perhaps, too hard on them?"

"I am tired to death of being patient all the time. I
wonder you are not as well. You must admit that Pendarly has treated you shabbily." As she continued, the last
night's brooding infected Althea with a certain evangelical
turn of phrase, and she spoke in a decidedly strong-
minded manner, which would have appalled Maria.

"Well, I have never been used to thinking in such a
fashion," Georgiana began cautiously. "I don't know if
Edward really treated me ill or no—I *was* ill and he was
lonely and you are pretty and so much more—more interesting than I am. I'm afraid that I have no spirit at all,"
Georgiana concluded sadly.

"You certainly have none if you cannot feel in the least
abused when your betrothed takes the opportunity of your
illness—just when he ought to be concerned only for your
welfare—to make advances toward some strange woman.
You have far more patience than ever I could muster,"
the "strange woman" said with fervor.

"To tell the truth, Mama has had so much spirit always
that I felt it best to temper what I had. Mama is so *very*

forceful, you know." Althea wondered if "forceful" was not a charitable word for Mrs. Laverham. "I know Edward really was not right in trying to make you feel warmly toward him. Were you much distressed when you found him out?"

"I?" Althea was startled by the question. "Do you know, I don't believe I have given it much thought since—well, I have had other matters to fret me since. I was angry, of course, but I cannot recall that I was very hurt. But what of you? Cannot you think of yourself? How did you truly feel when you learned that Pendarly was being enticed by some hussy lately come to London?"

Georgiana opened her mouth to reply that she had thought poor Edward much maligned, or that he was justified in seeking consolation while she was ill. But Althea had followed this train of thought and shook her head sternly.

"I felt—" Georgiana began tentatively. "That is, I was displeased."

"Yes?"

"And hurt?"

"I should imagine so!"

"And angry. And out of patience with Mama for enjoying having to tell me about the whole thing."

"Splendid!" Althea said in triumph. "Of course you were angry and hurt. Anyone less a saint or less fond of Mr. Pendarly would have sent him packing immediately." Georgiana shook her head and looked at Althea with alarm. "I am being an interfering wretch, and I am sorry. I am entirely out of sorts with mankind today, and have been trying to infect you with my displeasure, which is shameless of me. Let us talk of other things."

But Georgiana, relieved of the tension she had carried in her own anger, was now loath to depart from the subject of Mr. Pendarly's infidelities.

"I always thought it was wrong of me to complain of anything, but I never knew how much better it can make one feel. You are right. I was ill treated. And you, too, of course." Intoxication with her new freedom had put a becoming glow in Georgiana's cheeks, and her eyes had darkened indignantly. "You cannot know how good it is to speak this way. I hate to think how mealymouthed I have been previously."

Althea stared at her companion in some alarm. "I had no idea of despoiling your calm this way—only raising your opinion of yourself somewhat. I am so glad if that worked, but what an about-face you present me with!"

Georgiana calmed down a trifle under Althea's concerned eyes, but a militant light still shone from her own when she spoke. "I am sorry. It is just that it is such a relief not to pretend to myself that everything is well and suits me when it is not and does not." She sighed. "Mama always looks as if I have become a harridan if I dislike something. You can see that I count you as my friend for this. And as my fellow victim. Think how Edward would enjoy that thought. I think he would rather like to have a victim somewhere."

Althea smiled and thought of the other men who had been so much in her thoughts lately: her father, her brother, Francis, and finally, Calendar—always Calendar. "Why is it that men imagine they can play their nasty tricks and still be assured of our affections? Lord, I wish I had some game equal to their own that I could play in return that would vex them as mightily as they have vexed us. But I do not suppose there is any way we can do it. We can sit and net purses and paint watercolors, all the while praying that someone will keep us from the shelf. I feel like a pair of gloves to hear Mary talk of my success. I shudder to think what must have been my fate had Brummell not declared that I was in good taste."

"Your sister cannot come close to Mama. I wish I could picture for you her face the day Pendarly offered for me. As though the Kingdom of Heaven had been offered her. Of course, I suppose I looked just the same

way, but then, I was—I had learned to esteem Edward."
Georgiana's voice broke. "And he betrayed my confidence."

"He was too sure of you," Althea pronounced grimly.
"That is the whole problem of it. That was why I left
home, you see. Papa had been pronouncing my disinheritance regularly these years, all because he thinks that a
mere female cannot be as important as his heir. I showed
him what he had in me! If you could see his letters to
me—each a little more distraught than the last. He has no
more idea of how to run that household than to fly.
Should I return, I imagine I should be better appreciated.
Lord, but I sound vengeful," she added thoughtfully.

"But how could I make Edward appreciate me?" Georgiana stared bleakly into her teacup. "I cannot run away."
Althea nodded, and for some minutes she and Georgiana
sat with brows furrowed, pondering the problem.

"You _can_ run away!" Althea said at last with such
force that Georgiana made a very small ladylike jump
from her seat. "Not only can you—I mean _we_—but
you—I mean _we_—must!"

"My dear Miss Ervine—Althea—whatever do you
mean?" Georgiana asked nervously.

"I don't mean really run away, of course. That would
serve little purpose for either of us—"

"But I thought you had already run away," Georgiana
interrupted.

"That was merely from my father, and that was _only_
running way. But what I did was to make Papa feel my
absence. Georgiana, do you see? We shall contrive to
make them appreciate us, and to do that we must make
them feel the lack of us. And show them that others do
appreciate us."

"Who is _them_?" Georgiana asked. "Who else appreciates us?"

"Them is—them are—bother—_they_ are your Mr. Pendarly and my Sir Tracy. And why should not other people appreciate us? And I know just how to go about it—the oldest thing in the world, but we shall be more organized than any Greek or Roman comedy."

"Greeks? Romans? Are what—is what you are planning strictly—uh—*convenable?*" Georgiana asked. "I mean, are we to make them jealous in some way?" Althea nodded. "But that is ridiculous. Not for you, of course, but for me. Who in the world is there to make Edward in the least jealous? No one pays me the least bit of attention at Almack's, not since my betrothal was announced, and before that I think it was only my fortune."

"You are not to talk that way anymore," Althea said briskly. "Your attitude is all wrong. Besides which, I can think of one person at least who has been—well, not languishing after you, but studying you through his quizzing glass quite speculatively—I saw him do so last night at Almack's. I was very amused, for he used to squire Maria about, and now she is so taken up in her Darby and Joan relationship with Francis that she has not given him the least glance. He would never ever do for a husband, of course, but what an admirable flirt!"

"Will you please tell me who you are speaking of?" Georgiana pleaded in a tone between curiosity, trepidation, and laughter.

"One of Maria's old cicisbeos, John Wallingham. He thinks himself a famous rake, and is very good at romantic posing, so you see, if you could just carry on a flirtation for a little while, it would serve the purpose admirably." Althea smiled broadly. "Did you not say that Edward liked melodrama? Here is a fine one for him. I think he would be delighted in the picture of himself rescuing you from the arms of Rake Wallingham. Think what joy he would get from a duel."

"You cannot mean a duel!" Georgiana moaned.

"Well, if you think that he would cavil over the little matter of a meeting on a green somewhere before breakfast—" Althea relented at Georgiana's obvious distress. "No, please, I was only teasing you, although I maintain that the idea would appeal to him, if not the reality. But are you willing to try it?"

"You said we were to make them jealous," countered Georgiana. "With whom do you intend to whet Sir Tracy's interest?"

"You agree that I have a reason to be angry with Mr. Pendarly, do you not?" Althea began cautiously.

Georgiana agreed readily. "But you cannot mean to make him the object—oh, no, Althea, please. I know that Edward will never look at me again if you but cast a look his way."

"Will you please rid yourself of the notion that I am some Circe to entice him? I intend to make him mightily uncomfortable, and Tracy, too. Never fear me, Georgiana. By the time I have done, I will have led those two the chase they deserve—I hope—and I predict that your Edward will be so heartily sickened of me that, even if he doesn't suddenly discover how fascinating you are, he will flee from me to you simply as a safe harbor from my blandishments."

"You go too fast for me. Can we really hope to carry this scheme out?"

"Why not. 'Tis hardly an original idea. Are you going to the play tonight? Have you something very ravishing to wear? And believe that you are ravishing! That will accomplish more than a dozen bottles of Denmark Lotion and a score of hare's feet. Don't forget that John Wallingham was staring at you, and he is certainly not one to be caught admiring anyone who is not first rate. Now what is the matter?"

Georgiana had been toying nervously with her sash. "I am not sure I can fascinate anyone, let alone a—a rake."

Althea snorted. "Oh lord, Georgie, Wallingham is no rake—except in his own eyes. He's just another of those

slightly disreputable gentlemen hanging out for a fortune—and you notice that Mr. Willis always admits him
to the Assembly Hall."

"You think I will be safe then?" Georgiana faltered.

"If only you will take a little confidence in yourself.
For all my *fatal beauty*, you are the one with the golden
curls I always wanted. Smile! Will you take some more
tea?"

The conversation continued along these lines until Deb-
bens entered some fifteen minutes later to announce that
Miss's barouche had returned and was waiting outside.
Georgiana gave a guilty start and rose to her feet.

"I must leave at once. Mama hates it when I keep the
horses waiting, and besides, I promised to match some
ribbons for her and have clean forgotten to do so, so she
will be in a taking over that, too. We are due at my aunt's
for dinner before we go on to the play."

"You will be there, then. Try and see if you cannot
come to the box we have there between the acts. We
might as well begin our work at once. Please smile, Georgiana, and don't look so overset. It will work famously,
you shall see. Go home and tell your Mama, if she scolds,
that it is all my fault that I kept you talking so late."

With some misgivings still unvoiced, Georgiana agreed,
thanked Althea prettily for the tea, and returned to her
the shawl she had borrowed. Althea responded with equal
formality, and they parted laughing at the absurdity of
their excess of civility. Brimming with the subtleties of her
new campaign, Althea went upstairs to dress.

Maria returned home only a few minutes later. In her
own hurry to dress she forgot to stop at her sister's door
and deliver Calendar's message, and to inform her of the
sudden change in Francis's fortunes: there was a note
from Francis saying that he would accompany them to the
theater that evening, and in a cloud of dreamy content,
Maria dressed for the occasion.

During the first act of the play, which Althea enjoyed immensely, Georgiana contrived to catch her eye. They waved and smiled at each other, and each felt the charming excitement of having a secret with the other, over the heads of several dozen people. Georgiana had dressed with—for her—unusual abandon, although her good taste had limited excess to a circassian bodice and a garnet necklet. Her hair, also, had been done in a manner slightly less reminiscent of the schoolroom, giving her slight figure a surprising amount of authority.

When at last the break between acts came, Georgiana asked Mr. Pendarly to escort her to Lady Bevan's box. Mrs. Laverham, hearing this request, scowled fiercely at her daughter and said in forbidding tones that it was much better for dear Georgie to stay put and allow Mr. Pendarly to fetch her some iced cup. Georgiana blithely ignored her mother and took Mr. Pendarly's arm, much to his discomforture.

"Is there someone there you wish to see particularly?" he asked nervously as he attempted to make a path through the sea of people that separated him from what he regarded as imminent doom.

"Of course, else I should hardly have asked you to take me here," Georgiana assured him as they reached the door of the box. "I was introduced to Lady Bevan's sister yesternight—the dearest creature. She just caught my eye as the act closed, and I should like to speak with her," she finished airily.

Pendarly writhed.

In Lady Bevan's box they found, besides Maria, Lord Bevan, Mr. John Wallingham, and Miss Althea Ervine. Mr. Pendarly shrank back into the curtains while Althea and Georgiana greeted each other, but after a moment a peremptory command from Althea brought him forth. The friendship between the two women was so patently honest that for a moment Edward Pendarly wondered if perhaps neither was aware of what the other was to him.

"Dear Miss Laverham," Althea said enthusiastically, "here is Mr. John Wallingham, who has been admiring you since the play began. I am sure he could never tell us what the action on stage has been, so taken up has he been with watching you. Oh, and Mr. Wallingham, this is Edward Pendarly." Pendarly disapproved of John Wallingham on sight, unaware how much his dislike was obvious to the people around him.

Wallingham made a deep bow over Georgiana's hand. "If only I had the words to tell you how honored I am to have met you at last, dear lady. I regret that Miss Ervine has given away my secret; I suppose I shall now be relegated to the ranks of your score of unlucky admirers." His voice was low, with a curiously unpleasant timbre, and the attitude behind it so fulsome as to be almost oily. Georgiana dimpled and made herself reply in a flattered manner, while Pendarly watched her performance with a mouth that hung unattractively open.

"Mr. Pendarly, I vow I cannot have seen you in the last week and more," Althea said clearly. Pendarly blanched and moved closer to her in hopes that she would lower her voice. Georgiana seemed not to hear: she was happily engaged in a discussion of the play with Mr. Wallingham, and paid not a moment's attention to what her fiancé was doing.

"Can you be at outs with me?" Althea continued. "I wish you will tell me, for I cannot bear to have my particular friends alienated from me."

Pendarly stared at her in horror and made some sort of mumbled reply, all the while glancing over her shoulder at Georgiana. Mr. Wallingham had said something to make Georgiana blush. She was acting in a manner he had never seen before, and disliked intensely. Althea, in the meantime, asked several questions about his opinion of the play, listened to none of his replies, and repeated her question as to what had strained the friendship between them. He winced and attempted to answer in a manner that would not entirely compromise him with either of the ladies present.

Georgiana felt lightheaded, as if someone else were talking for her. She was aware that she had never behaved this way in her life, and was unable to understand why it came so easily now. She did not like Wallingham—there was something in his address that made her nervous—but whereas a week ago she would have made a weak smile at him and sunk into silence, tonight she was capable of anything. She babbled and laughed and babbled. Althea's advice seemed to be right, for Wallingham appeared to be enjoying the discussion. And Edward, she realized with relish, was entirely lost in the situation he now found himself in. The combined efforts of Althea and Georgiana were taking a definite toll: Pendarly was beginning to look years older and much harried.

"I cannot remember such a splendid evening," she chirped enthusiastically to Mr. Wallingham. "Even that dreadful woman in the puce does not bother me—she will poison the heroine, I make no doubt, and I shall not mind it in the least." She hesitated for a moment, then went recklessly ahead and batted her eyes at him in an admiring manner.

Mr. Wallingham, who had appraised Georgiana from across halls and considered her considerable fortune more than once, was surprised at how easily he had captivated little Miss Laverham. He had assumed that her manner would be as insipid as he privately thought her looks to be, but was agreeably surprised to find her quite amusing, for a wealthy and respectable woman. He found himself enjoying her company despite her regrettably blond hair and slight figure, especially when he considered the healthy figure she would bring with her to any marriage she made.

"You do the play tonight an injury," he said fulsomely, "for what mere mortal will watch the stage when he has you to gaze upon?" Pendarly, near enough to overhear every word, glowered fiercely at Althea; Georgiana only blushed and wagged her fan at her admirer. Althea continued her torturing friendliness toward Pendarly, but spared a thought in admiration of her friend's management in the toils of Rake Wallingham. She wondered if perhaps she had been wise in promoting their introduction, but, she thought fatalistically, it was too late now to worry. Georgiana was performing beautifully, and Pendarly was utterly confounded. She gave a gurgle of unintentional laughter in the midst of one of Pendarly's labored speeches. He looked at her so piteously that almost, for a moment, Althea thought of relenting, of letting him suffer over Georgiana without her interference.

"Lady Bevan, Francis, good evening." A voice from the rear of the box broke through her thoughts and Pendarly's conversation. "Good evening, Althea." Concentration all to pieces, Althea looked unwilling at Calendar. He was standing just inside the door to the box, looking immaculate and elegant in evening dress that made Wallingham and Bevan look like overdressed fops and Pendarly like a raw country squire. His manner was cool, a little wary, but except for the satirical curve of his mouth, friendly. Althea was entirely infuriated by it.

"Good evening, Pendarly," Calendar continued smoothly. "I see Miss Laverham is with you as well." He lifted his eyebrow slightly; the cynical look became even more marked.

"Evening," Pendarly choked. Althea was sure that this was the last straw for him: he was beginning to look panicked, and for the second time she thought of stopping the whole game out of pity for his predicament.

"Miss Laverham"—Edward looked piteously at Georgiana—"I think it is time we return to your mother—she has been alone quite some while."

At the sound of her name on his lips Georgiana turned quickly; just as quickly she controlled her eagerness and turned back to Wallingham to make a lingering farewell, regretting that their pleasant chat was to be so soon broken up. She managed a coquettish smile as she took her leave of him, then turned to Althea to make her farewell. A long look passed between them, and Althea said she hoped to return her friend's kind visit very soon. Tracy glanced lazily at Althea but said nothing. Edward Pendarly was, by this time, at the door of the box, wearing a look so earnestly desirous of departure that Georgiana cut short her thank you to Lady Bevan and followed him at once.

When they were gone, and John Wallingham, feeling he had made his point for the night, had taken himself off to dance attendance upon some other monied maiden, Tracy removed Althea's fan from between her gloved hands and began to fan her. In the heat she might well have been appreciative of the gesture, had not the gesture been an excuse for some not so gentle questioning.

"I shudder to do so, but I must ask you what plot you are hatching, my dear. I grant that you have a legitimate complaint against Pendarly, but need you rake him so publicly over the coals? And must you needs throw that little Laverham chit to the claws of a fox like Wallingham? It is all very well for him to dangle after your sister, who is a married woman, but an innocent like that girl is not proof against one like him." He sighed exasperatedly. "What are you playing, Ally?"

Since he had first entered the box Althea had felt herself become more and more out of patience with him. The feelings of ill use she had begun to nurture the night before, the fact that she was sure that he was unaware of these same feelings (no matter how reasonable that ignorance might be), and, finally, the fact that he was scolding her in public for a thing she herself had begun to fret over, overpowered Althea altogether. She dimly remembered a time—perhaps only yesterday—when she had remarked to herself how well she and Calendar were dealing together. That seemed years ago. She was seized with an almost overpowering impulse to box his ears.

"I play no games, Sir Tracy. I understand, of course, that you do, and make no difference in your dealings with *whom* you play." If Althea had expected this shot to go direct, she was disappointed; Tracy looked puzzled. "I am not at all sure I care for your implications about my sister, either. You have caused far and away enough consternation in my family without I mention this to Francis, who would doubtless dislike to hear you speak so of Mary." In fact, Althea doubted whether Francis would care to tangle with anyone who had the reputation with pistols that Calendar had, but she could not unsay the words, no matter how fustian they sounded.

"I have not the slightest idea why you are enacting me this bit of Cheltenham drama, Ally, but I wish you would make your grievances a bit more clear. And until you do, I wish you would have the kindness to keep an innocent like Miss Laverham away from Wallingham's addresses."

Althea felt a strong desire to cry. Instead she gathered her strength for one more assault on the enemy. "I am hardly Miss Laverham's keeper, sir. To hear you speak of her innocence, one would assume I had none myself, nor wit either. She is perfectly capable of caring for herself. And I am perfectly able to judge my own conduct without advice from you."

"I do not particularly approve of your conduct right now, Althea, and for your character, my love, I take leave to tell you that I am sure you have a ready enough supply of naïvité: I do not think you a stupid woman, Althea, but at the moment you are behaving like such a greenhead that I can only suppose it is your naïvité and not stupidity that occasions it." He pressed his lips tightly together. "I will speak to you tomorrow, perhaps, when you are recovered from whatever passion this is. But let me tell you, Ally"—his voice dropped—"that I do not care for machinations, and if I find that you have made that poor child unhappy to suit your own purposes, I will have a great deal to say to the point."

Althea started to retort that he had already said a great deal to the matter, but her voice showed a disturbing tendency to break and quiver, and all that she could do was turn her eyes toward the stage while Tracy made his apologies to Maria and Francis. When he had left, the Bevans were in close consultation for a few minutes. It was Francis who moved his chair close to Althea's and patted her hand in a clumsy, inefficient, but endearingly comforting manner.

"Ally, what's to do?"

She suppressed a manic urge to laugh. "Hardly anything at all, Francis," she murmured brokenly. "That man is the most infuriating person I have ever met." Francis looked a trifle perplexed over this, until he remembered a few occasions during his own courtship when Maria had professed to feel exactly the same way about himself.

"I know you rather like Calendar. Mary told me so, and he really is the best of good fellows. Can't have said anything so bad here at the theater."

"He is a wretched, preaching, prosing d-d-dandy!"

Francis was shocked. "Not a dandy, Ally. He's a great swell, certainly, and I wish I had his way with a cravat, but he only wears one fob, and never any tassels to his hessians." Having established, at least to his own satisfaction, Calendar's sobriety in matters of dress, Francis continued on to the other charges. "As for being wretched and deceitful and prosing and whatever else you said, Calendar's far too punctual in matters of *ton* to lie, especially to a lady, except if she ask him about her clothes, the way Lady Monkford did that time at—"

"Oh, for heaven's sake, Francis!" Althea hissed impatiently.

"Well, he doesn't prose, as I have reason to know. Don't know if Mary told you, Ally, but I got into some deep play with Calendar and—"

"Yes, yes, I know the whole of that!" Althea said bitterly.

"There, you see! Had a golden opportunity to prose like a father—Alvanley tried sure enough—should have listened, but I don't suppose it would have helped what with the pother I was in. But Calendar never said a word. It won't do to go creating scenes at Covent Garden, Ally," he confided.

"*I* did not create a scene. It was foisted upon me by that—" Words failed Althea at this crucial moment, and she turned toward the stage, trying to pick up the thread of the hopelessly confused dramatic narrative before her. "I suppose," she said a moment later, when she felt a little more composed, "that everyone in the entire theater is looking at me. Well then, they may stare as much as they vulgarly please to!" She dropped her fan, and in reaching for it bumped her head against the railing, which did nothing to improve her temper.

"Just you wait there a while until they finish with this act and we shall leave. Never did care much for the theater. Mary likes this stuff, and one must go anyway. It's all a lovers' quarrel anyway," he added obscurely. "I'll just go tell Mary what we plan."

His tone was so genuinely solicitous that Althea managed a weak smile and begged him not to spoil Maria's pleasure. To herself, she vowed that she hoped never to see Sir Tracy Calendar again. One could not, she reasoned, have a lovers' quarrel with someone one did not love. For herself, she only wished to be able to go home and be quietly miserable with a glass of warm milk in her own room. For the first time since her dusty arrival at the door of her sister's house, Althea wished that she was back in the boredom, solitude, and safety of Hook Well.

Chapter Thirteen

Mrs. Fulvia Laverham was displeased. Not with her own conduct, for of course there could be no fault there, but with the inexplicably difficult behavior of the rest of the world. Mrs. Laverham prided herself on her ability to right things that she did not like, so in her customary manner she studied the problems and set about trying to resolve them to her own (if no one else's) satisfaction.

To her irritation, since the meeting at Covent Garden three nights before, John Wallingham had begun to insinuate himself into Georgiana's company, and there appeared to be no way, short of tossing him out to the gutter, to indicate to this gentleman that his presence was not strictly desirable. Mrs. Laverham had gone so far as to lecture her child on the folly of encouraging the pretensions of a man of Wallingham's stamp: to be sure, his name and family were well enough, and his lack of money was no cynosure, but no Laverham was going to marry a shopworn piece of mischief like Rake Wallingham, Mrs. Laverham had thundered. It would without a doubt put her dearest Georgie beyond the pale. To which Georgiana had answered, with a laugh in her best flirtatious style, how such a thing could be so when Wallingham was received everywhere? "If he had a wife as respectable as I, Mama, it surely must only improve his credit, not damage mine. Not," she continued blandly, "that I mean to marry him, for I do not, but he is much more diverting that poor Edward, is he not?"

Mrs. Fulvia Laverham was not pleased at all.

That morning, when Mr. Wallingham again appeared, he found that Miss Georgie was not at home. Mrs. Laverham, feeling it about time that she was firmly in control again, had sent her child out on errands and lain in wait for such a visit as this. It was her intention to give the man as unpleasant a half-hour as was in her power. When the interview was over, she arose, serene in the belief that she had entirely confounded and intimidated Mr. Wallingham. It would have been a mortifying blow to her to learn that Mr. Wallingham had quit her house under the impression that he had charmed her completely, so that if and when he did approach Georgiana, it would be with her support. Satisfied with this piece of work, Mrs. Laverham spent the rest of the morning trying to work out how to restore Georgiana to her former docility.

Georgiana, sent after an entirely unnecessary length of ribbon and a book from the lending library, was puzzled as to why the maid sent to accompany her insisted on making so many small purchases as they went along. In fact, Mrs. Laverham had given the girl her orders to keep Miss Georgie from home an hour or more, under threats of dire punishment and possible dismissal. As for Georgiana, she went patiently traipsing behind the maid until all the purchases were made, then turned toward the lending library, where, it seemed, every other person in town had been drawn by the need for something to read. She stood by the wall for a moment, hoping the crush might abate, and was about to cry defeat and return home when a hand touched her shoulder.

"Miss Laverham!" It was Althea Ervine, with a pair of volumes in one hand and several small parcels in the other. "How fortunate to find you here. Are you just in or were you about to leave? And will you come back with me and take some tea? After battling this crowd, I think we both deserve it."

Georgiana was about to regret that she must return to

her home when the maid at her elbow spoke up and pressed Miss to go on—Madam would certainly want Miss to enjoy her afternoon a little. When Althea added her own voice, Georgiana shrugged helplessly and acquiesced.

Safely back at Grosvenor Square, secure in the morning room, with the maid sent downstairs to drink her tea in the servants' hall, Georgiana and Althea assumed the attitude of hardened conspirators.

"You can have no idea how glad I am to be able to talk in a rational manner!" Georgiana sighed. "Since we were introduced, I have been playing at being the most awful, flirting thing with your Mr. Wallingham. I never realized that being a first-rate is so dreadfully fatiguing."

"Is he very stupid?" Althea asked sympathetically.
"No, I suppose it is also to impress Pendarly. He *is* impressed, you know. I have been haunting him, and he has become more and more nervous in my presence, until he positively jumped last night when I spoke his name at Carlton House. He watches you now as if you were a pitcher of water and he a thirsty man. I only hope you can stand to continue with Wallingham just a little longer. I feel sure that all will end happily for you."

Georgiana blushed happily, but after a moment her frown returned. "I suppose I have no talent for it: this sort of beguilement comes very hard to me. He has the most awful way of making compliments—I cannot give a name to his manner, but he makes me very—very nervous."

Althea might have been able to put a name to what her friend was feeling, but she refrained. Instead, she voiced what had been bothering her since the argument she had had with Calendar. "You think you are able to handle Wallingham?"

Georgiana looked at her friend with surprise. "Why, of course. He is odious, and I wish that I did not have to torment poor Edward quite so much, but do not worry about Wallingham getting from leaders—I do not any-more. It is only a matter of seeing how much of his civility I can stand!" She giggled. "Since I have got to know him I have been able to see how much of his acts are merest posery. Oh, I am sure I can handle him." She paused thoughtfully. "How odd to hear myself speak so. Oh, I wish it need not be so complicated. How do you do with your plans?"

Althea had dreaded this question. Since the night of the play she had seen Calendar but twice, and both of these times he had come as close to cutting her as he could without causing comment. Even so there was some talk—a new *on dit* concerning Tracy Calendar could always find a place in Society, and Althea had, in her success, made a few enemies who were glad enough to see that what had looked like a conquest had turned to dust. In the Park the afternoon before she and Maria had met Calendar and Lord Petersham walking, and while Tracy had been civil—and Petersham quite voluble in giving Maria a message to Francis in reference to a new strain of snuff he had blended—Althea had felt the coolness in his manner, and had detected a definite lack of something in his treatment of her.

"My plans? They progress beautifully," she lied cheerfully. "And do you recall that I told you the other day that my father has been writing letters that grow more and more panicked? I received yet another this morning, and only think, he is actually come to the point where he will consider hiring a housekeeper. I shudder to think what sort of disrepair the house must have fallen into that he would contemplate such an expenditure."

Georgiana tactfully did not notice the change in topic. Instead she asked how much longer Althea thought their performance should continue. Althea considered this carefully for a moment before giving it as her opinion that it should go on for a few days more, perhaps a week—at least until Pendarly made some positive gesture to prove that their treatment had been efficacious. Even then, she thought it should continue a few days more, so they did not seem to relent too easily. "But I doubt that you shall have to continue the charade much longer. Lord, how desperate that boy did appear when last I saw him." Althea blithely ignored the fact that Edward Pendarly was several years older than herself.

"You think, then, we can have done soon?" Georgiana asked with relief.

Althea smiled a little bitterly. "I have no doubt we are almost finished as of now. Have a little patience. Is a week such a prodigious span of time?"

"I suppose not," her friend sighed. "I am so unused to any sort of prevarication—it is rather exciting, in a way, but I shall be so relieved when it is done. How does your sister do?"

The conversation became more general, which was fortunate, since not five minutes later Maria joined them, full of enthusiasm: only this minute had she received an invitation to a musical evening to be held on the coming Tuesday, and what would Althea wear? What would Miss Laverham wear? Of course Miss Laverham had been invited. And this was the most exciting part: there was to be a theatrical selection as well, and Lady Liverpool had asked Maria to play the part of the nightingale. "No, I don't know what the piece is, only that they want a nightingale and my looks are perfect for the part. Lady Liverpool said so. I know they are all a bunch of old Tories and she is dreadfully dull herself, but everyone will be there, and did I not always want to be an actress?"

Althea and Georgiana exchanged glances of amusement and let Maria prattle on about costumes and preparation; she asked Althea four times to be sure and help her learn her lines, and four times Althea cheerfully agreed to do so. When applied to, Georgiana said that she would be glad to help Lady Bevan with any special ideas she had for her costume: she had been used to sketching stick fig-

ures when in the shoolroom, and two of the dresses she
had designed in that fashion had actually been made up
for her. Maria, who had mastered the art of the water-
color sketch with the greatest effort of will, was quite
overwhelmed by this offer, and spoiled all chance Althea
might have had for a final private word with Georgiana
with her chatter and planning. At last Georgiana declared
that she must return to her mama, and sent for the maid.
That person felt that by now she had kept Miss Georgie
from home long enough to satisfy even Mrs. Laverham,
and she made no objection to returning homeward.

Within a few doors of the Bevans, however, they were
intercepted: Edward Pendarly waved urgently at Georgiana until she told the driver to pull over. The maid had
been given no instructions as to what to do should such a
thing occur, but she strongly suspected that it would be best
to stick by her young miss. Georgiana had time for a murmured adjuration to the maid to keep her tongue before
Pendarly joined them.

"I thought you would not stop for me," Pendarly said
slowly.

Georgiana, fresh from Althea's advisements, stifled in
herself an instinctive gladdening of her voice and
broadening of her smile. "Why ever would I do such a
thing? How do you do. I have not seen you much lately."

"I have been by, ma'am. It is only that I cannot seem
to draw your attention from others who please you better." Georgiana feigned a pretty puzzlement at this
speech. Pendarly continued. "I see that you and Miss Ervine are become very good friends."

"Oh yes, she is the charmingest companion, is she
not?" Georgiana watched him pale at the shot. "And today Lady Bevan joined us and we discussed a theatrical
and musical evening to be given next week at Liverpool's.
I think I shall be designing Lady Bevan's costume. Perhaps Wallingham will like to take me to the Pantheon Ba-

zaar tomorrow so that I can look for some materials to use."

Pendarly's face grew dark as it had been pale, and he asked in a querulous manner why Wallingham should be elected to carry out such an errand.

"Why, he has engaged with me to go driving, so it would only be the convenient thing. And he is a good companion, and so much in evidence these days." She laughed trillingly. "Was it not kind of Miss Ervine to introduce us?"

"You do not forget that you are—that we are to be—Georgie, I cannot trust that man," Pendarly stammered. He was unable to understand why he had so much trouble simply speaking these days.

"As for trusting," Georgiana replied, "why I do not trust him very far either. But trust is not something one looks for in a mere companion. Trust is more a quality one looks for in one's husband." Pendarly winced. "I am only looking to amuse myself for a while, until we are married, Edward," she said, contriving to make that marriage sound like a sentence to the direst tedium. "Then I shall be the most dutiful sort of wife, and if you cannot care for one of my admirers, I shall send him about his business. Now tell me, do you think that blue will suit Lady Bevan, or dare I try something striking in green?"

Pendarly answered he knew not what. This was a Georgiana he had never seen and did not much care for. He wanted back the quiet, prim girl he knew—lord, long ago, before Althea Ervine had arrived in town to complicate his life. It was all Wallingham's fault, he thought darkly. Vivaciousness and wit were all very well in someone of Miss Ervine's sort, but Georgiana was another matter. He did not care to be snubbed in favor of some rackety gamester either. While Georgiana kept up a flow of silly conversation about the ideas she had for Lady Bevan's costume as a nightingale, he continued the flow of resentful thoughts through his mind. Georgiana was growing tired of doing all the work in this conversation when the carriage drew up before her door.

"I will not ask you to come in, Edward, for it is late and Mama will be wondering where I have been all this time. Imagine! I only left the house to get a book at the library, and see how I have dawdled. Perhaps I will see you tonight? We go to a rout at Blessington's. No? Well, good day, then." She allowed him to help her from the carriage, and started to move toward her door, but strangely, he did not relinquish his hold on her.

"Georgiana," he said, "what has happened to you? Why are you behaving in this strange way? Perhaps I haven't been very fair to you—the amusements I pursued while you were ill, but—"

"No, Edward? I find that hard to believe. There is nothing that has happened to me," she answered coolly. "I think that this is hardly the time or the place for you, of all people, to read me a catechism on my behavior. Perhaps some other time. *Good day.*"

Georgiana fled inside the house and was almost to her room when the tears she had forced back broke forth in torrents. Behind her the startled maid followed, wondering how she would ever explain the scene she had just witnessed to her mistress. And outside the house Pendarly stood, his mouth slung open, watching the door through which his betrothed had disappeared. That finished it, he thought grimly. She knew All, and had resolved to punish him. The fact that the punishment might be well deserved occurred to him, but it was far easier to nurture feelings of ill use and indignation over the mess she was making of him and his feelings. She had no proper regard for him at all. It was in this state of picturesque and romantic frustration that he returned to his rooms.

Georgiana had succeeded in avoiding her mama; the maid had not been so lucky and was engaged in explaining in agonizing detail the events of the last half-hour to Mrs. Laverham while Georgiana wept and began to change her dress. The fact that she herself had wondered at her own behavior did not make Edward's scolding any more palatable. He thought that *perhaps* his conduct had been a little less than correct indeed! He had the nerve to scold her for her amusements, which heaven knew were innocent enough! After all the work of amusing that odious oily John Wallingham, Edward acted as though she were going after wickedness with mad abandon. It was not to be borne. It was not to be borne at all. She did not stop to think that his speaking to her that afternoon was as much of a capitulation as she was going to receive from Pendarly. In any case, had not Althea, who had more experience of this sort of tactic than she, said plainly not to relent too easily? A few more days of uncertainty would not hurt Edward at all. Georgiana sighed mistily. Thank heaven, only a few more days of smiling at John Wallingham's everlasting gallantry! With this consoling thought, she burst into another bout of tears and, feeling much relieved, set about choosing her gown for that evening.

Chapter Fourteen

Calendar had considered leaving town for a few days, to give his own temper a chance to cool, and to see if Althea would not abandon whatever this latest folly was without his intervention. He certainly had not meant to quarrel with her as he had, let alone to be as unfriendly as he had felt himself becoming in the last few days. Every time he

saw her he remembered her words to him at the theater—he was not without pride, and some of the things
she had said had cut close. He could not account for her
behavior at the play or for the way she had been behaving
since that time; he had seen her in company with Pendarly, when she tormented that gentleman without mercy;
with Wallingham, when she was as cool and appraising as
any marriage-minded mother in London; with Georgiana
Laverham, when she was almost enthusiastic about
wrongheadedly leading her friend into acquaintance with
Wallingham.

"Damn it, if Ally hasn't the sense to keep from making
a botch of her own affairs, she might at least leave someone else's alone," he said savagely under his breath after
meeting Althea and her sister in the Park one afternoon.
His companion, Lord Petersham, was happily engaged in
some animated discussion of snuff and paid no attention
to Tracy's mutterings. It was observed by certain
knowledgeable passersby, however, that from the black
look on Calendar's face there was certain to be trouble in
some quarter, and soon.

He made some effort, when in company and likely to
meet Althea, to escape before his tongue betrayed him
into saying things he had no intention of owning publicly.
He could not see how to bring about a reconciliation until there was some issue from whatever Althea thought
she was doing. So he thought seriously of retiring to his
seat in Lincoln and waiting there for a while.

In the end he dismissed this notion. There was still,
despite all else, the damnable wish to see how it all came
out. So he stayed in London and tried to restrict himself
to his clubs and to such social events it appeared Althea
would be likely to pass upon. His aunt shrewdly guessed
at what had happened, but asked no questions, preferring
to wait until he volunteered some information of his own
will. At last her Joblike patience wore thin, and when the
dowager had for the third time that evening interrupted

the long thoughtful pause, with a question he did not reply to, she asked him to come out with the matter and stop his melodramatic manners.

"A quarrel with Althea," she stated for him. He looked at her with respect.

"I swear you know everything, ma'am. Which of your spies informed you of it?"

"No spies at all, dear child. I have eyes in my head and a reasonably well functioning mind that can still add two and two and come up with four. I must say that I have been impressed," she added thoughtfully.

"With what, ma'am?"

"With Althea, for inspiring such affection—I've never seen you take any set-back in such a fashion, Tracy! Next I'll see you rending your locks and going about with your collar askew like that German fellow—who was that? oh, yes, young Werther. I do dislike people who take themselves so dreadfully seriously."

Calendar bowed in his aunt's direction. "I regret to discommode you, Aunt Peg."

"Fiddlestick. I admire Althea for making you feel so, and I am glad of it, dear. I used to wonder if watching the chasings and comings and goings of that frippery set you grew up with had soured you completely upon the subject of women, or if you would ever bring yourself to care for anyone at all. So now, what is to be done?"

"I cannot think of a thing, save to wait and watch, Aunt."

"A wise dictum, Tracy, but do you think you can support it for long? Or better still, do you think that I can support watching you support it for long? I no longer have your stamina, dear one."

"I don't think I have much choice in the matter, ma'am," he said ruefully. "Ally is set upon some sort of revenge on Pendarly, and she seems to have made Miss Laverham a part of it. What bothers me is that she has introduced Miss Laverham to John Wallingham—"

"Not that dreadful son of old Wallingham—the one who brought his convenient to church incognito! What a turn-up that was. So Ally has promoted a flirtation between this Wallingham and Miss Laverham in order to discomfort what-y'may-call-him?"

"Pendarly, Aunt."

"I know, I know!" the old woman snapped. "So they have this Pembroke, or what have you, they have him tied up over his Miss Laverham's defection, and confused by the attention I imagine Althea is showing him—oh, dear me, what a lovely plot. If only you didn't see quite so much, or rather less of it, dear." She clucked merrily to herself under the exasperated glance of her nephew.

"I was able to understand everything you said until that part at last—although why you scruple to ask me for details when you know as much or more of what has gone on than I do I cannot fathom. What more or less am I supposed to have seen?"

"Your maddening lack of consequence, Tracy!" Lady Boskingram chided. "You suppose that this plot is all for Pendarly's benefit! Something—I have no idea what—has decided Althea that you needed a lesson of some sort. Tracy, dear stupid male that you are, she has been hanging on Pendarly's sleeve as much to annoy you as to worry him. Lord, love must be blind, for it is all clear as daylight to me."

"What?" The black look returned to his face, complicated by a lingering aspect of confusion. His dark brows knit into a straight threatening line over his eyes, and Lady Boskingram shrank a little from his glare. What occasioned his wrath, as much as the fact that he had a genuine dislike for machinations of this sort, was the equally important fact, and one that he had only just realized, that the plot had been successful. Even when he knew how she must dislike and distrust Pendarly, there had been in the back of his mind a maddening thought that perhaps her affections had been more deeply engaged than she knew. He had been, in short, very jealous, and completely unaware of the fact.

"I wish you would not stare at me in such a ferocious manner: you petrify me absolutely. Think a moment if you can: at least the gamble you spoke to me of once has paid off—more successfully than you knew. Only a woman who has some—shall I say interest—in a man will play such a charade. Especially a woman of Althea's wit."

"It seems a confoundedly difficult way for a woman to inform a man that she is—interested in him," he muttered. "And I do not bother to apologize for my language—you taught me everything I know of it."

"So I did. But Tracy"— Lady Boskingram reached her hand out to him—"do not be too hard on her. Who knows what sort of nonsense she has been supporting from that bird-witted sister of hers, or from that deadly dull pompous father—she told me all about him—not to say this strange situation in which she has found herself. She seems to attract furor as honey attracts bees, and you will have to accept that fact if you wish to marry a heroine. But consider that she has spent her life in a little Lancashire town with no society to speak of before you judge her too harshly."

There was a long pause. "I think that I had best go think over all you have said, Aunt Peg," he said tightly.

"Meaning you will go to your club and get foxed and sit in some overstuffed chair all evening and brood and snap the head from everyone who comes near you. Your uncle used to do just the same."

"Correct as always, Aunt Peg," he said admiringly, and stalked out of the room, looking, she thought, terrifying enough to startle any well-intentioned friend he should meet. Lady Boskingram sighed deeply and shook her head.

True to her word, Georgiana had, after some consultation with Lady Liverpool, taken over the design and execution of Lady Bevan's costume for the theatrical. Althea dutifully kept Maria from impeding progress on the costume by hanging over the shoulder of the seamstresses and making nonsensical suggestions by drilling her sister in her few lines. Georgiana wanted to achieve the suggestion of a nightingale without the feathers, paint, and jewels that Maria imagined necessary to such a toilette, and was devoutly grateful for the time Althea kept her sister out of the sewing room.

The morning of the day set for the theatrical found Maria trailing about the library speaking her lines to Althea, who was paying no attention at all, reading instead *Tristram Shandy* and trying not to let her amusement disturb her sister's tenuous train of thought. Georgiana was upstairs, directing the seamstresses in the last details of the costume, a sheer white crepe gown embroidered with pailettes, which in the light contrived to suggest feathers.

When the knocker was dropped several times in furious succession Althea was shaken from her book and Maria from her recitation. Upstairs, Georgiana dropped her pincushion, picked it up again, and said a brief prayer that it would not be the everlasting Wallingham. It was not. Even before Debbens could step to the door of the library and announce the arrival, a young man, prodigiously fine in a bottle-green coat matched unsuitably with buckskins, and slightly greasy top boots, and with a film of dust over all, surged into the room and stood before the amazed sisters.

"Merrit!" they exclaimed in one voice.

The boy gave a cheeky grin and advanced to kiss his sisters.

"Come at last. Father said it was time I went after you to bring you home, Ally. Things are in a sad state, with Cook threatening daily to leave, and lord knows what-not. But don't think you need take any great hurry in getting back, m'dear," he said easily. "I don't fancy returning home just yet."

"But how are you come, and why did you send me no notice!" Maria squeaked. Debbens, still standing in the doorway, wondered if perhaps that was not the usual manner of travel in Lady Bevan's family—he still remembered Miss Althea's arrival too well for his comfort. Since the young gentleman was obviously not to be turned from indoors, Debbens decided that he had done his duty and could return to polishing his brasses.

"I say, Mary, who's the dasher I saw at the top of the stairs? Pretty thing in a stuff gown with a pincushion in her hand. Blushed like fury when I smiled at her and ran off down the hall."

"Merrit," Althea said reprovingly, "you will stop thinking whatever it is that you are thinking. The girl is Miss Laverham, and she is a good friend of mine, and she is here helping Maria with her costume for a theatrical tonight—you will come, won't you?—*and* she is engaged to be married."

"Well, that scotches that, don't it? All right, Sis," he said easily. "Mary, where's Francis? I count upon him to show me some of the city before I have to return to Hook Well. The devil's in it that I'm on damnably short purse strings—Father's had to pay some duns for me, and I'm afraid that he wasn't much pleased. I don't suppose either of my kind sisters could advance me just a little of the ready?" He smiled charmingly and threw himself into a delicate chair, which shuddered under his impact. Maria had opened her mouth to offer some assistance when Althea stopped her with a cautious hand.

"Cannot let good nature overcome good sense, Mary. Merrit, it seems that the last time I advanced you any money, you vowed upon all points to repay me by the new quarter. That was all of two years ago, and I still am wondering when I am to be paid."

"Never said which new quarter I'd pay upon, did I?" Merrit objected cheerily. "Come, Mary, surely you have a little pin money tucked by for me. . . ."

Maria, strengthened by Althea's refusal, gave one of her own. "You know, dearest, that if I could depend upon you to pay me back, I would, but things have not been so easy financially, and I am sure you would go directly to some dreadful hell and there would go all my chance of reimbursement."

"Is it my fault that my luck is damnable? Besides, it ain't for the tables I ask—I simply need a new rig-out. Can't show my face in town with these rags I'm wearing."

There was a certain truth to what he said, Althea reflected, but she was of the opinion that Merrit's idea of new furnishings would only be a newer, more spectacular version of his present outlandish costume—very expensive, depressingly bandboxy, and ridiculously extreme as to cinched waist, padded shoulders, and collar points. "You do have your evening dress, don't you?" she thought to ask.

"Brought it, but I'm damned if that means you'll be able to drag me from Almack's to the opera, or any other dull-as-ditch-water functions of the like. As long as I'm here I intend to make good of it—Father told me I should acquire a little town brass. He also said I wasn't to spend my money too freely, but that's Father all over." Merrit was the first to look up when a gentle rapping sounded at the door. "The seamstress, I'll be bound," he whispered wickedly. Althea made a threatening motion as Maria called for Georgiana to enter.

"Excuse me, Lady Bevan," she began. "I thought you could try the headdress now that the glue is dried on the peacock boas." She stood in the doorway with a tentative air. "I would like to see them on you and adjust their size if it is needful."

"Of course, I'll come straightaway." Maria dropped her book and started for the door.

"It appears that I am the only person in this family who has manners enough to be admitted into Society," Althea said rebukingly. "Merrit, for pity's sake, stand up.

I care not how tired you are. Georgiana, this rapscallion is my brother Merrit. Merrit, this is Miss Laverham. *Now, Maria*"—she turned to her sister—"go try on your peacock feathers. I'll come upstairs in a little while and see." Georgiana and Maria retreated from the room and went to deal with the headdress. In the library Merrit surveyed his sister doubtfully.

"You've not got it in mind to scold me, have you, Ally?"

"Have you anything to be scolded for, love?" Althea closed *Tristram Shandy* and settled herself back in the chair. "I was just wondering if Papa had the thought to send you for me, or if it was all your own notion."

"It was Father's idea, Ally, I'll swear that. I don't deny but that I did my best possible to make him send me, rather than going himself. Thought you'd rather be spared his prosing for a while than not."

"And that you'd make more of London that he would? O selfless brother, your motives stick out a mile! But tell me, are things in such a bad case at home?"

Merrit stretched one dirty boot out before the other and perused the toe thoughtfully. "It ain't very happy there. Father's in one of his gouty moods. Had a turn-up with one of his straw damsels—don't frown at me!—and that's put him about, too. So he's been in a fighting mood, and anyone without the sense to stay out of his path gets lambasted thoroughly. He's fired and rehired Cook three times to my certain knowledge. Doctor Phillips tried to put him on a diet of barley water and weak gruel for a few weeks—you can picture the turn-up that produced! And Andrew and young Will say Father has been poking into the stables again, which you specifically promised them he would not do. And Firth has been trying to keep the maids to their work, but he don't seem to have the knack of it— don't know how to handle them the way you do, and Cook has them stirred up against him now. I'll tell you something, Ally: if something ain't done, Father will end in Bedlam, and probably old Firth will be with him."

Althea could not laugh: it all seemed eminently probable to her. "I suppose I ought to return home for a little while at least—if naught else than to engage a housekeeper for Papa."

"A housekeeper! Ally, you know that Father would rather live in a sty than pay an extra salary when it wasn't needed."

"Merrit, has it never occurred to you that I may not always be there to keep house for Papa, and much respect as I owe him"— a derisive noise from Merritt—"and much love as I have for him, that I may not want to spend the rest of my life soothing Cook and luring Papa away from the stables and implementing Doctor Phillips' physics?"

"Why not?" Merrit asked obtusely.

Althea laughed in despair. "Merrit! If you have no courtesy, you might at least affect some! Has it never occurred to you—or my father, for the matter of that—that someday I might follow Maria's example and set up in an establishment of my own?"

"No," Merrit answered simply.

"Merrit!"

"I can't see you setting up as a bountiful lady and visiting the poor with baskets and that sort of nonsense. With all the books you've read I used to think you might make a fair don, but that certainly wouldn't do. Even if they'd take you, Father would never permit it."

"Merrit, has it never occurred to you or Papa that I might marry?"

"No," Merritt said interestedly. "Never thought you very partial to any of the bumpkins round Hooking, and I *never* thought of you setting up housekeeping with one of them."

Althea made an effort to control her temper. "You and Papa have a delightful picture of me dwindling into my

declining years at Hook Well keeping house for Papa, and
then for you, until you displace me with a wife and I am
relegated to the position of helpful maiden aunt. Good
God, I'm of a mind not to return there ever. Even here
there are some people who think I am worth more than
that!" A thought of Calendar, up to now a thorn in her
flesh, came to her as a vast comfort. She dwelt on the
thought for a minute until her temper was cooler.

"I suppose I cannot expect much more from my father's son," she said at last. "I had some hopes that you
would not be quite so silly as Papa, but—oh well, I suppose I might as well return to Hook Well anyway. Who
knows," she added darkly, "but what it might serve my
purpose to do so. A quick escape might be indicated—after the mess I have made of my affairs here." She made
herself smile. "All right, Brother, I will return home—and
perhaps I shall wind up setting up as a lady bountiful
despite your doubts. That's not to worry about now. I will
need a few days to settle my affairs here, though," she
said, thinking of Georgiana.

"Did I not say to take as much time as you like? I
didn't travel over some of the worst roads in the kingdom—remind me to tell my father that that chaise needs
new springs—well, I haven't come to London just to drag
you back home. Where is Francis anyway? I want him to
tell me where I may find the man who makes his boots."

Althea sighed and released her brother to search for
Lord Bevan, suggesting that he might try the office in the
rear of the house. "But beware his temper. He's doing accounts today, and I doubt he'll be in a good frame of
mind." Not, she thought, with the debt to Calendar still
hanging over his head.

Merrit stood in the doorway. "That little thing is
promised, is she? Damn shame—she's quite a taking little
article."

"Merrit!" his outraged sister cried as he escaped the
room. She reflected that she would have to warn Geor-

giana of her new admirer before they met again. She then returned to *Tristram Shandy,* with rather less attention than that book deserved.

It was as well that she was not able to go far with her reading. Five minutes after he had gone, Merrit returned with Francis, who was without doubt relieved to have any excuse to take him from the accounts. Merrit announced that they were off to see a bootmaker and a haberdasher and anyone else Francis could recommend who was prepared to make a young gentleman into a Tulip of the *ton.* Althea reserved her doubts on that score and merely reminded them that they dined at home tonight, and earlier than usual because of Maria's theatrical debut. Five minutes after they were gone, arguing what color Merrit's new coat should be, Georgiana came down to ask Althea's opinion of the costume. Althea dropped her book with a sigh and followed her friend up the stairs.

One of the back bedrooms had been converted to a sewing room, and two round-faced young women sat in one corner appraising their handiwork with critical but approving airs. In the center of the room Maria stood, resplendent in white crepe almost wholly covered in blue paillettes, padded shoulders, and three filmy overskirts that gave the impression she had wings. Atop her curls was perched a delicate headdress of white feathers and one or two peacock feathers, skillfully placed on a slender band of silver that circled Maria's head.

"It is beautiful," Althea said reverently. "Georgiana, I had no idea you had such talent! Mary, if only you will contrive to remember your words, you will have all the audience at your feet, and Lady Liverpool will not need to bother with the rest of the program."

"My lines!" Maria said in some alarm. "I have forgot them already, I'm sure. Miss Laverham, I am more grateful than words can say, but now I simply must rest and try to recall my part. Oooo!" Heedless of the management of her skirts Maria started distractedly across the room, and was only stopped by Althea and one of the maids, who anticipated disaster.

"Here, then, Miss, you just let us take that dress and the head thing and keep 'em fresh for tonight, and then you go along." As she spoke, the maid coaxed the feathered diadem from Maria's head and Althea began to unfasten the dress. When Maria was safely out of the garment and into a dressing saque, Althea sent her off to her room to rest for the night's excitement.

"Poor Mary," she murmured to Georgiana. "I misdoubt that she will be able to remember above half her words, but she will be gloriously pretty, thanks to you, and that should make it easier for her. How did you learn to design so?"

"I never learned it," Georgiana admitted. "It started when I was in the schoolroom: I think my governess found it easier to let me play with paints and stuffs rather than try to teach me anything."

"This is a craft," Althea admired. "You could even keep yourself with it—I have nothing that would support me if my circumstances were reduced—except my wits."

"I should never have the daring," Georgiana said sadly. "I am not at all a daring person, you know."

"I suppose not." Althea smiled. "Oh, listen, I wanted to warn you—my odious brother has decided that he is smitten with you, and will probably try to make you the object of some of his heavy-handed gallantry. You know best how to deal with such a thing, but I felt it only fair to warn you. He is a nice boy," she said thoughtfully. "He is good-hearted, but I am afraid that he really hasn't two thoughts to rub together, and I begin to have the awful notion that he will be just like Father when he grows a little older."

"Althea," Georgiana said hurriedly, "I am going to end the charade tonight. I really cannot be civil to Mr. Wallingham another day, and I *miss* Edward. . . ." Her voice broke. "He scolded me for being so much in Wallingham's company the other day."

Well, thought Althea, it was just as well that Georgiana came out of the scrape with success. After she had scotched her own hopes so abysmally, what right had she to suggest anything to Georgiana? She had not seen Tracy in almost a week, had not heard a word from him, and was, all the time, thinking of him. Francis, when he had caught her in private about the house, had taken a moment to tell her that it did not do to prolong lovers' quarrels, and at first she had staunchly denied to herself that love had anything to do with it—just that odious insufferable man trying to put her in her place. But she was too honest not to feel the justice in what he had said, and she was too honest to deny that the lack of Tracy's company made her angry, sullen, and miserable by turns. Deprived of it, she found herself reviewing every word he had spoken to her, every meeting they had had, and found herself, when she admitted it, loving him as much for the times when he had been most irritating as for his moments of compassion and gravity. There was no reason for him to forgive her, to reinstate her in his good graces, or to treat her with any respect at all, she thought bitterly. He had offered for her to provide himself with an heir, with a suitable hostess for his home, to make up to her what he thought was the loss of Pendarly. (Which was not so deep as a ditch, Althea thought wryly; how could she have been so stupid? And poor Georgiana, she wanted to marry that man.) He had offered for her because he had thought they could deal together, and now she had proved to everyone's satisfaction that they could not.

For a moment Althea recalled the kiss he had given her under his aunt's supervision.

Mere amusement. He had had for her perhaps a friendly regard, and she had shattered even that. Thank heavens I never allowed the announcement of our engagement to be published, she thought. Georgiana might suspect, but Maria and Lady Boskingram were the only ones who really knew that it existed. She could cut her losses and break off the betrothal without anyone being the wiser, and go back to Hook Well without a trace of scandal. And grow old and miserable in just the bleak future she had detailed to Merrit earlier. Delightful.

She made herself smile. "I don't know if there has been any purpose to all this," Georgiana was saying, "except that I don't mind so much being out in company anymore. Why, if I can amuse Wallingham, I must be a better prevaricator than I thought. But now I only want to make all right between Edward and me and to go back to being a little white mouse—for a while at least. Who knows but that I have become used to my dissipations."

"Hardly dissipations." Althea laughed a little unsteadily. "A little frivolity, perhaps, but not dissipations."

Georgiana looked at her friend. Over the past week she had seen a shadow—cunningly hidden but a shadow nonetheless—over Althea's face. "Don't fret so, love. I am sure he will come around soon, whatever your quarrel was."

Althea was suddenly too exhausted to feign ignorance. "It makes no matter," she said quietly. "My brother is come to take me home. Did I not tell you? My father is at his wit's end, and has sent Merrit to fetch me home before the cook leaves and the gardener prunes the roses to extinction and the housemaids forget their duties altogether. I am sure I'll have a busy time of it when I first return to Lancashire. So whether I am forgiven or no, it makes little difference. Besides, I have had my gaiety! Had I not taken it into my head to run away in the first place, I should have wasted away at Hook Well and never known what it is like to dance with the Prince or be confronted by the Patronesses at Almack's or see the Botanical Gardens, or any of the mad *dissipations* that have come my way." She laughed a little hysterically.

"When do you return home?" Georgiana asked solemnly.

"I shall not leave until I know that all is well between you and Pendarly," Althea promised. "If he is difficult, even if I have to shake him myself, I shall make him understand what is what. But I doubt you will have any trouble, Georgiana. Then I shall collect Merrit, who I hope will not have had enough time to get greatly into debt, and I shall be off for home. And you will invite me to your wedding, and I will come and weep a little, and go home again and rule my family with an iron hand and write dissertations on Greek poetry," she finished brightly. Georgiana was not in the mood to be amused.

"I don't like it that you should be unhappy, Ally."

"Nor shall I be," Althea insisted stoutly. "I am used to have the ordering of things at home, and I shall have the house to run and the estate to watch over, and my studies to attend to. I can imagine the messes I shall have to unsnarl when I get back. It is exactly what I am used to, and I shall be quite content with it. I forbid you to worry over me. And tonight we end the game and you and Edward will be as happy as if I never had come into your lives at all."

"You are the first person I ever could talk with this way. I shall miss it."

"Then you must school Edward to talk with you more. I've a notion he will prove very good at it when he understands the idea of it." Althea bent to pick up a pincushion from the floor. "You and your mother dine here tonight, am I correct? Then I collect you will want to go home and get away from the Ervines and the Bevans and rest yourself a little. We dine early. Maria informed Lady Liverpool that our party would arrive early on account of her participation. Lord, what with twelve people in her cast, I think half of London will appear there in the wake of the performers before the doors are even officially open."

Together the girls left the sewing room, talking of the party as if there were no weightier matters in the world to be discussed, quite as if their hearts were whole and un-breakable.

Chapter Fifteen

Dinner that evening might have been a lively affair had it not been for the exceedingly sober and virtuous presence of Mrs. Laverham. But, as Maria remarked petulantly to Francis, there had been no help for it: Georgiana had to be there to help with final adjustments to the costume, and one could hardly invite the girl without inviting her loathsome mother. Francis, in his turn, told Althea that he was sure he had not seen Maria so done up over any-thing since the day of her presentation at court: "And a fine thing that was! Went through the whole ceremony without a fault, then came home and fainted in the but-ler's arms. Don't understand why women get so upset about these things."

Althea did not try to explain the dynamics of her sister to her brother-in-law.

They sat down eight to dinner. Aside from the Laver-hams, there was, at Althea's insistence, Edward Pendarly. Maria would have excluded him for her sister's sake, but Althea reminded her sternly that the man was still Geor-giana's fiancé. John Wallingham had also been invited—altogether at Maria's instigation, since she had no idea of the plotting that had occurred around her. The Bevans, Althea, and her brother made up the party. No one

seemed particularly at ease: Maria was wrought into a
state of sublime frenzy and insisted upon repeating her
words *sotto voce* during the soup. Georgiana, who was
settled between Wallingham and Merrit Ervine, spent the
meal nervously turning aside the gallantries that assaulted
her first from one side and then the other, while Edward
Pendarly watched angrily and pretended to listen to Mrs.
Laverham's comments upon a variety of equally insipid
topics. Althea was too dispirited to try to tease Pendarly;
instead she focused her attention somewhere on the
middle of the table and tried not to think on anything
more than the quality of the soup. In all, when the last
dish was removed and Maria remembered that it was up
to her to lead the ladies into the other room, everyone
breathed a little more freely.

Althea more than once exhorted herself to behave a
little more socially, no matter what the effort, but it was
not until the party had arrived safe at Lady Liverpool's,
and she, Maria, and Georgiana had gone up to the tiring
rooms, that she was able to affect enthusiasm. Even then
it was a peculiarly feverish sort of cheerfulness that she
feared must be as transparent as her sullens. Luckily her
two companions were both taken up in their own anxieties
and did not notice anything in Althea's manner that was
out of the way. When finally the headdress had been ad-
justed for the fourth time, the skirts of the gown had been
arranged to everyone's satisfaction, and the requisite number of compliments had been paid the gown and its
wearer, Althea and Georgiana left Maria on her own to
recite her words over and over, while they went down to
join the throng of people who had come with the performers in advance of the rest of the guests.

Georgiana, whose object for the evening was to cool
Wallingham's affections and to try to regain Edward's approval, was utterly at a loss to know how to begin. Even
this problem was destined to be complicated by the fact
that Merrit Ervine *would* hang about her, allowing her no

opportunity to speak with either Wallingham or Pendarly. She adopted with him the same empty-headed manner she used with Wallingham, and laughed, rather preoccupiedly, at his comments, while raking the crowd for Pendarly *or* Wallingham. Her mother was nowhere to be seen, and Georgiana was not sure whether that was a blessing or a curse. In the growing crowd she became surer and surer that she would not see Pendarly all night, and without even Althea to torment him, how would she ever know where he was or with whom he was consoling himself?

She need not have worried. Although she herself was paying less than no attention to Merrit Ervine's importunities, to the world at large she appeared to be vastly entertained. Georgiana did not realize the picture she made until Pendarly himself, with the brow of a wrathful Apollo and a voice tight through clenched teeth approached her. She blanched and very quickly dispatched Mr. Ervine for a cup of punch—or anything, so long as it was cool and would take some time to fetch.

"So," Pendarly said at length.

Georgiana looked up at him beseechingly, and almost, for a moment, he was ready to relent. But only for a moment. Then full consciousness of his abominable ill use came flooding back to him, and he began again.

"It is not enough that you must let that—that dandy gamester, that flash cull, that unscrupulous hound follow in your tracks, or that you encourage him. No, now you work your wiles upon some new mark. Has no one ever explained to you that a betrothal is supposed to imply some manner of commitment between two people? Have you no more respect for yourself—not to mention me— than to make yourself cheap by flirting with the first dashing face that appears before you?" Pendarly continued wrathfully onward, altogether unaware that he was convicting himself as he accused her.

"What has come over you, Georgiana?" he asked finally. "All of the sudden you are grown out of my knowledge—so trivial, as if you were any girl out to win a husband." He abandoned his softened tones. "I owe myself something better than a wife who will make me a spectacle before the world. I give you warning. Either you abandon this path or we are quits and your mother can direct a notice to the *Gazette* announcing so!"

Before Georgiana could speak a word in her own defense he had stalked off, leaving her crushed and helpless in his wake.

After five minutes' reflection Pendarly came to the realization that perhaps he had not been quite fair in refusing to listen to anything she could say in her own defense. After ten minutes more he considered returning to her side—or possibly wresting her from the arms of Wallingham, or Miss Ervine's fatuous brother—and speaking more rationally to her, making her understand his devotion to her. He had wondered in the last weeks whether both Althea and Georgiana knew of his behavior during Georgiana's illness: they had been so often in each other's company that he was sure they must have pieced it all out: another five minutes' deliberation decided him to seek her out and beg *her* forgiveness—to see if she could not be persuaded to forgive him and accept his devotion to her. As he started across the hallway to the room where he had left her, a uniformed lackey impeded his progress and inquired if he was not Mr. Pendarly. He replied impatiently that he was and continued to look impatiently over the man's shoulder for Georgiana.

"Well, sir," the footman said carefully, "I have a note here for you from a gentleman, sir." He presented an envelope to Pendarly with a pompous flourish. Pendarly took the note, thanked the man briefly, and continued his way into the main room, where he searched for some fifteen minutes without success for Miss Laverham. He then canvassed the rest of the public rooms, going so far as to inquire of one of the ladies retreating from the tiring room if she had seen Georgiana within. The music had

started and much of the noise of the gathering in the main
room had quieted. He returned there, where most of the
occupants had found chairs and were listening with care-
less attention to the program of music being served up.
Again he searched the rows of chairs for Georgiana's
face, and again he missed her.

At length he dropped into an empty chair and sat, de-
jected, until the envelope he had pocketed, which was
now jabbing him unpleasantly, recalled him to the fact
that he had received a message. He retrieved the envelope
and opened it. It was written in a bold untaught hand.

Sir:

   You may consider your arrangement with Miss Laverham at an end. I have undertaken to ensure her happiness and my own. By the time this reaches your hand
we shall be in pursuit of the border, and will be married
at Gretna.

   Any attempt to stop our progress would be ill advised,
as this elopement is as much by her wish as by mine.
Pray convey my compliments to Miss Ervine. My own
consolations go to the loser of the prize.

                                                    J de MW

Pendarly stared at the missive for a few minutes in utter shock. Then, without thinking what he did, he sought
out Tracy Calendar.

When Edward left her, Georgiana stood, paralyzed, altogether brokenhearted. She looked around the room
sightlessly; Althea waved from across the room and received no answering signal, but she was so situated that
she could not go and question her friend. After a moment
of this unseeing search Georgiana found that she had regained the limited use of her limbs, and sought a chair

somewhere out of the way. What she finally found was a settee carelessly left behind a group of ornamental statuary and curtains, and there she sat and waited for tears. She did not have long to wait before her solitude was disturbed and Merrit Ervine discovered her. He had the appearance of a man returned from a great battle—not altogether successful, but victorious at last. In his hands were punch glasses, miraculously half full; minute stains on his formerly reproachless inexpressibles testified to his struggles.

Georgiana did not take in this spectacle—after she had identified the gentleman with a glance, her head dropped low again, and to all his solicitous inquiries she replied with a whimper or a choke. Merrit considered taking her in his arms and banishing her misery, but he had a lurking suspicion that even in London that sort of behavior, if found out, could have dire consequences. So he sat for some few minutes chatting about various equally inane subjects, and finally, as Miss Laverham stubbornly refused to be amused from her blue-devils, he asked her pardon and left.

Which left the area clear for Wallingham. He had been about to accost Miss Laverham when Pendarly had swooped in like an avenging angel. Now, with the fine judgment of an expert, he waited until he judged her ready to listen to his suggestions. He had not planned originally to make such a final move so early, but certain gentlemen in the City were becoming increasingly impatient, and here was Miss Laverham, ripe, as the expression went, for the plucking: considerably farther along to being under his spell than any of the other women he had an interest in. So, with a little regret for other fortunes lost, Wallingham decided to effect an elopement, since even with Mrs. Laverham's favor (which he firmly believed he should eventually have), it might be a little awkward to wed in London, at a church, with Pendarly frowning over the proceedings.

He advanced upon Georgiana, and with practiced solicitude, said nothing, but set himself down beside her and
took her hand. Georgiana did not want to speak to
him—the cause of her misery—but years of training had
made it an article with her that one was not impolite to a
gentleman; and in any case, once he saw how distressed
she was, he surely would not expect her to speak with
him.

His first assurance was that she need not speak if she
did not wish to; he knew enough not to tax her for words.
But if he might speak—and Georgiana merely listen—for
the space of five minutes? Georgiana could not begrudge
him that, and besides, whatever he said, if she was not required to answer, then she need not pay any attention at
all. So while Wallingham began to introduce the subject
of marriage, his heartfelt admiration for her, and elopement, Georgiana busied herself with cheering thoughts of
how truly miserable she was, and heard not a word of
what he said. Had Wallingham tried to besmirch Pendarly's character, she might have awakened from her
stupor, but the man had too much sense, and so nothing
called her away from her morbid thoughts while he continued his declaration of love. He had gotten so far as the
elopement, and was describing their triumphant return to
London, when a word caught Georgiana's ear.

"Home?" she repeated dully.

"Yes, Miss Laverham," he said patiently. "But now?"

"Oh, yes, please." Georgiana looked at him beseechingly.

Wallingham had a good idea of how Miss Laverham
was thinking, but any gentlemanly impulse he might have
felt to explain to her what plans he had been laying at her
unnoticing feet was scotched by the memory of the fellow
who had promised to wait on him within the next week
should he prove unable to pay his debts.

"Stay here, my heart, while I procure your pelisse and
tell your mother. There is certainly no reason that she

should disturb herself." Georgiana nodded listlessly and did as he instructed.

If it were possible to have shouted his relief in public, Wallingham would have done so. All was working out splendidly. He even stopped to watch a moment of the theatrical presentation now getting under way: Lady Bevan was, as expected, bungling her words, but looked so pretty that it really made no matter. He went first in search of paper and pen, and having found them, wrote notes to Mrs. Laverham and Pendarly. The first was filled with overblown phrases describing his burning love for the lady's daughter; the second was an insolent note to a rival. This duty discharged, he found Georgiana's pelisse and returned to her.

Now that she was resolved to go, Georgiana affected a certain purposefulness of manner. She left her hiding place upon Wallingham's arm, looking for all the world as if there were nowhere she would rather be, and walked with the gentleman to the door without a backward look. Once in the hackney he had procured, however, she began to shiver and look pale again.

Wallingham had been faced with the problem of how to get his captive willingly from the hack to a post chaise, so that they might effect as speedy an exit as possible from the city. He knew that his note to Pendarly had been ill advised, but he had never been a good winner, and the temptation to rub his parsonical adversary's beautifully chiseled nose in the dirt was too strong. The hack they rode in was so drafty that Wallingham decided it would serve as an excuse for changing carriages. From the first moment (after he had instructed the driver of the hack to head for a certain posting inn where he was well known) Wallingham complained loudly of the draft, and was equally loud and indignant in his fears for Miss Laverham's health. When he saw that they were within a few houses of the inn, he instructed the driver to stop, and explained to Georgiana that he could no longer countenance her riding in the hack in such chill. Georgiana paid no attention to where they were going, and as he had made a remark about how slow the traffic was—"everyone of the *ton* must be out tonight"—Georgiana did not wonder that it was taking them so long to go from Lady Liverpool's to her home. Once the carriage had drawn to a halt, Wallingham sprang from it with an assurance to Georgiana that he would go only so far as to procure another hack for them. Then, leaving her alone to consider her misery in cold and silence, he went around the corner to the inn and demanded a chaise and four.

Georgiana, when he had been gone perhaps five minutes, began to be afraid. She had ventured a look out the window and knew none of the buildings she saw by dark. She had no money with her with which to hire her own hack, and even had she had some coins, she would not have known how to hire a hack, or how to go on at all without a man's protection at that late hour. When Wallingham finally returned, she was so relieved to see even his face that she immediately burst into tears, and was taken from one vehicle to the other without the slightest idea that she was entering a traveling carriage. In the new vehicle there were several warm rugs, which Wallingham immediately piled about her; in another moment he had paid off their first vehicle, and installed himself across the seat from her. His manner remained so kind and solicitous that she felt herself obliged to cry again, and strangely, going from cold to warmth and then to crying, she finally came to an uneasy kind of slumber. The driver of the chaise, who had traveled this route before, turned his coach toward the north, in the general direction of Gretna Green.

It had not been Tracy's intention to place himself in any position where he would see Althea. This party could not be helped: besides certain courtesies he owed his host and several of the players, he had promised to make his appearance there long before. If he could not avoid seeing Althea, the next best thing would be to avoid looking for her, so from the moment that he arrived at the party, he was conscious of scrupulously avoiding glances at any part of the room where she might be lurking. This encompassed such a great amount of space that shortly he felt the ridiculousness of his resolve and decided it was better that he should watch the crowd for Althea's face than that he should cause remark by studying the floor for the entire evening.

He endured the music, which was nicely performed, and watched some part of the theatrical offering before boredom overwhelmed him. He saw Althea's sister make her entrance, looking very like some pretty, affected little bird, and sounding rather like a scarecrow, for her voice was so harsh with repeating her part that she sounded more like a rook than a nightingale. When even this became too much for his sense of humor to absorb, he decided to leave, and made his way toward the hallway. He had begun to make inquiries after his hat and topcoat when he became aware that someone was addressing him. He turned and found Edward Pendarly, white as a ghost, clutching a sheet of paper in one hand—and, by the looks of things, keeping himself from tearing out his hair with the other by main force of will.

"May I have a word with you, sir?"

Tracy looked bemusedly at Pendarly. "Of course. What have I done to put you in such a state?"

Pendarly had the grace to look pained. "Not you, sir, and if I ever seemed to bear you some ill will, I wish you would forgive and forget it now."

"Well then, has it to do with the letter you're holding?"

"It has." Pendarly proffered it to his companion. He had no idea why he had sought Calendar out, except that somehow he felt the man was involved in this mess, and he could think of no one else who would stand by him. Tracy read the letter through twice.

"Has anyone else seen this?" he asked. Pendarly denied it. "She did not go with him willingly, I imagine. I misdoubt that Miss Laverham would have a taste for this sort of adventure. I wonder what he did to inveigle her into it?"

Pendarly started to remark that he was not sure that Georgiana had needed any encouragement, but Tracy disabused him of this notion rather harshly in a few short words, then told him not to waste time in feeling sorry for himself.

"They are for Gretna, of course," he said. "Look here, Pendarly, you go change into something you can ride in and I'll meet you at my house—Cavendish Street—in an hour and we'll go after your Miss Laverham. I have one or two things to attend to here before I leave." Pendarly made an impatient *moue*. "They are traveling in a chaise, and even the fastest chaise cannot go so fast that we will not overtake it this night. One hour at Cavendish Street." He dismissed Pendarly with a curt nod and turned back toward the assembly room with a glare of undeniable purpose in his eyes.

He found Althea among the audience for the play, smiling to herself at her sister's absurdities. Without salutation of any sort he grasped her arm; she looked at him with a flush of pleasure for a moment—until she saw the look on his face. From the red of his hair to the black scowl in his eyes, everything about him was cold. Involuntarily she shuddered and attempted to withdraw, but his hand on her wrist admitted of no retreat. After another second's resistance, he spoke under his breath, biting off each word as if it were to be used as a weapon.

"If you do not wish to be involved in a very public scene I suggest that you take my arm without delay, and come with me," he said slowly. "I have something to say to you. Now."

Althea felt the futility of trying to break away; any sort of resistance would immediately call attention to them.

She rose and took Calendar's arm, following him to the curtain-enclosed area where earlier Georgiana had been hidden. When he had placed her unceremoniously on the settee there, she looked up at him questioningly, ashamed and infuriated by the way her heart changed its beat in his presence.

"What can be of such moment that you draw me away from my sister's performance? Bad I must admit it was, but I owe her the loyalty to attend to it. And since you have been able to prevent yourself speaking to me this week and more, why do you choose this particular moment to go into one of your tempers?"

He said slowly, "Althea, do not push me. I have a weak enough hold on my temper as it is. I thought that as the author of the situation you might be pleased to know that Wallingham appears to have abducted Miss Laverham. I warned you before of the folly of allowing that stupid chit to dandle upon Wallingham's knee, but you assumed that you knew best. I take leave to tell you that you knew nothing. I hope you are proud of your handiwork. For myself, I go now to see if I cannot undo some part of it," he finished. With no more than the most cutting of nods did he leave her, and with an equal disregard for ceremony Miss Ervine hid her face in one of the curtains and wept.

Chapter Sixteen

When he saw his sister removed summarily from her seat in the audience by a tall red-haired gentleman dressed with such exquisite simplicity that even he, whose taste ran more to padded shoulders and a profusion of fobs, had to admit the man's superiority in fashion, Merrit Ervine's curiosity was roused. This, aside from Miss Laverham's pretty face and the amusing spectacle of Maria trying to remember her speeches, was the first interesting thing he had seen that evening. As he had assured his sisters earlier, a musical evening was no more than a tepid sort of amusement to him, and although Francis had promised that after the *musicale* they should go on to something more amusing, that hardly helped now, in the midst of the most damnably boring evening he could remember. Althea's movements with the stranger were intriguing to him, and he set himself the task of spying upon the couple as they moved from the banks of chairs to the same area where Miss Laverham had been settled not long before.

From his vantage point he did not hear what was said, nor could he see the faces of the two while they were within the confines of the curtains, but less than five minutes after they had disappeared therein, the gentleman emerged, looking like thunder, and Merrit caught a glimpse of Althea's face. He had never, in his twenty-three-year acquaintance with his younger sister, seen Ally's face so totally bloodless, nor her expression so par-

ticularly horrified, and the sight of her was enough to
make him—not precisely spring into action, but amble
over to the curtains. Althea looked up with a startled,
weepy face: she had been crying. When she saw who it
was, her face relaxed a little and she did not try to pretend a composure she obviously was not feeling. She said
weakly, "Oh, Merrit," and then her voice dropped off into
little hiccups of sound.

"Who was that sharp swell, Ally? I'll make him sorry
for troubling you, right enough." Merrit swore roundly,
putting his arm about his sister's shoulders. "But look
you, it don't do to have crying fits at soirees, ain't the
thing at all."

Althea shook herself furiously from his arm. "I am not
crying!" she sobbed. "And you needn't trouble Tracy, for
he was in the r-i-ght of it all along, and I was w-w-wrong.
Now I shall never be able to face him, l-l-l-let alone—and
p-poor Georgiana!" Althea burst into another bout of
tears.

"Georgiana?" Merrit asked quickly. Althea, had she
had her wits about her, would probably not have told her
flighty brother anything of the situation, but her wits were
not about her, and without realizing what she said, she
gasped out the story of Georgiana's disappearance. Now
Merrit *was* galvanized into action. With unwonted
sternness he regarded his sister and ordered her to cease
her crying at once and repeat the last part of the story.

"As near as Tracy gave me to understand—and he
didn't say much, only stormed at me and stalked off,
which he was perfectly right to do; I'd have done it myself had it been me—anyway, Georgiana has been abducted by Mr. Wallingham, that odious man who sat
between her and me at dinner, and they are off to Gretna
so he can pay his debts out of her pocket. But she swore to
me that she could handle him. How could she be so hen-
witted as to let this happen?" Althea had stopped crying
now and submerged her overwrought conscience in bitter-

ness and recrimination. Her expression was particularly
unattractive as she ruminated upon her own part in the
drama.

"I'm off then," Merrit said suddenly.

"What?" Althea was shaken from her reverie and
looked mistily at her brother.

"Well, aside from its being the most tremendous adventure, I can't let that poor chit be savaged by that flash
cull, can I? You said the tall fire-thatch would chase after
her? Where do I find him? And has Bevan a horse I can
ride?"

Althea gave him the information Merrit requested, then
rose shakily to her feet. "Have you seen Francis?"

"What's he to the purpose?" Merrit asked abstractedly.
"He's over by the potted palms."

"He and I shall have to keep this from becoming generally known of, as well as fobbing off Mrs. Laverham
with some story as to Georgie's absence. You go ahead,
Merrit. I won't make a cake of myself anymore. And
please, once you know she is safe, come back straightway
and tell me. Better still, bring her back to Maria's when
you find her."

They parted, and Althea went in search of her
brother-in-law. She found him at last at the back of the
crowd, admiring his wife. With a sort of bloodless effi-
ciency Althea apprised Francis of the situation and enlist-
ed his help. To his credit he immediately offered himself
her conspirator and between them they managed to make
Georgiana's apologies for an indisposition that had forced
her to retire to the Bevan house. Mrs. Laverham, deep in
a hand of silver loo, muttered a darkling "Yes, yes," and
otherwise ignored Althea when she tried to explain to her.
All that remained was to persuade Maria to leave the
party early. This seeming impossibility was achieved by
Francis, using Althea knew not what domestic diplomacy.

In something under ten minutes Francis signaled that
all was ready, and Althea, impressed with his dispatch,

was handed into the barouche waiting outside the door. Maria had already been installed there in one corner, and sat looking, to Althea's surprise, neither furious nor triumphant but small and shaky and white.

"Ally," she moaned softly.

Dear lord! Althea thought wearily. Not yet another crisis! I shall not be able to endure it. But she very calmly slid over to her sister's side and bid to be told what the matter was.

"I was dreadful. I was awful. My voice broke over that simple little song, and I couldn't for my life remember my words, and I have never ever been so mortified! Oh, Francis!"

From the seat opposite Francis solicitously assured Maria that her performance had been everything he liked to see, and that her appearance had been enough to knock the eyes out of anyone with eyes to see her. By the end of their ride Maria was tolerably comforted and submitted to be led up to her room and handed over to Bailey's care, while Francis and Althea continued to the morning room for further councils.

"Mary must be told at once," Althea fretted. "She'll have to know what our story is, and after that I depend upon you to keep her silent about this night's work."

"Don't you trust your sister any more than to have to put such a rider on it?" Francis asked indignantly.

"I have known her longer than you, and while I have found her lack of regard for the secrets of others severely trying on some occasions, I will trust that you have some influence with her. Just tell her how vital it is. And I hope I can council Merrit to keep his peace as well, although I can see him bursting to tell his boon companions at Hooking how he rode off his first time in town to rescue a female in distress. I shall have to impress upon him the facts. . . ." Althea sighed wearily.

"Shall I tell Mary?" Francis suggested.

"Let us both go up—Bailey will have given her some

milk, and perhaps a glass of hartshorn and water, so
Maria should be a little more composed."

"You don't appear too composed yourself, Ally," Francis said as they climbed the stairs. "Look as though you
were studying to go into a deep decline."

"Not until this is all resolved, my dear. Then I think I
may be entitled to a very small decline, do you not
agree?" She smiled wanly and studied the hem of her
dress. "I cannot tell you how much I feel my part in this
business. That poor little thing gone racing off with Wallingham, and I at root to blame. I am altogether mortified
with myself."

"Come, now," Francis said brightly, "can't show that
Friday face to Mary! Heaven knows what she'd assume
was to do with you."

Althea smiled a very little at this, but studied to arrange her face in less alarming lines. It took only a few
minutes for the skeleton of their plan to be drawn for
Maria's benefit. She was already sleepy and therefore
quiet enough to listen to their questions and plans without
raising any sort of fuss at their narrative. When Althea
had finished with the tale she said drowsily, "But that is
terrible. She is to stay here tonight? I never thought that
John Wallingham had such an ill nature. I will do exactly
as you bid me tomorrow, Ally, but just now mayn't I
please go to s-l-e-e-eep?"

Althea could hope for no greater assurance of compli-
ance from her sister in this state, and so she left Maria to
the ministrations of her husband. For herself, she vowed
not to sleep until she knew that Georgiana was safe. If
Georgiana was brought back to Grosvenor Square after
her rescue, someone would need to be about to have the
ordering of things. Althea returned to the morning room,
stopping in the library to retrieve her neglected copy of
Tristram Shandy, and proceeded to attempt to finish the
book. Even the scandalous characters of Sterne's novel
had no power to distract her attention, and after an hour

or so Althea gave up the pretense of reading. Instead she tried to sew, to sketch, to braid, to finish a beadwork reticule Maria had begun some weeks before—in short, to occupy herself in any manner that might conceivably make thinking impossible. In none of these things did she find the needed diversion, however, and ultimately she found herself staring unseeingly at the wall opposite her chair, mesmerized as much by anxiety and contrition as by fatigue and overexcitement.

Georgiana Laverham was ill, and John Wallingham was forced to admit that eloping with a lady—he refused to permit the word "abduction" to enter his mind—was not nearly so easy or so adventurous as he had imagined. At first he had felt altogether exhilarated. His ruses had worked excellently, and he was sure of a good two-hour lead-off, should anyone undertake to follow him. He was not much troubled by the thought of pursuit. Pendarly would be offended enough by the note he had sent, he thought, to stay home in bed, and there was no other person so directly concerned with Miss Laverham as to make Wallingham apprehensive. Mrs. Laverham, once she discovered the truth of the matter, might let loose a hue and cry, but he doubted that she would be so harebrained as to alert the entire party at the Liverpools' to what had happened: she would sit tight and pray that it would come off with not too ill an odor, and Pendarly would retire to watch for another wealthy woman to pay his relatives' debts.

After this promising beginning things began to go awry. Georgiana had slept until they were perhaps an hour out of London, then had awakened, chilled and fretful, and, when she got her bearings well enough to realize her situation, highly indignant.

"Why am I still in this coach, sir?" she had asked. "I should have been home above an hour ago—I beg your pardon that I fell asleep—naturally I would never have done so had it not been—an exceptionally—that is—a very upsetting and unpleasant day." There was a catch to her voice as she remembered her scene with Edward.

"But what is this!" Wallingham had breathed, full of feigned amazement. "Do you mean that you do not re-call—but surely you must!—your protestations of love! The moment when I declared the full of my passion for you and, to my infinite joy, you told me that you recipro-cated! Do not say that you have forgotten all that." The throb in his voice was wholly artificial, but momentarily convincing, and for the space of a second Georgiana won-dered if she could have taken leave of her senses so far as to—no, it was clearly impossible. She could not have for-gotten Edward in such a fashion as to permit such pro-testations, and in a closed carriage, too.

"You must have misinterpreted me, sir," she said severely. "I would never have said any such thing. In fact, I do not remember anything of what you say, and I strongly suspect that you are pitching me a—a Banbury tale. I am not so lost to the proprieties, sir; we cannot go on. I wish to be returned to my house as quickly as pos-sible, and I will endeavor to forgive and forget this ep-isode, and I am not feeling well in the least." The vulgar truth was that Georgiana was prone to become ill on long trips by coach, and the motion of the chaise had begun to make her feel very peculiar. Wallingham had never con-sidered the possibility of such an inelegant malady imped-ing the progress of his elopement, and was thrown into confusion by this reality. "If only I could have a little bit of air," Miss Laverham gasped weakly, and he immedi-ately opened the curtains, so that there was an influx of fresh cold air into the chaise. Georgiana gasped with relief and chill and sank back into the cushions.

When next she spoke, every vestige of that spirit she had manifested only a moment before had vanished, and she felt herself the same Georgiana she had been when she emerged from the sickroom, the Georgiana who had never spoken a cross word to anyone in her life.

"Please, sir," she entreated in a voice made shaky by the motion of the chaise, the suggestion of tears, and the curious, unsettled feeling in her stomach, "I dislike greatly to be a bother to you, but I am afraid that I am going to be very ill. I assure you I never held you in more than friendly regard, and I *beg* that you will take me home."

The first statement was the one that most concerned Wallingham: he leaned out the window and desired the driver to pull over for a few seconds, and Georgiana regarded him for a moment with something like gratitude, then began to sneeze violently. Wallingham regarded her with a peculiar admixture of astonishment and loathing. Never had he heard of an abduction conducted in such an irregular manner. Finally Georgiana looked up, white-faced, and said that he might continue, and that she devoutly hoped that it would be back to London that they traveled. Wallingham thought quickly, then presented what he considered a very beautifully thought out plumper.

"That is a thing I cannot do, in all honor, until we are wed, Miss Laverham," he said solemnly. "Can you not recall what day this is? Yesternight we left town, and if we were to return to London now, it would still be four days you had spent alone and unwed. Only consider your reputation, and then I am persuaded that you will be moved to take the protection of my name for your own. I beg you will consider how you are circumstanced."

Georgiana blanched. "I cannot remember anything after we changed coaches. Are you serious in telling me that we have been abroad—that I have been absent since yesternight? Ooohhhh!" With an anguished cry Georgiana turned her face into the wall of the chaise and began to sob in earnest now. Wallingham approached her with some notion of attempting to comfort her—to make her resign herself, even, to the inevitability of their marriage.

He picked up her hand—and dropped it at once, for it was hot with fever. He drew away from her and placed a handkerchief to his nose.

"Perhaps," he said through the folds of linen at his face, "we should retire to an inn. I fear you are more unwell than you know. After you have had a good night's rest, all will look different to you, I am sure." He added as an afterthought, "Please remember that I hold you in the greatest esteem, and wish only for your happiness. If I thought that another could procure it for you, or that there was a way less revolting to you to reclaim your reputation, since you are so suddenly"—he heaved an aggrieved sigh—"an unwilling participant in this adventure, you may rest assured that I would do all in my power to help you. But do at least recall that I hold you dear to my heart."

Wallingham congratulated himself on this speech and wondered how soon he could lay his hands on her money. The mere fact of his marriage to her fortune would assuage some of the less ambitious of his creditors, but some would demand a small show of faith, in the form of a token repayment at the least. Georgiana had not been swayed by the logic of his words, and was trying to stifle her weeping as she huddled in the corner, murmuring Edward's name like a talisman. With a suspicious eye on her, Wallingham leaned out the window and instructed the driver to stop at the next posting inn.

The landlord of the Red George, one of the smaller inns along the Great North Road, was not at all pleased to have visitors arrive at such an unseasonable hour, particularly when one of them was a mewling sick young lady. Still, gentry was gentry and usually paid promptly, and the Red George did have a reputation to maintain, so with sullen obsequiousness he called for his wife to show the young lady to a room, and offered to mix up a tankard of good strong punch for the gentleman, who looked in need of something reviving.

"My God, yes!" Wallingham said when this proposal was made to him. He was directed to the empty taproom and beseeched to make himself comfortable there while the landlord busied himself with brewing the potation. With a sigh of relief Wallingham threw himself into a chair near the fire and gave some thought to whether he should call in a boy to assist him in removing his boots. That any youth to be found here would undoubtedly have dirty thumbs and thus mark the boots irredeemably, he was certain. Still, they would have to come off at some point, and as it was Wallingham's sincere intention to become as drunk as possible and thus gain *some* good of the evening, he decided that it were best done while he had the power to direct the operation.

Fortunately, at this moment the landlord reentered with a tankard of steaming, fragrant punch. Wallingham accepted the tankard and gave the proper orders regarding the boots, which the landlord assured him would be well tended to, since *he* knew the likes of the gentry. After a few more of these assurances and a hearty draught of punch, Wallingham wished for something convenient to lob at the man's head, but nothing came to hand, so he merely ordered another round of the punch and sat back to consider his ills.

When he was halfway through the second tankard, and considering muzzily whether or not to inquire after some brandy, the landlord's wife entered the room a little diffidently and stood waiting to be observed.

"Well, what do you want?" he growled at last.

The woman was a plump, motherly sort of person, and while she had been no better pleased at being called from her bed to attend to these folk than her husband had been, she was by nature of a better temper. The folds of her face were set in an aspect of timidity and concern both. "It's the young lady, sir," she started. "She's a-running a fever something terrible, sir, and tossing about like fury. I mean to make her as comfortable as I know how, but I thought you'd better know."

Wallingham stammered out a stream of interesting oaths and then, with the courtesy peculiar to the very inebriated, thanked the lady and sent her back to Miss Laverham's side. When the woman was gone, he returned his gaze to the bottom of the tankard and, finding that his view was somewhat obscured by the remaining punch, drank it off so as to afford himself a clear prospect of the tankard's base. By the time the innkeeper arrived with the bottle and glass, his guest had regrettably lapsed into a stupor so deep that he could not be roused from it. The innkeeper, being a philosophical man, left the bottle and glass and settled himself on a pallet behind the door, so as to be handy when the gentleman awoke and wanted his own bed.

Perhaps two hours later the landlord was awakened, but by a determined pounding on the front doors. Roused from a pleasant dream for the second time that evening, he suppressed his feeling of ill use and went again to answer the door.

There were three gentlemen, each with a look so stern that he immediately fell back a pace. The tallest of the three demanded in an even voice that should not have sounded menacing but somehow contrived to, to know if a man and a girl had changed horses there that evening.

"Changed horses, sir? Why no, sir," the man stammered. "That is, *I* should hardly know, sir. Ask the ostler, sir."

The shortest of the three, a fair-haired young man with a look of ferocious excitement, peered over the first man's shoulder. "That's no good. He sent us to you—said you'd know of 'em. Don't try pitching us any gammon or you'll find yourself fair and far to the—"

"Quiet, Ervine," the tall man said briefly. "Have you any idea of such a party? Tell now: we three are on a short fuse tonight, and it will be better for you to deal honestly with us."

The landlord, having made some rapid calculations about the influence of the first gentleman and that of his present guests, decided that it was in his own best interest to oblige these men in any way possible. "There are a young lady and her—uh—brother, sir, is what the man said—staying the night. The young lady was monstrous ill—my wife has been tending her these last hours—but the gentleman has been in the taproom since his arrival—drunk up two tankards of my punch and now has a bottle of my best brandy by him."

"Where is he?" said the first and the second gentleman. "The young lady, where is *she*?" cried the third man, who had been so silent before.

"The gentleman is in the taproom, sirs, and the lady is upstairs in the best back chamber, sir." Almost before he could finish this report the three had split apart: the silent gentleman made for the stairs with a bound, while the other two made straightway for the taproom.

John Wallingham was awakened rudely by the din in the hallway. It took him some seconds to remember where he was: in a country inn on the Post Road, eloping with an heiress. It took him another minute to remember which of the heiresses he had decided to elope with, and another second after this to conclude that he had been pursued and that his plans were overthrown. There really was no point to causing a scene, he thought wearily. He poured himself some brandy, gulped it down quickly, and as he poured another became aware of a singing in his ears and a throbbing in his head. He groaned and dropped his head into his hands, and it was in this dignified posture that he was discovered by Sir Tracy Calendar and Mr. Merrit Ervine.

Chapter Seventeen

Georgiana, while not so ill as she had let the landlady give out to Wallingham, was feeling very uncomfortable, and this discomfort, when added to her fears, her shock, and her absolute certainty that by her own folly she had lost Edward Pendarly forever, contributed largely to her distraught appearance. Aside from sending the landlady down to the taproom with the information that she was deathly ill, there was nothing she could do but sit and stare at the wall, unable to cry, awaiting some sign that would direct her future for good or ruin.

It was some time after the landlady had bid her a sleepy good night that Georgiana, out of the dreamy, gloom-filled contemplation she had fallen into, heard a stirring below. She could in no way tell if it was one voice or twenty that had caused the noise, and although she dared hope that it was a deliverer, or even deliverers, she shrank against the wall, fearing that it was Wallingham preparing to come up and see if she was really ill. On her last visit the landlady had informed her that the gentleman downstairs was a-drinking deep, and heaven only knew what the gentleman would be like to do when he was concerned, as it was, and begging Miss's pardon. These words came back horribly to Georgiana now, and she began to dwell on them. There was hardly time for her to ruminate too far, for the door was opened, and in the darkness of the hallway Georgiana could just discern the face of her visitor.

"Edward!" she sobbed, and straightway fell into a faint.

When she came to herself again Georgiana was conscious of being held against a shoulder, while one of her hands was chafed and a soft murmuring of endearments was made into her hair. She opened one cautious eye and was delighted to learn that the hand holding hers was Pendarly's.

"Edward!" she repeated softly. The patting stopped and the murmuring voice returned to its normal register.

"Are you quite recovered now?" he asked sternly.

"Oh, now you are come, yes, yes, I am all right. Oh, Edward, I am so happy to see you!" She rubbed her cheek against the cloth of his coat. "I was so very afraid. Oh, Edward, I have been so—so criminally silly, and all because I wanted you to love me just a little."

Mr. Pendarly had resolved to be stern with Georgiana before relenting, but he was not proof against this artless speech, and he was able to say, with a perfect belief that it was the truth, "I have *always* loved you, Georgie. I thought you were—I thought you had a *tendre* for that fortune-hunter downstairs." Concern suddenly replaced forgiveness and wrath infused his face and tone. "Did he hurt you? I swear by all that's holy if he laid one finger upon you I'll—"

"No, no," Georgiana said hastily. "He has done me no injury—except to wrest me away from you. The landlady here has stood my friend, and since we arrived, he has been downstairs drinking punch at the fire."

Assured of Georgiana's safety, Pendarly returned to the more interesting matter of forgiveness, apology, and reconciliation. He felt it behooved him to scold before he relented, however, and went about it at once, the better to finish the scolding and get on with the reconciliation.

"If I seem too dull for you, I will gladly drop my pretensions to your hand, rather than embarrass you with them," he started out coldly. "I have always been unswerving in my devotion to you—"

Georgiana had it in her mind upon the utterance of this plumper to remind Edward of Althea Ervine, but some prudent instinct told her that it would not be advisable to assault her betrothed with the inconvenient truth at a time like this. "Oh yes, I know I was wrong," she said instead. "But oh, Edward, I don't want anyone exciting or glamorous if he isn't you. Won't you find it in your heart to forgive me? And maybe love me a little?" She looked at him with so much pleading in her eyes that Pendarly would have had to have been a much harder man to have resolved against her wishes. The proximity between them made it convenient that he should lower her head and give her a kiss of forgiveness. The next kiss was an assurance that he would probably be able to love her very dearly for a long time to come. Their third kiss was a celebration of this fact.

At last Pendarly drew a shaky breath. "Georgie darling, we shall have to join Calendar and Ervine downstairs in a moment. Shall you dislike it excessively if we insist that you drive back to London immediately? We have given out, or rather Miss Ervine has given out, that you were to stay at Bevan's tonight, to help Lady Bevan with her costume. You can see the necessity for it."

Georgiana assured him that there was nothing she would like better than to return to London as soon as possible. "And you say that Sir Tracy and Althea's brother are with you also? Oh, I hope that Sir Tracy has not taken Althea to task for my disappearance! I have a notion he understood all of what was going on and disliked our plans so excessively that he and Ally quarreled."

Pendarly stared at his betrothed. "Calendar and Alth—Miss Ervine?"

"Why yes, of course. Since the day she found out that you and I were betrothed," Georgiana said airily, "they have been—I imagine that if they are not promised, that at least he has an understanding with her. They will be excellent for each other, too, if ever they are able to patch up their differences. And poor Ally has been pining for him all this last week." All this was said in such a matter-of-fact way that Pendarly had the grace to look a little abashed. Georgiana smiled lovingly at him. "You need not look so aghast, Edward. I shall simply undertake not to become ill from now on. And besides, I misdoubt that Sir Tracy will brook any interference with Althea in the future. Shall we go down now?"

Taking his arm, Georgiana led the speechless Pendarly out of the chamber.

The interview then occurring in the taproom was proving not so much dangerous as amusing, at least to Tracy Calendar's way of thinking. Wallingham seemed to regard their arrival as the fitting crown to a hopeless evening. He stood rather shakily on his feet and invited Calendar and Merrit Ervine into the taproom for a draft of punch before they returned to London with their prize. Young Ervine was not to be so easily dissuaded from his adventure, however, and cheerfully offered to draw his cork for him, if only Wallingham would have the goodness to raise his dabblers. Calendar looked pained at this lack of finesse, and said sternly, "Ervine, for the last time, contrive to have a little sense. Sit down." It was to his credit that Merrit knew a voice of authority and at once dropped onto a nearby bench.

"I take it this enterprise has not been so fruitful as you had hoped," Calendar said dryly to Wallingham.

"Deuced unpleasant, Calendar. The chit came up ill on me, and now you come barging in—don't know when I'm to have a little peace. Got the devil of a head as well. You might as well take your ease—don't see how the chit is to travel in the state she's in."

Tracy raised an interested eyebrow. "Really? And what is that?"

Wallingham lifted his hand defensively. "Nothing of the sort. I told you—she took ill in the carriage. Motion, I suppose, and besides, it was damned bad sprung and drafty as well. All of the sudden the gal was a puling wreck. I certainly couldn't have driven on with her in that state, could I? To tell the truth, I'm damned if I ain't glad you've come. Somehow I didn't think that an elopement—"

"An abduction!" Merrit interjected hotly.

"—didn't think that an *elopement* went on in this fashion," Wallingham finished. "I suppose you've taken some care to invent some story for her so that she can return to London with impunity?" Calendar nodded. Wallingham sighed deeply. "Just as well. I shall have to return to London myself and see what can be done there—chase another wealthy woman and hope that she's got a stronger stomach—hope I can turn up something before the creditors get me. If not, I'm sunk."

"I propose a slight alteration of your plans," Calendar said evenly.

"Oh, aye, I supposed you might have something to say to the matter." Wallingham beat his tankard against the table to summon the landlord. "More punch here!" he snapped. "Oh, and give these gentlemen whatever it is they desire."

Merrit was about to repudiate this hospitality, but when Calendar calmly spoke for a tankard of punch, he followed and requested ale.

"Well, what is your alteration, sir?" Wallingham asked, when he had calmed himself with a taste of the punch.

"I believe that it would be—uh—impolitic for you to return just now. It might distress Miss Laverham if she were to encounter you about town, and I should dislike that distress to become the source of a quarrel between you and me," Tracy said reasonably. "I understand also that you have certain debts that you are afraid you will be unable to meet. What I suggest is that you take a vacation on the Continent for a while, thus avoiding all these un-fortunate consequences. I care not where you go there or what ladies you seduce or elope with or abduct, but I feel certain that it would be inadvisable for you to return to London at this time." Tracy gave Wallingham a look of great portent, which was not lost on the gentleman. He sighed again, lengthily.

"Why did I not think of that? Just the thing for my—my health. And who knows but what my luck might change—God knows but it could hardly be worse. Then I will take my leave of you gentlemen here, or you may take your leave of me, for I've a mind to stay a day here and recover my strength. This has been a taxing day." He slunk down into his chair and turned his feet toward the fire. Merrit had hoped for more action than this adventure was supplying; this sitting about discussing things in a ra-tional manner over tankards of ale was hardly to his taste. But Calendar seemed satisfied with the night's work, and Merrit had the disappointing notion that the night's ad-venture would end in their delivering Miss Laverham to Bevan's house and themselves to their beds. He sulked a little until another opportunity occurred to him.

"I shall have to leave directly," he announced happily. "I promised Ally I'd come back straight to tell her the outcome of things." He rather fancied the picture of him-self riding *ventre à terre* to collapse at his sister's door and gasp out the happy word "Safe!"

"I think, if it is all the same to you, that I will play the messenger tonight, Ervine." Tracy quashed the younger man's hopes. "You are, after all, a latecomer to this drama, and really should have the courtesy to let the prin-cipals act it out among themselves."

Merrit opened his mouth to say that he wanted no part in the drama at all if he could not play a good one, but his retort was cut off by the arrival of Pendarly and Geor-giana from upstairs. Again Wallingham rose to his feet, this time keeping his right hand firmly on the back of his chair in hopes of not tipping over entirely.

"Well, madam, I understand I am to wish you joy?" he said precisely.

"You may, sir," Georgiana said falteringly. Behind her Pendarly was bristling furiously.

"Needn't look daggers at me, boy," Wallingham addressed him. "I am quite undone, overthrown, and you have won the day. Have a little charity for an older man." He dropped back into his chair in a manner that demonstrated to his audience that he was very much disguised.

"Don't concern yourself with Wallingham, Pendarly," Tracy advised. "He is about to start out on a journey through the Continent to see what change his luck may take there. I believe by next week?" he suggested.

"Just so," Wallingham answered owlishly. "Sorry, Miss Laverham, to greet you in this fashion, but I've eaten Hull cheese, and that's the truth of it. Hope you are recovered from your indisposition, ma'am."

Georgiana managed something to the effect that she felt much recovered, and then fell silent, clutching Pendarly's sleeve nervously.

"Thought you weren't one of those drooping little schoolgirl things, but a man is entitled to a mistake, ain't he?" Wallingham addressed the bottom of his tankard. There was a long stretch of quiet in the taproom, broken only by the whisper and cackle of the fire. Then Calendar drained the last of his punch and rose.

"I suggest that we all start homeward now. Ervine, you and Pendarly can escort Miss Laverham back to London. Miss Laverham, you are expected at Bevan's, and if necessary Lady Bevan can send your mother some excuse saying you are indisposed to come home for a day or so, if you like. I will do your duty," he informed Merrit, "and inform your sisters and Lord Bevan that all is well."

Georgiana stood forward shyly and held out her hand. "Thank you, sir. I haven't the words to properly thank you for your help to me tonight, but if you will promise one thing to me?" He nodded agreeably. "Don't be too hard on her, sir."

Tracy regarded Georgiana with respect. "Ma'am, I do not propose to be hard on her at all." He bowed over her hand, nodded to the gentlemen, and left the room.

Merrit stared after him in amazement. "But I understand!" he insisted. "I understand it now. Calendar's soft on Ally! Ain't that the damnedest thing you ever—beg pardon, Miss Laverham, I forgot you were here." Still shaking his head in wonder, Merrit followed Pendarly and Georgiana out to where the chaise was waiting.

If Calendar did not precisely ride *ventre à terre* to London, he was at least very speedy in his return. He outdistanced the chaise at once, and arrived in Grosvenor Square perhaps an hour and a half in advance of the party. He surprised the footman at the Bevans's household, who had certainly no expectations of admitting a gentleman calling at the unlikely hour of four in the morning, but before he could be turned away by an insistent man who reiterated that the master and mistress were not receiving at this peculiar hour, Lord Bevan and Miss Ervine emerged from the library to greet him.

Tracy was shocked by Althea's appearance. She was not only bleary-eyed from lack of sleep; worry and the course of a few tears had left their marks on her face. Her gown was badly crumpled, and her hands, pressed tightly into fists beyond her power to unclench, testified to the origin of some of those wrinkles.

Bevan led them back to the library and closed the door. He and Althea faced Calendar as one might face an enemy charge.

"Well?" Bevan asked.

"Safe," Tracy said briefly.

All the strength that had heretofore supported Althea disappeared in a minute. She swayed where she stood, but when Tracy and Francis moved to help her to a chair, she waved them aside and managed to seat herself without aid.

"She'll be coming here, I hope," she whispered.

"They should be here within the hour or so. I congratulate you on the story you gave out—Merrit explained it to me as we rode out. Very neat."

"Yes," Althea said bitterly, "I have a perfect genius for neat plots and convenient tales." She looked up at her companions. "I'll see that her room is made ready before she arrives. And, Tracy: how is she?"

"Blooming: she is united with Pendarly, who seems to have discovered a novel diversion in the fact that he is genuinely attached to her."

"With such a chance to play the hero I should wonder he'd have time for such a novel discovery. He may never have the chance to be so gallant again. I beg your pardon—I *am* being uncivil, and with no excuse—I cannot claim fatigue when you have been up as late as I, and with more to fatigue you in a ride like the one I am sure you must have had. . . ." Her voice was shaking, and she hardly knew what she said anymore. "I'll go up now," she murmured, and rose from her seat, managing with effort to appear collected.

"Bevan, will you give us a few minutes?" Calendar asked. "I have a message for your sister's ears only, which Miss Laverham charged me to carry before I left her." Francis rose obligingly and left the room. Althea wanted of all things to avoid being alone with Calendar, but could not for her life think of leaving until she knew if Georgiana blamed her for the abduction. For a moment he said nothing at all.

"The message, sir?" she asked pointedly.

"There was none," he admitted. "But you might let a man catch his breath after a ride such as I have had, Ally."

"At least you were doing something! I was here, left to

my own thoughts, indeed, quite unable to avoid them! All I have been able to do is run through my mind images of the perils that faced poor Georgiana—my God, what images! I had rather have been riding all night than sitting here spoiling embroidery patterns and trying not to think."

"I sincerely wish you would not take quite so much blame upon yourself," Tracy said mildly. "You were hardly to know what straits Wallingham was in, or what he had in his head. Miss Laverham, who was certainly more in his company than you, had no idea at all."

"You *are* magnanimous, sir," Althea said hotly. "When I consider that only last night you were happy to lay the blame at my door for my lack of sense in even introducing Wallingham to Georgiana—and now you are proven right and I admit it. I wish you the joy of your forgiveness. I shall not find it so easy to forgive myself."

"Althea, stop playing at tragedy and behave like the rational woman I know you to be," he scolded.

"Perhaps I cease to be a rational woman between the hours of two and eight in the morning. I can see very little but my own folly at this hour. And that is not a sight it pleasures me to indulge in." Her voice filled with tears as she turned her back to him and addressed the wall. "I wish I had never come to this horrible city! I wish—lord, how I wish that none of my friends had ever heard my name here, let alone that I ever had the power to hurt them." Her voice broke, her shoulders shook. "I should have known better than to leave the home I was used to. From the day I entered London—from the morning when that lunatic in a phaeton ran my chaise off the road—I should have realized that I was out of my mind!"

"What was that?" Calendar's eyebrows rose. "When exactly did you arrive in town?"

Althea gave him the date abstractedly. "What can that matter? The only thing that concerns me now is when I leave." Calendar, bemused by his own calculations, missed the bitterness in her tone.

"My God," he cried, with a mixture of horror and delight, "that could not have been you in the chaise that day? Aunt Margaret will be delighted to know it! It will utterly confirm her opinion of me as a racketing nabster with more hair than wit." He began to chuckle to himself. Althea turned to him hotly, forgetting the tears on her face, and demanded to know what was so overwhelmingly funny. He advanced to take her hand; she drew it from him sharply.

"Only this, sweetheart: we *must* have been destined for each other—I am very much afraid that it was *my* phaeton that ran *your* carriage off the road. I was driving for a bet, you see, and couldn't stop to see what damage I had done."

"And that is funny? It confirms only what I had thought: we should never suit. Fate had us clashing from the outset—even before we knew of each other's existence!"

"Althea, please spare me your melodrama! Can't you see the humor in all this?" Tracy was taken in his fatigue by laughter; Althea was taken in hers by morbid melancholy. His chuckles became laughter he could barely control. When he saw Althea turn and make for the door in a determined fashion, though, he did control it, and went to grasp her arm and turn her toward him.

"We really haven't anything to say, Tracy. I am sorry if I ever made you think that you could like—could stand to be—could marry me—I won't hold you to your promise. Goodbye." She was not crying anymore. Her eyes were stony dry and her face set in lines of miserable determination.

"Once and for all, will you stop this fustian nonsense? I see it is no use to talk to you now, but I will be back later, my dear." He released her and made to open the door for her. "Georgiana did say something to me—per-

haps that was her message to you. She begged that I
would not be too hard on you, and I told her I had no intention of being hard on you at all. But don't you be too
hard on yourself, love. I shall call later today. Get some
sleep and the world may begin to look more the thing."

He was still close enough so that he could bend and
brush his lips across her cheek before he left.

Althea stood stock still for some time after he had
gone—it might have been five minutes or half an hour:
she knew not. Her first coherent thought when she had
regained the use of her limbs was: I must pack. I must be
ready when Merrit arrives home. In a flurry of mindless
organization Althea went up to one of the second bedrooms and made sure it would be ready to receive Georgiana when she arrived. Then she went to her own room
and began, pell mell, to pack her clothes. Only the morning and round gowns, her habit, a few traveling suits did
she pack (somewhat inexpertly) in the first bandboxes
that came to hand (they happened to belong to Miss Banders). The evening and opera gowns and similar frivo-
lous articles she left for Maria, with a note that made it
clear *she* would not need them again. A few tears were
dropped upon that note, which sent her best love to both
her sister and brother-in-law, begged them to make any
excuse they liked for her sudden departure, and to ask
Georgiana's forgiveness when they thought best. For Banders she left a note explaining that she was returning to
Lancashire, and that Banders could follow when and if
she wanted—with no fear of trouble from Sir George. "At
least I am sure that I can still manage Papa without ruining anyone else's life!"

At a quarter past seven a carriage arrived at the back
and deposited what looked like two gentlemen and a very
large bundle composed of sprigged muslin and plaid
woolen blanket. Althea had warned one of the maids, a
good girl who could be trusted not to share the morning's
adventures with her friends, that Mr. Ervine and Mr. Pen-

darly would be bringing one of her friends in early in the morning, so the gentlemen and their parcel were admitted with no trouble, despite the oddness of the hour. Althea was there to greet them in a moment, and to direct Pendarly, who bore Georgiana in his arms as if she were a Ming vase, to the bedchamber prepared for her. If she expected some change in his manner of greeting, she was disappointed. His concern for Georgiana, and her avid desire to avoid conversing with any of the principals in the night's drama, coupled with her intention to leave the house as soon as possible, made their communication rather a brief one, and she considered that she might have been mistaken and missed less enmity than was truly there.

Georgiana was settled—still asleep—with as little fuss as possible, and Miss Banders given charge over her. Pendarly made a grave adieu to Althea and took Merrit's hand in a gesture of fellowship that Merrit felt at least a small recompense for the lackluster quality of the evening's amusement. When the door had closed behind Pendarly, Althea turned to her brother and announced that they were leaving.

"What? But I only just got back, and even at that, I only just arrived in town anyhow. I told you there was no rush to get back to Hook Well—not for a day or so, a fortnight even. I've just begun to see some adventure: last night was something out of the common run of things in Lancashire, I can tell you."

"Merrit," Althea said dangerously, "we leave within the hour."

Merrit regarded his sister with the respect born of many years' close association with that same tone.

"Yes, Ally," he said.

Chapter Eighteen

"Well, boy, where are you off to?" Lady Boskingram surprised her nephew as he made for the door. It was late in the afternoon, and he had been sleeping since his return that morning. Having cornered him, his aunt had no intention of releasing him until she knew the full story of the previous night's adventures. As quickly as he could Tracy sketched the story for her. At the end of the narrative the Countess applauded. "Delightful outing. And what time did you return here this morning?"

Tracy yawned extensively. "I arrived at Bevan's in advance of the party, soon after five, to inform Althea and Bevan that all was well—Pendarly and young Ervine followed behind with Miss Laverham in a chaise. That gave me ample time for a set-to with Althea—I swear, ma'am, I have never met any woman so determined not to be happy!"

"Are you sure she knows that you are where her happiness lies?" his Aunt Peg asked shrewdly.

Tracy sobered. "I'm not sure of anything, ma'am. I know that I love her and would endeavor to make her happy. What more can I say to her? But also, you have not seen her as she was last night. I fear I raked her down pretty harshly at Lady Liverpool's, and this morning I was too tired to think, let alone deal with her self-recriminations. I never thought she would take what I said so to heart. She's been tearing at herself, Aunt Peg, and that is what I must put a stop to. Good God, the nonsense she spoke this morning! About her foolishness and my patience—if you will!—and releasing me from my promises and God only knows what other fustian."

"I should never have taken her for such a peagoose," Lady Boskingram regretted.

"Nor should I, but you will admit that the circumstances were extreme—she was very tired, and stretched tight as a drum with worry. I'm afraid that I was hardly at my most conciliatory this morning either: the journey had made me a trifle lightheaded, and I think I began to laugh somewhere in the middle of the interview."

"Now that is unforgivable," the dowager reproved. "I shall be much impressed with Althea's charity if she speaks to you again before a fortnight. Laughing at her tears! I begin to think all my earlier estimates of your worthless character were correct."

"No doubt," Tracy said dryly. "But, Aunt Margaret, I have just recalled it—I thought of you when I learned— do you remember the day you arrived on my doorstep?"

"What? Well, of course I do, but what is that to the purpose of anything? You do occasionally bewilder me, Tracy."

"Only occasionally?" He raised an eyebrow at his aunt. "Stop interrupting me for a moment. You recall that I made my race to Quinlan's seat and back that day. And it was the day that Althea arrived in London."

" 'Tis a marvel to me that the city of London could withstand so much excitement all in one day," Lady Boskingram volunteered.

"Quiet. You recall the chaise that I was so ill mannered as to push into a ditch as I went along?" The dowager nodded. "It was Althea in the chaise, ma'am."

He waited for her laughter. There was none.

"Boy, you go to the most confounded lengths to snarl up your courtship, do you not? I suppose you announced this to Althea? All the tact of a Piccadilly cutpurse.

Thank God you never aimed to be a diplomat—we'd surely all be French by now."

"I assume you don't find this a jest," he said stiffly.

"What matters it if I do? The question is how it would take Althea. And if what you have told me of her state last night is true, Nephew, I cannot conceive that she would see much humor in it. Oh, fiddlestick, must I conduct your courtship for you? Go to her and speak quietly—quietly, mind,—and don't for heaven's sake press on her any suit. Even a heroine must pine for a little quiet and peace now and again."

"If that is your prescription, wisest of my aunts, I will follow it. Perhaps I shall see you later in the evening?"

"But you hope not," Lady Boskingram retorted to her nephew's retreating back. "Give her my love." When he had gone from the house she gave vent to an enormous cackle of delight. "Ditched her carriage before he even knew of her! Oh, Tracy, what was I about to have had a stick of a son like Richard, when all along it was you I should have been raising?"

"But both of them are gone, sir," Maria said peevishly. "And Ally left me a note filled with the greatest stupidities about how grateful she was to me and how kind I was and how kind *everybody* was, and that she hoped I would visit her at Hook Well sometime. . . . Well, I may be a widgeon, sir, but I never wrote such fustian in my life." She folded her hands and looked plaintively at Sir Tracy.

"You have no idea when they left?"

"The note was found only half an hour ago. Francis told her maid not to bother her until she awakened, but we are engaged to dine tonight, so I sent to wake her, and there she was not, and only this stupid note and one to Banders."

"Banders?" Tracy asked blankly.

"Her maid. Actually, our mother's maid, but Althea has been her pet forever, since Mama was taken from us.

The notes were only *just* discovered, in any case, for she placed them among the bedclothes, and they were almost taken to be laundered with the sheets, and then think of the pretty pass, with ink on my sheets and no idea where Ally had got to."

"You said your brother had gone with her?" Calendar interrupted.

"Of course! Papa sent him here to fetch Ally back, although I had no notion that they would be leaving so soon. Papa is not very good at managing," Maria confided, "and I think he wants Ally back to untie the knots he has got the household into. Ally is terribly smart." She sighed.

"Your sister seems to be terribly smart about everything except dealing with a man who loves her," Tracy said bitterly. "On that score she is as like to run and hide as to give encouragement."

Maria clapped her hands gladly. "Then you love her! Oh, I am so pleased, for she never really thought so: I suppose that is why she's been so dreadfully mopey of late. Did you ever tell her so?"

"Did I ever tell her so?" Tracy stared at his hostess with amusement. "Dear Lady Bevan, even if I never said so in so many words, I should think that my actions, my very demeanor, would have indicated it to her. As you say, she is certainly not stupid."

"No, of course not. But think, Sir Tracy. There was that stupid Pendarly vowing his devotion when he was all the while engaged to Miss Laverham—oh you have not inquired for Miss Laverham. She is very well, and has gone home to her Mama in great spirits. Mr. Pendarly took her home."

"I am no end relieved to hear it," Tracy said impatiently. "But would you have the goodness to finish the thought you began a moment ago?"

"Oh dear, which thought was that?"

Tracy suppressed a shudder of annoyance and told her,

word for word, through clenched teeth, exactly what she had been saying.

"Oh, yes. Well, Pendarly had been hanging after her in the most flattering way, and he really is terribly handsome, and he may even have said that he loved her for all I know—and then he betrayed her. So naturally she could not trust people as easily after such a humiliation. And if you never told her that you loved her—why, it is really very shocking. How was she to know you hadn't decided to marry her for the convenience of it, and because she *suited* you. And Ally didn't feel suitable for anyone after she had let herself be made such a game of. Even I saw it—although I didn't understand all of it—and I am really very silly," Maria finished proudly. Tracy watched her for a moment, dumbfounded.

"You mean, ma'am, that she honestly thought I would offer for her simply to get myself a housekeeper and furnish myself with an heir? I must be mistaken in your family: I cherished the idea that your sister was passably intelligent."

"Oh, but it's the smart ones that always end up in a coil," Maria assured him.

"Lady Bevan," Tracy insisted sweetly, "do you think that I should go after her or not? I have the most striking vision of my wedded life: pursuing my notional bride over the countryside."

Maria considered. "Could you follow her very slowly? If she could have a few days back at Hook Well with Papa to realize how awful he and Merrit can be when one is confined to their society—I love them both dearly, but they can be a dreadfully trying, even to a nature as sweet as Althea's. And if you do go, will you take her a note from me? I really cannot use the gowns she left for me—with my coloring, can you imagine a mulberry satin pelisse fitted in sable, or yellow muslin with sand-colored ribbons? She *must* come back to town or the waste of those gowns will quite break my heart."

"I would be delighted to carry your note." Tracy smiled. "How long do you think I should give her to consider her situation?"

"Well, you know best how long the trip into Lancashire will take you. I suppose two days will suffice. She did cry over the note that she left me, and that I think is an excellent sign, do not you?"

"If *you* think it is, I shall bow to your knowledge, ma'am. I have very little idea if it is or no." He raised his eyes heavenward. "Thank God a man need only once go through this business of courtship. I could never survive a second essay. You see, your sister will have to take me."

"Oh." Maria considered this. "Do you know, no one has ever told me I had any knowledge. It's rather nice. But please do call before you leave and I shall have my letter ready for you."

Sir George Ervine took an unaccustomed seat in the office of his house, one morning, several days after he had dispatched his son to plead for his sister's return. He did not expect their immediate appearance, but as he eyed the number of papers upon the desk, he could not keep from hoping that Althea could be persuaded to leave the dissipations of her town life with reasonable alacrity—the business of running a household was turning out to be more complex than he had ever imagined. So he sat in the office and tried to look as if he were not only busy, but busy with something he fully understood. The effort was hardly successful.

"Father, what are you doing here, of all places?" The voice was, unbelievably, that of his daughter. She stood in the doorway, dressed in a modish but somewhat rumpled traveling suit, her hair differently arranged from when he had seen her last, but with a familiar look of tolerant amusement on her face.

"Althea, my dearest child!" Sir George sprang up from

the desk and embraced his returned lamb. "You are made so fine I hardly recognize you."

"And you are grown so busy I hardly recognize you. Sitting in the office on a fine morning like this when I am sure you had much rather be out riding. Oh, shame, Papa, it is quite out of your character." She clucked chidingly as she went toward the desk, untying her bonnet strings in a businesslike fashion. "I see that some work has piled up for me to tend to—how *thoughtful* of you to save it for me, Papa dear."

Sir George smiled fondly. "Well, I know you never did like others meddling in your accounts so I tried to keep as much intact as I could for you, m'dear." He cast a look of impatience toward the door. "Are you much fatigued from your journey, my child?"

"I slept the greater part of it, much to poor Merrit's disgust; he is upstairs changing from his clothes now, but I expect he will be down in a moment. Perhaps," she said wickedly, "you would care to sit with me a while and explain what changes you have made in my organization while I was gone?"

Sir George coughed nervously, acutely aware of an overwhelming desire to remove himself from the office as soon as possible. "I'd be delighted," he lied. "But perhaps now is not the proper moment. I was just about to ride into the village—got some urgent business there, and—"

"Enough," Althea conceded. "Papa, I can see the office holds no particular charm for you. Go, and I will see if I cannot manage to untangle what is here on my own."

With an alacrity almost unbecoming in a gentleman of his years and dignity, Sir George sprang for the door. Althea watched his exit bemusedly: she was depressingly certain that soon enough she would be frowning. She had slept almost entirely through the journey homeward—had insisted that they make no overnight break in the trip. By traveling in this fashion, Althea found that she was largely able to avoid thinking of her London stay. Now, by immediately plunging into the fascinating task of trying to unsnarl her father's accounts and the domestic crises of Hook Well, she hoped to further delay those thoughts. By contrast with her remembrances of the last few interviews she had had with Calendar, even the running feud between the cook and the butler was a matter for celebration.

She had not had the opportunity to sort out the bills at the desk, let alone turn her attention to paying them, when the door opened and disclosed Cook, two housemaids, the youngest of the gardener's sons, all apparently come to give evidence against Firth, the much maligned butler. Cook preferred to wait until the others had done to parade her woes, but Sarah and Annie had tales to tell that made that loyal, elderly retainer sound like the greatest fiend in history, and as for Davy, who generally transported his father's flowers from hothouse to kitchen, he had a tale that should have made Althea's hair white with horror at what he had submitted to by way of beatings, scoldings, and threats. Since Althea was reasonably sure that all three of them had deserved any and all scoldings received, she clucked, nodded, promised nothing, and dismissed them from the room under the impression that they had accomplished their purpose.

"Well, Miss Ally," Cook said when her supporters were gone, "you may turn the others aside as hasn't the grievances I have, but you shall have to listen to how that man has used me." Althea did not seem impressed by the direness of this tone, so she tried a different tack. "But hasn't Miss Mary been feeding you down there in London? You're peaked and thin as a pole. You'll just go to bed with a bowl of my barley water and gruel this very instant."

"Cook, I am no thinner than when I left, Maria fed me more than well, and if you think to turn me up sweet with gruel and sympathy, you have sadly forgotten me in my absence, so pray go on with your accusations. The stories

I have heard so far do not convince me of anything but that Firth has been sadly outnumbered in this household."

Cook, much aggrieved by this address, plunged into her story, which was the most complex of the accusations, involving, as nearly as Althea could tell, Firth's refusal to allow Cook to defend herself when Sir George sent some of her gruel (ordered on Doctor Phillips' instructions as a cure for the master's gout) back to the kitchen with a message both insulting and untrue regarding Cook's culinary skills. If only the sainted Lady Dorothea was still among them, Althea was assured, she would never have brooked such treatment of such old and devoted servants.

By the time this diatribe came to an end, Cook was nearly drowning in her tears, and it took almost half an hour for Althea to calm her, assure her that her sacrifices would not be overlooked, and that she would attempt to live up to her mother's standards as a housekeeper, with the help of those old and devoted retainers who still recalled that worthy lady. This last comment was not overlooked by Cook, who resolved at once to be Althea's preceptress in all things; with a sense of mission she departed for her kitchen, tears dried, cheerfully unaware that Althea had promised no action against her arch enemies Sir George and Firth.

Within three days Althea had finished the worst of the office mess, to the occasional accompaniment of quarrels from the servants' hall and her brother and father's bickering over everything from backgammon to the sugar in their tea. The music of home, the tranquility she had longed for in London, was now becoming the same old commonplace drone: her father's prosing and her brother's wheedling. This was, she reflected grimly, the price one paid for refuge. This morning, however, with her figuring done, Althea felt it time to make a tour of the house and see what had been most grossly neglected. Since this was likely to be a messy chore, she donned her

oldest, most faded gown, made a turban for her hair with
a scarf, and ascended to the attic to begin there.

As she had expected, all was in a disarray ranging from
mild to severe. She had had the foresight to equip herself
with tablet and pen, to make notes of what stood most
direly in need of repair. By noon she had swept through
half the house, and had begun to work on the public
rooms below. With reckless abandon she noted chairs that
needed reseating, drapery beyond all hope of repair, and
rugs that needed immediate attention. She knew her father would rebel vigorously at the cost of the work she
planned, but while she still had some power as returned
prodigal, she intended to make use of it.

She had planned to stop at noon and partake of some
sort of nuncheon. When a glance at the watch pinned to
her gown assured her it was some minutes past the hour,
she unwound the scarf from her head and shook out her
curls, which were full of dust despite the turban. She
made to look over her list of the most immediate projects
to be done, and did not look up when the door opened.

"Is the nuncheon ready, Firth?" she asked abstractedly.

"I really haven't the slightest idea, love," said Tracy
Calendar.

Chapter Nineteen

"I wish I understood why it amuses you so to provoke
me," Althea said crossly. Her face was hidden from his
view by a spray of roses conveniently located on a table
between them, and her voice conveyed such a combina-

tion of feelings that Tracy could not define her emotion. Still, finding her there, in health and active enough to be cleaning the house, cheered him somewhat and renewed his confidence.

"I wonder if perhaps it doesn't please you just as well to plague me. We will be a frightening pair, love: all London will go in terror of us. I can only hope that the Bevans will provide us with an example of how a married couple goes on." He advanced around the table to her. "But we won't be bored, I imagine, if these last weeks can tell anything at all. Of course, I will not answer for an occasional urge to throttle you, but I am sure that that, too, can be managed—you handle almost everything in the most admirable way, my dear."

Althea said nothing, but hung her head, scarlet faced.

"And of course, if you should become bored in between fending off my destructive tempers and attempting to instill the usual virtues in our children, you could always take up writing scholarly dissertations on the insipidity of Cowper, or the infinite superiority of——"

"Dreadful!" Althea broke in, willing to argue anything rather than attend to the plunging feeling that had hit her when he had spoken of *their* children. "You think that I could not write dissertations? Or something of the sort?" she flashed back.

"I have the utmost confidence that you can do anything, love, except possibly answer a declaration in form. But we shall see to that."

"I will not marry you," Althea said flatly.

"This is a shame. Why not?" Tracy asked with maddening calm. Althea was spared the necessity of an answer to this trying question by the appearance of her brother and father at the garden door. They were arguing over something, and Sir George's face was a choleric red.

"I will remind you, sir, that I am your father, and the master in this house, and an indulgent one at that! No need for me to listen to this disrespectful hogwash! If I hear one more word on this disgraceful subject, I shall be—oh, what's all this, hey?"

It had dawned upon her father that Althea was not alone in the room.

Merrit spared a peevish glance and a nod for the visitor, then returned to kicking the leg of the sofa.

Sir George, on the other hand, crossed to his daughter with a look of pompous cordiality, not unmixed with suspicion, on his face.

"Well, Ally, who's this? Got one of your London beaux to visit, hey? Well, sir, I'm the gal's father. You may address all inquiries to me. Who're you, hey?"

Althea blushed for her father. She could be sure that even Sir Tracy's fancied partiality for herself would not keep him from thinking her father excessivly ill bred.

"My name is Calendar, sir, and my intentions are honorable. My family is good—I am remotely in line to an earldom, which I am thankfully not likely to ascend to at any time. I have a good income, several seats, and drive a phaeton. And I intend to marry your daughter."

"No you don't," Althea gasped.

Sir George seemed a trifle taken aback by the wealth of information provided him, coupled with the blunt manner Tracy had adopted in speaking to him. "Now, sir, why don't we just go into the library? It don't do to let the womenfolk know too much of these arrangements: gives 'em notions and nothing is more ruinous to their looks. Knew a lady novelist once—only published one volume, but it made her absolutely fubsy faced. Thinking will do it. Just this way through to the library, sir."

"There is no reason for him to follow you, sir, I promise you. I will not marry him, even if I have to become a novelist to avoid it."

"But no, love, did I not say that I expressly wished that you should write, if you would like to? Of course, I thought you would prefer to do literary critiques, but if you had rather write a novel, I could always suggest a plot myself."

"I imagine you could suggest several," Althea said.

Sir George chortled. "That's the way, sir. Humor her now, but don't never let her bother her mind with notions. Looks couldn't stand it. The library, sir? Merrit, go see what Firth has done with my port."

"No port, Father, until Doctor Phillips says that your gout is completely done. And in any case, I forbid you to speak to this man. I am not going to marry him, and even if I was"—a long, shaky breath—"I am above age, and what I do need not concern you in the least. I shall show Sir Tracy out, and that will be an end to it. You may continue to argue with Merrit if you like. I believe that I have the headache, so I shall be retiring to my room directly. Or, if I don't have it now"—a wrathful look at Calendar—"I am sure that I shall have it by and by. Father, do please go away."

"You forbid me? You are ordering me about? You forget yourself, my girl! I have forgiven you often enough for your disrespect to me and your brother, but you will recall who is master in this household! Or else, by God, I shall scratch your name from the Bible and forbid you ever to darken my halls again."

"Oh, go ahead, Father, you've done it often enough before." Althea sighed. "And it will only mean that you will have to hire a housekeeper. Only think of the expense."

There was a long pause while Tracy and Merrit studied the father and child and Sir George strove to understand exactly what his daughter had just said to him. Realization broke like dawn over the sea when he understood that this was just another of his daughter's unaccountably disrespectful remarks. His face darkened and he bellowed something about insolence and ingratitude. He was about to banish her forever from the house when the second part of her statement occurred to him with renewed force, and he recalled anxious hours bent over the ledgers. He croaked something about leaving Althea to consider her outrageous behavior and, gathering his dignity and his son to him, left the room with an injured air.

Althea sank rather limply to the sofa. Tracy observed his beloved with some concern; her face was pale and there was a bleakness in her expression.

"If nothing else could convince you, Tracy, this must. I cannot marry you. It was perfectly all right for Francis to marry Mary, that was merely a case of one widgeon marrying into a family of equally silly people. Francis even thinks that Papa is, in his own words, 'a devilish good 'un, albeit a trifle high in the instep!' How could I inflict my father and my brother upon you? You have already been much involved with the foibles of my poor sister, and believe me, she is quite the best of the Ervines."

"Not quite the best."

"Please don't be gallant. It rather unmans me, you know. You are concerned for me, I suppose—we were become friends in London for a time, despite the muddles and stupidity, and one cares for one's friends. I'm very glad that I had such a friend there. But how could you possibly explain to your aunt that you'd married such a one as Sir George Ervine's daughter? You know that I love Lady Boskingram dearly, but even if she didn't cavil at my family, Boskingram would, for you know that within the week Papa would begin to speak of 'Calendar, my girl's husband—the heir to Boskingram's title, you know.' "

She swallowed, then continued ahead, rather fiercely.

"I know just how vulgar and pompous he is, and to myself I make fun of him no end, but he is my father, and I will not have other people laugh at him. Nor should I care to make you a laughingstock among your friends on account of my family. Oh, for pity's sake, Tracy, go back to London and leave me alone!"

She attempted a laugh. "You can have no idea what has to be attended to here. Papa lets things become so dreadfully snarled up. It was no idle threat when I told him that if I left he would have to engage a housekeeper; as it is, I shall be quite frantically busy for the next few weeks." She stopped speaking and became aware that Calendar was observing her with that rather inscrutable, vaguely amused glance that she had first noticed at the Fforydings' party.

"I think your father has the right idea," he said at length. This declaration so startled Althea that she was unable to think of a suitable rejoinder except to croak out a faint "What?"

"I think your father has suggested the best thing. He will cast you out on the mercy of the world and I shall, of course, be there to catch you. Although I realize that that is not quite what he had in mind. So he must needs engage an housekeeper anyway. And while I really cannot continue to allow you to stay in a household where thinking is held to be injurious to your beauty, I also think that you have been thinking in entirely the wrong way if you can come to such ridiculous conclusions. In any case, I find it far more likely that you might kill one of your own family than that you and I should do each other any irreparable harm." Althea had begun to smile unwillingly so he allowed himself to continue in a more serious tone.

"I do respect your feelings very much—if I didn't fear to sound like that pompous fool Pendarly, I would say that I honored your feelings. Up to a point. But do you imagine that I am such a weak sort of fellow that I would allow your relations to annoy me? You have a foolish father, but I have my cousin Boskingram, and worse than that, his estimable and wholly unbearable wife, Amalia. So if I attempt to overlook your father's deficiencies, cannot you overlook those of my cousins?" He sat close to her on the sofa. "You know, Ally, the only reason I can think of for your refusing to have me is that you cannot love me. If *that* is the case I wish you would tell me so, and I will not importune you any more."

The silence that followed was oppressive in the extreme.

Althea sat with her head bowed, examining her fingers as she knotted and reknotted the scarf she had removed from her hair.

"Do you know how much I hate to be in the position of saying missish things? All my life I have tried to avoid it, but in the last weeks I have said more horridly missish things than I can remember—and always in your company, so I knew that you would be sure to notice it." She gave a particularly fierce tug at her scarf and the corner came away with a rending noise.

"Althea. Do you love me?"

"You are a fine one to speak of love! To marry to establish your home, or to get an heir, and oh, to rescue me from Papa, and because you think I have been ill used, and because you think that we could go on together—although where you acquired that notion I am sure I cannot tell!—and because I thought such dreadful things of you, and perhaps because you don't like to be thwarted, and lord, I don't know what. And then to speak of *love* to me! I don't know why you offered for me in the first place, although I need not scruple to say that *I* know *you* know why I accepted your offer."

"I offered for you in the first place, my love, for the same reason that I offer for you now. I love you." This admission startled Althea from the examination of her torn scarf, but her reaction was quite other from what he had hoped. She stood up suddenly.

"No Canterbury tales, Tracy."

Sir Tracy sighed wearily, but stood up also.

"My love, you are behaving in the most tiresome way," he said, and kissed her. Althea felt as if a great weight had been lifted from her: she drew her arms up around Tracy's neck and surprised herself with the response she gave. A moment of timelessness, while Tracy answered her cooperation by tightening the hold he had taken on her. At last, breathless, she emerged from the embrace, satisfied as to the truth of Sir Tracy's declarations.

"Will you always punish me so when I am tiresome? If so I fear I shall grow more and more tiresome."

"Hush," was all Sir Tracy would say.

Some minutes later, when they had retired to the garden in hopes of attaining a little privacy from her family, as they wandered aimlessly arm in arm, Sir Tracy Calendar renewed, and Miss Althea Ervine accepted, an offer of marriage. Not only did they renew their troth, they spent some time discussing their household, the number of children that should grace it, what their names would be—in short, they planned every facet of their domestic felicity.

"Here's proof of love indeed!" Althea declared at length. "The mighty social lion discussing nursery and governesses as calmly as he might speak of snuff or lacquered boxes."

"No, love, it's Petersham for snuff and Brummell for old lac. I have an interest in chinoiserie."

"That sounds positively improper. What a thing to say to a woman so newly betrothed!"

"And will you much mind being married to a fribble, love?"

"Not if you are a very good fribble, Tracy. I should hate to see you second rate at anything."

"And you, my dear, are going to be content to be a married woman and have no more adventures gadding off in the middle of the night? Think how their father would feel, explaining to the children that Mama has run off yet again."

"If their father treats me as he does now, I shall have no reason to make any moonlight escapes. They pall after a while, anyhow." Althea sighed and allowed herself to rest more heavily on his shoulder. Tracy realized that she was very weary.

"Poor honey, have they been very hard on you these last days?"

"If we really are to be married, Tracy, and I suppose we are, now you have compromised me so dreadfully—and in my own garden, too! have you no shame?—I must and shall cure you of this habit you are developing of treating me as the veriest child. Not that I dislike the sentiment, but I am three and twenty and certainly no small, weak little thing, and even you have been so kind as to say I was not entirely loathsome in appearance. . . ."

"Did I say that? I lied," Tracy interjected nonchalantly.

"Abominable man," Althea scolded.

"And I will have to cure you of parrying my questions, sweetheart. You are as brave as a lion, but you are also a little wan, and I imagine that you have had quite a time of your return here, if you have truly been extricating your father from his housekeeping tangles. Either he throws you out this minute and I carry you back to London and away from his worrying, or we are wed within the week by a Special License. I suppose there is no excuse for such havey-cavey behavior except my own impatience."

"In point of fact, Tracy, it has not been so bad here as I expected. The bills were in a shocking way, and the household not much better, but it was all as I had expected. I shall have to find Papa a good housekeeper and an agent. You are marrying an organizer, Tracy, and I am afraid you shall have to adjust to that fact."

"I know well enough. I shall endeavor to suffer as a Christian should," he said meekly.

"O noble man!" Althea laughed. "But if I look a little fagged, I suppose it was the journey, and sitting up that dreadful night wondering what I had done, and thinking about—about all the things that had happened during my stay. About you, I suppose, most of all. I have been so stupid in my management there it is a wonder you still speak to me." Althea's voice lowered and there was a more sober cast to her eye. She continued more brightly, "And there was Papa—although he was on his best behavior until this afternoon, and I suppose I must count that lapse somewhat to my own account. I have been positively *bustling* trying not to think of you," she finished shyly.

"Fool." He kissed her ear briefly. "Why were you so stubborn in refusing to believe me when I said that I loved you?"

"It seemed so very unlikely!" Althea cried. "And there was the whole business of the wretched money, and Lady Boskingram implied that settling down was your duty— she said your cousin had been trying to settle you suitably any time this last five years. And she said she was glad that you were showing some sense in that line."

"I owe Aunt Peg a little something for that bit of mischief." Tracy spied a marble bench cunningly hidden under a cluster of sickly rhododendron, and guided his lady there.

"She didn't mean to cause any trouble, Tracy—I do like her so much! But it seemed so—so illogical that you should care for me, especially after I had made such a fool of myself over Pendarly—and I didn't care tuppence for him after all, so never mention his name to me! I have conceded as much as I am about to on that score. Even when I knew I—liked you, I could not see why you should care for me except in an ordinary friendly sort of way. Then there was all that business with the money, and Francis and Maria, and Georgiana and Pendarly. It all sounds so stupid now, but at the time it seemed so awfully reasonable."

"What is this money you mention? I cannot for my life recall any monetary exchange in this tangle." They were seated upon the bench now, with Althea's head comfortably established against Tracy's shoulder, and the ribbon in her hair was tickling his chin most umercifully.

"Why, that dreadful sum that Francis lost to you the

night of the Ffordyings' ball!" Althea said in some surprise. "It caused Francis to quarrel with Mary, and then to go away, and heaven only knows what economies they shall have to study to meet it. Of course, Mary does tend to exaggerate, but it must have been a prodigious sum of money."

"It was," Tracy assured her. "But I absolved Bevan of that debt quite early on in the intrigue. Had no one thought to inform you, sweet manager? And I had no idea it had caused such a furor. I only played with him that night because he was foxed"—Althea gave an indignant squirm, but was kept in her place by a ruthlessly strong arm about her waist—"I saw that he was foxed, and I didn't want him falling into the toils of someone less charitable than I. You see, Ally," he said ruefully, "even then *I* didn't want you troubled—least of all by Bevan's ruin. And if I ever saw a man hell-bent for ruin, it was Bevan that night."

"He and Mary quarreled," Althea said.

"I know. But do you believe in the purity of my motives now, O cynic?"

"I believe. Tracy? I do love you." If she had mentioned this vital fact before, Calendar did not seem visibly perturbed by its repetition. He addressed himself instead to replying to the statement as sensibly as he could.

"And believe," he murmured in her ear, "that I loved you when I first offered for you. See what an unscrupulous brute I am, love? I would have married you first and then allowed you to have come to the realization that you loved me."

"I am shocked," Althea reproved. To remove any impression of callousness on his part that she might have formed, Tracy was again forced to persuade her of the sincerity of his intentions.

"You see how everything is worked out, Tracy." She laughed after a few minutes. "It quite undoes me to consider it. Mary and Francis happy again, Georgiana has

her Pendarly (and I'm sure I wish her joy of him!), Sophia and Mr. Tidd seem to be well on the way to marrying and producing a gaggle of blushing offspring. And
then there is us . . . it is all wonderful."

"Do I understand that you feel this is all to your
credit? Which recalls it to me: I was charged to give this
to you right away."

"You are a trifle tardy, but I will not give you away.
What is it?"

Tracy produced Maria's note. Althea received the letter, written on heavy notepaper in her sister's large,
looping, imprecise hand, and scanned it three times. Then
she read it aloud, spelling for Tracy's delectation the more
delicious of Maria's spelling mistakes. Georgiana and Edward were happy again, and Mrs. Laverham was as-
suming an air of triumph at having assured her daughter's
happiness, as she thought, by her own hand. And as for
Maria and Francis, they were happier than anything, as if
Althea couldn't guess! For her sister had had no time to
confide it, but they were setting up a nursery. Everything
was altogether delightfull, and the Prince was having an
enormous dinner to celebrate his Regency at last, so Althea must certainly head back to London at once to plan
her toilette! In a postscript Maria added that if she had
ever said a word against Sir Tracy, she wished her tongue
had been cut out, for he was perfectly amiable, and she
was sure Althea would be marvelously settled in no time.

Tracy expressed no surprise at any of the news, including Maria's condition. "There is a look that women acquire when they are breeding—I know it well, since
Amalia has been increasing continually since she wed
Boskingram. Very glad to be approved of, at last. I cannot imagine why Lady Bevan has suddenly developed the
opinion that I will not beat you—which I am not sure is
so true! You led us a damnable chase, Ally." A rough
note crept into his voice. "I shall have to keep a close
watch on you, and keep you by me."

"As if I needed watching all the time!" Althea bridled indignantly. Where this altercation might have taken them they did not discover, for out of the bushes came a thin hallooing: Merrit's voice.

"Ally, are you about here? Ally?" He broke through the bushes and landed, unkempt and grubby, in the clearing before them.

"Merrit, must you insist upon ruining all of the gardener's work by crawling through it as if you were a fox?" Althea sighed.

"Careful, Sister—that's what got you exiled last time," Merrit said carefully, with a speculative eye on Sir Tracy, who still had his arm about Althea's waist.

"I was never sent away: I escaped. But what is all this yelling and fussing and *invasion of my privacy?* Sometimes I swear you think you are still playing games back at Eton."

"I came out to find if Calendar had gone yet, or if you'd decided to take him, after all. He's a bruising rider, Ally," Merrit recommended. "Hope you take him."

"She will," Tracy said briskly, none too pleased with the interruption.

"There's good work, Sis. But what I came to tell you is that I've finally learned why Papa would not countenance my going down to Lancaster. It's the shabbiest thing I ever heard of. He's a convenient down there and he don't want me to meet her, though there's little likelihood of that. Don't think the old man cares to have her know he's a son my age. Don't suppose that you'd have a little blunt you could lend me until next quarter, Ally?" He had managed to ingratiate himself by squatting down, at no little risk to his already begrimed pantaloons, and brushing the dirt from her sandals.

"Merrit, I hope to have you for a brother soon, and I hope that I shall never presume to manage my wife's affairs—when she is my wife, and stop kicking at me, you shrew!—but I think that I speak for her when I say that she will be in no position to loan you any money. She has her bride clothes to consider, and after that, I expect her to support me in a suitable fashion—I am afraid all *my* funds will be tied up for my heir, you see." Tracy allowed his voice to trail off insinuatingly.

Merrit, to Althea's surprise, did not sulk or go into a tantrum, but directed a rare, cheeky grin at Tracy. "I see. Well, Ally, I think that you two will suit down to the ground, and I shall contrive to get to Lancaster somehow. Hey, if you write a book, don't use *our* name for it, please. I couldn't stomach owning a sister who was bookish in public." With this exhortation, the heir to Hook Well dove back into the bushes, leaving his sister and future brother-in-law to stare after him in amusement.

"Tracy," Althea said thoughtfully, sometime later, "was it really your phaeton that ditched my chaise that morning?"

"It pains me to admit it, my dear, but I'm afraid that it was. What machinations are you concocting to revenge yourself upon me?"

Althea eyed her love reproachfully. "Revenge? Do you really think me such a mean creature as that?"

"Well, after seeing Pendarly in your toils, I have some notion of what a woman scorned may do," he answered philosophically.

"There's the difference, you see. There I was a woman scorned. In the other instance, I was merely a woman overturned. Two entirely disparate things, although I do think you might have had some concern for a fellow traveler cast pell mell to the winds. Or at least into a ditch. Do you know it took all morning to have that wretched chaise repaired? It was very bad of you, Tracy. I hope you made a great deal of money over it." Althea turned aggrievedly from Calendar's shoulder and fixed her gaze somewhere into the shrubby distance.

"Althea," Tracy said dangerously. She did not turn. "Althea." Her back remained resolutely turned from him.

"I suppose I shall have to wed you by Special License to-morrow, for if we go on this way, I have no guarantee of even having you to wife. Althea, turn around," he commanded in a voice that brooked no denial. Althea turned slowly to face him, eyes lowered, a muted smile hovering at the corner of her lips.

"No cure for it," Calendar said fatalistically. "I had best wed you immediately, for who knows how much discipline I shall be forced to administer to you."

"Yes, please," Althea said agreeably.

Norah Lofts

Norah Lofts weaves a rich tapestry of love, war and passion. Here are her most entertaining novels of romance and intrigue. You may order any or all direct by mail.